LUCID

LUCID SERIES: BOOK 1

Kristy Fairlamb

wool
street
press

LUCID

First Published by Lakewater Press 2019

This edition published by Wool Street Press 2020

Copyright © Kristy Fairlamb 2019

Cover design by Robin Ludwig Design Inc.

ISBN: 978 0 6487845 0 0

www.kristyfairlamb.com

For my daughter Ajah,
I wrote this just for you,
now we get to share it with the world.

—1—

D REAMS ARE THE DOOR to the soul, although, in my case, the door led to someone else's – someone whose life just ended. My feet pounded the secluded dirt track on the edge of town, as if I could stomp away my last nightmare. Blood rushed through me, the endorphins buzzing to the outer inches of my body. Why did she have to die? If she were five more metres down the road the rock would've missed her. She was gone before she knew what happened – the only blessing in an otherwise senseless disaster.

I stopped and hunched over, my hand resting on the rough tree trunk. Battered breath in. Aching breath out. I squeezed my eyes closed, trying desperately to rid my mind of the image. Thick auburn hair covered half her young face as she lay there, blue eyes wide open, blood pooling and coating her cheek.

I kicked the tree. Damn it.

'Get a grip, Lucy,' I whispered into the trees. 'You've seen it all before.'

I tightened my hands into fists and launched my feet forward. I loved this track and the crisp gum-scented air that breezed past my face and cleared the relentless smog in my mind; a camera reel of the worst news headlines, shown in full, high-definition, blood-splattering clarity. Why couldn't my dreams be filled with flying or snowboarding? Hell, I'd even prefer a constant recap of my maths lessons with Mr Blythe. Sadly, there was never any flying, only an eternal loop playing the end of life, arrival of death, and a series of last breaths.

Tree branches encroached onto the path as I raced through dense brush, and then burst into the clearing. The scrub dispersed into farmland and empty hilly paddocks, before melting into a backdrop of mountains towering our small town. I stopped at the flimsy wire fence and caught my breath. The rhythm from my earphones slowed, mirroring my heartbeat. The harmonious tune and soft breeze enveloped me, gave me comfort, peace. I inhaled, sucking it all in.

Beyond the fence, one of the three black-and-white cows lifted her head and acknowledged me, this thing that had interrupted her solitude. I stared back until she bent for another mouthful of grass, and then I spun toward home, my thick, dark ponytail whipping my warm cheeks.

The last of the track merged into road and part of the residential area of Antil Springs. I paused at the top of the steep hill stretching into town, where we came with our sleds on the rare occasions it snowed this far from the mountains. A bland row of half-empty houses lined either side of the street, patiently waiting for their winter inhabitants to bring them back to life. At the end of each winter the streets were like a slow evacuation – only the truly committed stayed behind.

Antil had a lot going for it, even if it was a tiny blip on the map. Tiny might be a slight exaggeration, but with only one set of stop lights, one lowly supermarket – which used the lack of competition as a green light to bump the prices sky high – and one high school, it was fair. Although the copious amounts of restaurants and cafes did lend to an appearance of something larger and more alive than what we knew for most of the year. We were a tourist town, the four backpacker hostels and six real estate agents shouting 'Come live here!' were evidence of that.

Winter was our attraction, and outside of that we slipped back into the quiet-town shoes we felt most comfortable in – even with no hospital, no library, and terrible internet coverage. With two hundred kilometres between us and the east coast of Australia, we were close enough to the busy cities if we needed them, but far enough away that we tried not to.

I started down the hill, my feet moving in time with the easy beat from Of Monsters and Men's 'Slow and Steady'. A flash of hair, the colour of my strong morning coffee, caught my attention. A boy climbed into a green removalist's truck, and waves of familiarity coursed through me.

I stopped running, hands on hips, and caught my breath as I tried to place where I'd seen him. The truck sat reversed in the driveway of a red-bricked house across the road. The large 'For Sale' sign pegged into the dying front lawn now had a 'Sold' sticker plastered across its front.

I didn't know anyone from out of town, except my grandparents, aunts, and uncles. Maybe he resembled someone from a dream. I remembered all of the victim's faces. Obviously he wasn't one of those, and yet I recognised him. Why?

He slid out of the truck, his strong forearms wrapped around a large box, muscles bulging at the weight – *nice*. In tight black jeans and a denim shirt, sleeves rolled up to his elbows, he strode up the driveway. A smile tugged on my lips when I took in the black low-top Cons on his feet – my favourite. Tendrils of wild hair poked up haphazardly and flicked down one side of his forehead, awakening that unyielding familiarity again. I could almost guarantee someone in a dream had hair exactly like that. I needed to know who. For no more reason than not letting a question go unanswered. As much as standing there appraising him appealed,

I suddenly itched to get home – I knew exactly where to look.

Walking down the hill, I turned back as he stepped through the front door, shouting, 'Mum! You want this one in the back?'

THE SECOND I OPENED our front door and turned off my music, my senses shifted into overdrive. The TV blared in the lounge room; Dad reclined on the couch, his feet propped on the ottoman. The tangy spices of dinner filled my nostrils, a scent that told me my shift-working Mum hadn't left for the hospital yet.

With a sigh I swiped the back of my hand on my sweaty forehead and slid off my sneakers. The air inside was stifling after being out in the fresh breeze. Holding my shoes, I crept past the kitchen. *Please don't spot me.*

No such luck. 'Hey, honey. Mind helping me with the last of dinner when you've cleaned up?'

I'd just as soon scrub the toilets; besides, I had a mission. I inched closer to the stairs. 'Can you ask Jake or Ollie?'

'Ollie's still out and Jake's working on an assignment.' Who says I didn't have one, too? A 'find out who the new kid around the corner was' assignment.

Mum spun from the sink with a handful of tomatoes and tipped them onto the chopping board. 'Please, honey.'

My shoulders sagged. 'Fine, sure. Give me ten?'

An apron covered Mum's nursing uniform, her greying hair pulled back into a tight bun, ready for her shift. 'Can you make it a speedy ten?' She reached for a knife. 'I'm trying to do too many things tonight.'

She always did. But her good intentions meant she raced against the clock to prepare it all before leaving for work. And I swear she never realised she needed me until she saw me. I ought to try harder to stay hidden, like Dad and my brothers.

Once in my room I tossed the shoes on the bottom shelf of the bookcase with the rest of my sneakers and Cons. The white bookcase sat beside a small, square window and held a vast array of books on art and dreaming, even books about dreaming *in* art. I didn't read much fiction. Most of my entertainment occurred in my dreams – that was enough. But give me a book about art, historical paintings, and the interpretation of the ancient arts, or anything on dreaming, and I'd be lost for hours.

I placed my phone and earphones on the round table in the centre of the room. Mum and I found it at a garage sale for ten bucks last year, after I'd had a disturbing dream where a man sat with his back to the door. It didn't end well for him, and I'd woken with a desperate need for a new desk for my room. Oblivious to my reasons, Mum suggested a round table – better Feng shui apparently. We found it. Old and round with the white paint peeling off the legs and top.

'It's shabby chic,' Mum said, laughing, but I didn't care about the design, I was more concerned about the purpose. Eyes on the door – don't get murdered. Once we got it home, I piled it high with paper, pencils, and laptop; it wouldn't have mattered if it had green and purple stripes.

I sped through dinner and retreated to my room, intent on discovering the reason the boy looked familiar. I yanked the stack of sketchbooks from the bookcase, dumping them on the table, and slumped in my chair. Dragging in a breath, I opened to pages and pages of faces I'd drawn from my dreams.

Granny Tess had suggested I record them. The day I discovered her own set of books was the first I knew she'd once been like me.

'You have a gift,' she said, as if it were a good thing. I couldn't fathom why she'd call something as extraordinarily normal as closing my eyes a gift. But she was my own personal cheerleader, encouraging me in a sport I never wanted to compete in.

As a child I had more imaginary friends than Mum could fit into seatbelts. My dreams filled my days as much as my nights, but the best and worst part of my affliction was the lucidity of my dreams and waking with the ability to recall every single detail.

Granny Tess had sighed and held the books to her chest. 'This is all I have of my dreams now. But whilst they may plague you and make you terrified to sleep, they can be a good thing. Draw the people you see, make notes of any details, it'll help.'

And so I did. Not like Granny Tess's; hers were colourful and abstract, where mine were realistic and always in lead. I stared at the first face I'd drawn, a young man I'd watched die in a bike accident four years ago. I flipped the page; a little girl – car accident.

My phone vibrated on the table. My best friend Max's name flashed on the screen, and I placed the phone against my ear.

'Hey hon,' she said.

'What's up? How'd training go?'

She groaned. 'Same as always. Coach pushed us hard, and I'll pay for it in the morning.'

'Do you ever learn?'

'Well that's the point,' she said. '*Learning*. I won't let those bars beat me.'

'Like they did me?' I joked. I gave up trying to perfect the uneven bars years ago, and then gymnastics altogether. It was no secret I'd been terrible at it. Max on the other hand – superstar.

'Totally,' she said with a giggle. 'So hey, you finish that English assignment yet?'

'Only like two days ago.'

'Yeah, thought so. I'm so screwed.'

I curled the corner of the paper under my thumb and forefinger and turned over the page; a teenage boy – anaphylaxis. I sighed and closed the book. 'What do you need?'

By the time I finished helping Max I no longer felt like rehashing the faces from my books and the curdled feelings that came with them.

I had enough to battle with my latest victim, the young lady who'd been in the wrong place at the wrong time. Hopefully I could redream an alternate ending for her tonight. Alter the moments before the rock hurtled from the bridge, give my mind a nicer image to hold on to. I did that with most of my nightmares. By way of a slight change in events, the flicker of a second, enough to bring them back to life. Desperate to save each and every person – even if only in my dreams.

Without any freshly disturbing news stories, nothing had me on edge as the darkness encroached. But no matter how reassured I felt as I lay down, I could never foresee a peaceful night's sleep any more than the nightmares. Predicting would lead to hopes being dashed, and I never hoped. Still, my eyes closed with little effort and I drifted to sleep.

VIBRATIONS RUMBLED THROUGH ME *as an aeroplane flew overhead. A tinge of pink lingered in the dull light, the barest hint of dawn slowly departing like the planes on the runway. The frigid air from the night clung to me, refusing to let go, and I rubbed my hands vigorously together.*

I scanned the area. I stood near the pick-up and drop-off zone. The cars flowed like worker ants in a nest, weaving in and out of one another with the flurry of travellers. A horn echoed in the enclosed space.

An elderly, silver-haired lady climbed out of a black BMW. Her eyes were hollow and shoulders slumped as if too heavy to hold up.

She hugged the man who'd dropped her off, a tender, lengthy embrace. As he drove away, she extended the handle on her small suitcase and ambled toward check-in. Her foot hooked on a crack in the concrete, and she toppled forward, landing on her knees. The suitcase fell with a thud, and her hands splayed out on the cold ground. People stopped and stared, but damn it, why didn't anyone help?

Without hesitation, I rushed forward. At the same time a boy around my age, sixteen maybe, headed for the lady, his light brown hair flicked over half his brow as he strode toward her. He was a fair distance away and stopped when I reached her first.

I squatted beside her. She looked up; I was visible – she saw me.

'Are...are you okay?' I hesitated, always on edge when people saw me in their reality. 'Do you need some help?'

'Thank you, dear. That would be most kind.' She didn't quite manage a smile, but the beginnings of one drew creases around her eyes.

I held her elbow, and she released a long breath as she struggled to stand. I gathered her fallen suitcase and placed it into her trembling fingers.

'You gonna be all right?'

'Yes, I'll be fine now, thank you again, dear.'

'You're welcome,' I said, and she shuffled away. My heart ached for her; she was alone yet clearly needed someone by her side.

I lifted my gaze back to the boy. His dark, piercing eyes fixed on me. Squirming under his stare, my pulse quickened.

I admired him with a courage I rarely had in reality, but I couldn't drag my eyes away if I tried; I was being sucked into the depths of his gaze like quicksand.

The spell broke, and his face took on a different shape. The sharp lines of his chiselled cheekbones softened as his lips rose. My feet urged to close the fifteen-metre abyss between us, but before I got the chance, he ripped his stare away. Disappointment poured through me, but it didn't stop me appreciating the sight of him. He wasn't overly tall but wouldn't be the shortest kid in class either. My eyes raked down his grey hoodie, skinny jeans – and Cons. Hell yeah.

A couple, probably his mother and father, embraced, a small overnight bag sat on the ground by their feet. They broke apart, and then came together for a short kiss, her face lighting up as the man whispered in her ear. The boy stood to the side. He brushed his fingers through his unruly hair, and with an eye roll in my direction we shared a silent laugh. Yes, definitely his parents.

The woman climbed back into the car, and his dad said something, which the boy answered with a nod and words I was too far away to hear. They shared a brief hug, and the man grabbed the bag at his feet, threw it over a shoulder and walked away.

My dream pulled at me as the boy jumped in the front seat of the car, but I couldn't avert my eyes, not yet. The car drove out of the parking bay, and he turned, giving me one last smile, moments before I was thrust into the next part of my dream.

My hands gripped the armrests as strong as any Olympic weightlifter. I winced at the seatbelt digging into my stomach, struggling to keep me in my seat. The plane dipped forward. Deafening wails of the passengers sliced into my ears.

The intimate knowledge that I, alone, would wake from this tragic reality did nothing to quench my fear. I was about to die, and the only thought rushing through me was, 'I better bloody wake up'.

The lady by the window in my row was still, staring straight ahead, eyes fixed on the chair in front of her, resigned to her fate.

Between us sat the silver-haired lady. She mumbled the same words over and over. 'My daughter needs me, she needs me.' Her eyes pleaded with mine, as if I could somehow help, but I couldn't relax my fingers enough to offer her any consolation. Guilt seized me, churning in my stomach, because, why else was I here, if not for that? She needed reassurance, and I had none to give her.

'She needs me.'

I shifted my attention toward the woman sitting diagonally from me, *hunched over the child beside her.*

The middle-aged man across the aisle held his hands in his lap, almost as still as the lady by the window. Smoky black hair gathered in curls on top of his head, and his slim nose was far too small for his face in proportion to the broadness of the rest of him. His eyes were closed.

I was about to turn when his eyes opened and stared straight into mine. He sat silent and resigned, the worry evident by the slight furrow on his wrinkled forehead. Before he looked away his mouth lifted in a disturbingly crooked smile, but the hint of light in his eyes made me feel less lonely. We flew alone, but we were in this together. My lips lifted ever so slightly before a lump caught in the back of my throat and a solitary tear slid onto my cheek.

The plane jerked upward. I was thrust back in my seat before it tipped, jarring, and sent me sliding forward again. I clenched my hands tighter onto the armrests and held on for dear life.

The aeroplane speakers crackled to life. 'Brace for impact.' There was a pause before the captain repeated. 'Brace for impact!'

I lowered my head to my knees and gripped my shins with shaking hands. My heart pounded against my thighs, and my breath thundered in my ears even though it was difficult to breathe at all.

The screams around me dulled, moments before they were abruptly overwhelmed by the deafening sound of explosive metal as it crunched closer. Flames engulfed me, scorched my skin, and my mouth opened in a silent scream.

—2—

T HE DARKNESS BECAME BLINDING light as I opened my eyes and instantly closed them again, resisting the golden glow that blasted into my room. My pulse vibrated at a high frequency, and I inhaled deeply to bring it down. I wished I could stay in bed. All those deaths to contend with, I wasn't sure I wanted to face the day. Maybe Mum wouldn't notice if I was a no show.

As though she heard my thoughts, her voice crept into my room. 'Lucy Cate Piper, get up. Coffee's brewing.'

I tugged the covers over my head with a moan, before flinging them back again. Rubbing my eyes, I reached into my bedside drawer, and lifted my well-used A5 sketch book onto my lap. I flipped through the pages searching for one particular drawing: the one I'd pencilled the last time I'd had that same dream. It was nearly a year ago when news of the tragic plane crash swamped the television. It wasn't unusual to have recurring dreams. Sometimes events stayed with me for days, forcing the images on me, making me afraid to fall asleep. Thankfully I'd never repeated the plane crash dream...until now.

Faces peered from the page; the strange man across the aisle, the old lady beside me, the boy at the airport. The same boy who'd moved into the house around the corner.

'Holy cow.' My heart rate accelerated, like it did whenever I tried to piece together the puzzles from my dreams. But those pieces had never collided with real life before.

Forty minutes later, after I ran a brush through my unruly hair, gathered it into my usual high ponytail, and added an extra coat of tinted moisturiser under my blackened, sleep-deprived eyes, I downed my coffee and stepped out into the fresh morning air. I wrapped my arms around my body as anticipation crept through me at the thought of the winter easing its descent upon us. I couldn't wait for the wind in my hair, the feel of thick powder under my board, and my favourite time of year: that first week when it felt like we were the only ones on the mountain.

A horn blared and I rushed to jump into the front seat of Jake's '92 Toyota van. Moments later, my younger brother, Ollie, always ten steps and three years behind me, clambered in the back with a grunt.

"Bout time,' Jake said, tapping the wheel. Jake was taking the school year seriously, repeating his final year in an attempt to earn higher grades and pursue medicine. He regularly threatened to leave Ollie and me behind if we weren't ready, and I'd been tempted on more than one occasion to let him go without me. Jake bought the van almost solely for the purpose of transporting as many people and snowboards as possible. It had grunt to get us up the mountain, but not a lot of charm.

I leaned my elbow on the armrest, put my earphones in, and played with the beaded jet bracelet around my wrist, recalling all the lives lost in last night's dream. It was a long time ago now, but the guilt after waking up when they didn't hung heavily on my shoulders. And why had I witnessed the crash again after all this time? Biting my fingernails, I focussed on the mountain tops, unease rippling over my skin. Did it have anything to do with dream boy moving in around the corner? I yearned to know more, my usual need for answers prodding at me, cramming into my stomach, refusing to budge until I figured it out.

*****

My hand glided across the paper, sketching the fine lines of his cheekbones and his full lips. They were nothing short of perfect, and I did my best to draw them as I remembered. The shadow from the fall of his hair made his eyes appear almost black. Brown perhaps – I hadn't been close enough to see – but I wasn't drawing in colour so it made no difference.

Who was he? The lady in the first part of my dream had been killed on the plane, and I always thought he was simply an innocent bystander.

At the easel beside me, my close friend Amber groaned as she tackled her own portrait. That was normal for her in art, but I found myself with an equal amount of angst today as I attempted to draw dream boy exactly as I'd seen him. He reminded me of James Dean, the eyes and the cheeks, maybe the hair too. I only knew this because Granny Tess was a huge fan and, despite my protests, I'd grown up watching his movies. He stared back from the page, and I drew in a deep breath.

'Everything all right?' Amber whispered. She always flitted about like a kindergarten teacher, as if everyone's happiness was somehow her responsibility.

'Yeah, just admiring.' I hadn't taken my eyes off his face.

'Why wouldn't you, he's a tad lovely,' she said.

'Only a tad?' I could stare at him all day. But Amber was serious with Cal, one of my oldest and dearest, if not craziest, friends, so she clearly appreciated a different type.

'Hey, is he the new kid?'

'Who?' I darted my eyes to her.

She flicked her hand in the direction of my picture. 'Him. Looks like the new kid. You've met him then?'

I resisted glancing over my shoulder as if he were standing at the back of the room. My pulse pounded against my chest. The boy who'd given me goose bumps from a single stare was at my school? I hadn't been expecting that when I woke up. Who starts at a new school on a Thursday anyway?

'Lucy?'

'What? Uh no...'

She scrunched her brows, examining my picture.

'I mean, I haven't met him, I saw him before school.' Of course, I hadn't really seen him before school. Well I had, just not in real life.

'You saw him one time and drew him that accurately?'

'I usually do.' I didn't mean for it to come out so abrupt, but it was true. I swallowed and shifted to take in her picture. 'How you going with yours?' Amber had drawn some seriously furrowed eyebrows on her portrait of an ageing lady.

Amber whined. 'I can't get the eyes right.'

'Looks great,' I said. 'She looks really angry.'

'Exactly.' Amber tucked a loose strand of honey blonde hair under her lace headband. 'I was going for mildly irritated.'

'You can't change it?'

'I've tried, but I might have to go with this now before it becomes a big smeared mess. I should just stick to photography.' She turned back toward my drawing and tilted her head. 'How do you do it? You get it perfect every time.'

'Not always.'

'Yeah, and I'm the most popular girl in the school. Looks pretty good to me.'

I inwardly disagreed. I had a clear picture in my mind, but some elements didn't transfer seamlessly to the page. A wrong angle, a misplaced line, and it wouldn't be the same person.

I'd seen this face twice now, and both times it'd held my attention, but this was the first time I'd drawn it properly. I wanted to get it right. I clenched the pencil. Oh my God, he was here. Part of me wanted to search the school grounds for him; the other half eyed the art store room and the lock above the handle.

Mrs Mac appeared behind me, her hands on her broad hips. 'That's coming along really well, Lucy. I love the intensity in his eyes. Makes me wish I knew what he was thinking.'

Yeah, I'd thought that myself.

I GRABBED MY BOOKS in one arm, slammed the locker door shut and spun around to make my way back to class. I'd forgotten my books for PE and ditched Max so I could sprint to my locker before Ms Furness noticed me missing.

A girl just ahead swung open the double doors, and I dodged around her and slipped through before they shut. In my carelessness, I whacked into her arm. Without slowing, I shouted an apology and ran full pelt into someone coming from the other direction. Before my brain had a chance to comprehend the impact, my feet were in the air, the books too, and I landed with a massive smack against the concrete.

'Shit.' I placed my hand on the back of my head as a searing pain made its way from my shoulder to the nape of my neck and shot into my skull. Damn. I squeezed my eyes shut momentarily, and then remembered why I'd been rushing in the first place. I sat up as fast as my pained body would allow, my head down, and waited for the spinning to ease.

'You right?' The voice was smooth and deep.

'Yeah, you?' I lifted my head.

'I'm fine–'

From around soft strands of hair, familiar dark eyes peered out, widening as they met mine.

I couldn't breathe.

It was *him*. So much for searching him out. Now he stood in front of me, all I wanted to do was race back and lock myself in that store room.

'You sure you're okay?' He rested a hand on his knee and leaned over, running his fingers through his hair.

Where was my voice? Not wanting to witness the humiliation, it'd apparently packed up and shipped out the moment the panic set in.

My pulse thundered in my ears as I spoke. 'Perfectly fine.' My voice was hoarse, as if I'd just run a marathon. I collected the books beside me, and scraped myself off the ground.

I scrunched my brow and looked at him again. Tears stung the back of my eyes, but I couldn't tell if it was from the sharp pain in my head or because for the first time in my life I stood face to face with someone who I'd only ever seen in my dreams. He held out one of my books, a tentative smile on his face.

I extended a shaking hand, grabbed the book, and backed away. I lowered my eyes, mumbled a thanks, and, still struggling to take a lungful of air, barrelled away from him.

—3—

M Y VISION BLURRED, THE buildings warped, and I couldn't see the ground below my feet, but I kept running. I blinked rapidly to clear my eyes so I wouldn't end up on the ground again. My head throbbed, a cocktail of pain and anxiety. Of shock. I was expecting it, but the impact of actually seeing him slammed into me like a ship into ice, breaching my core.

And he'd looked almost as startled at seeing me. Why? He couldn't possibly remember me from the airport, I'd only ever been there in my dream. My hand trembled as I covered my mouth, swallowing back a wave of nausea.

I darted into a small alcove between two buildings, the dull orange bricks looming above me. I dropped my books, lowered my hands to my knees and inhaled slowly. This made absolutely no sense. He'd been in my dream, I'd been in his reality; but he shouldn't recognise me. I tried to shake off my uneasiness, but it wouldn't budge. I wiped at my still moist eyes, picked up my scattered books, and staggered back to the gym.

'What took you so long?' Max peered nervously over my shoulder at the teacher. 'I said you had to go to the toilet, but that cover was starting to look embarrassing. Hey, you okay? You're all pale.'

'Good, that'll go well with my cover story.' I avoided her question.

'Yeah, but I know you're not sick, what happened?' Her voice was laced with concern.

'Lucy and Mackenzie,' Ms Furness called. 'You two, court four, you're up against Karla and Abby.'

'Aren't we doing theory?' I asked Max.

'Yeah, later, apparently.' She rolled her eyes.

I'd known Max since we were in nappies. She'd been part of so much in my life, she was like my birthmark – always there, as much a part of me as I was her – and we matched strides as we marched from the gym, grabbing our rackets on the way out.

'Spit it.' Max bumped her hip against mine.

'I saw someone unexpected, that's all.'

'So unexpected you look like you've seen a ghost?' She grabbed my arm, staring more closely at me. 'Hey, have you been crying?'

'No, I'm perfectly fine.' I waved my hand in front of me before stupidly deciding on a truth so absurd it would probably shut her up anyway. 'Okay. I literally just banged into someone that I dreamed about last night. I ran into him, fell on my ass, and smacked my head on the ground. I made a complete moron of myself in front of someone who, only this morning, I thought was a figment of my imagination. Now, say I'm not crazy.' I giggled, trying to dismiss the queasy misgivings rumbling in my stomach at admitting the truth to Max.

She wasn't laughing; her eyes narrowed, lips turned upward. Dark hair swayed around her face, highlighting her light brown skin, one of the best assets her Fijian father gave her. 'Did you say *him?*'

'Seriously? Out of all that and you want me to clarify *that* part?'

'It is the most interesting bit...well, maybe after the crazy part.' She grinned boldly as we reached the courts. Abby and Karla stood on the other side of the net, waving their arms and racquets in animated conversation.

'Ready?' Abby called. We positioned ourselves and she threw the ball in the air, delivering a perfect serve. Max lunged on long legs and hit the ball squarely over the net, it landed out of Karla's reach.

I picked up a spare ball, bounced it on the court, and belted it into the air. Max and I were in flawless sync, a fusion of white and navy dancing across the court. The ball flew through the air, and Max gracefully sent it soaring back.

'So, you dreamed about him, *then* saw him in the flesh. That's pretty cool. *And* crazy. You sure you haven't seen him before? The school's not that big.' Max did always go for the logical.

Yeah, in the dream a year ago – but I couldn't tell her that. *Whack.* The ball bounced off my racquet. 'Maybe I saw him without realising it.'

'That or you're destined for the loony bin'.

'That's what I'm afraid of.' I missed the ball as it flew past my head. 'Damn!'

Max placed a hand on her hip, breathing hard, her chest heaving against her tight polo. She looked me in the eyes. 'Hey, I'm kidding. You're only crazy if you believe it, so stop. It's not possible you dreamed someone up. Like, you know how insane that sounds. I mean, the possibilities sound fun, but also insane.' Her mahogany eyes glimmered.

This was what Max did. She wasn't the friend who validated my feelings – she told me not to feel what I felt, with the notion it helped.

It didn't.

My feelings, doubts, insecurities, whatever you wanted to call them, weren't a light switch to be turned off so easily, no matter how insane they sounded. Confiding in Max and her telling me to stop my train of thought only reinforced why I kept my dreams to myself.

When I was younger, my brothers had gathered around me each

morning to listen as I recapped the previous night's dream over breakfast. Their pancakes grew cold, and untouched cereal turned to mush as I recounted the events I'd experienced in my dream life.

They were good memories, but, like anything worn and old, my dreams turned into a darker, less desirable kind. I was thirteen when Mum replaced her smile with wary eyes and small shakes of the head. She ignored my brothers' protests, afraid my recollections would be too grim for Ollie, never mind if they were even worse for me. So, ever so slowly, like the shift of the tide – not noticed until it's gone – I spoke of the dreams less and less, until one day I couldn't remember the last one I'd shared with them.

Seeking to replace my loss I'd turned to Max. She hated horror stories, but didn't seem to mind mine until I suggested my dreams were things that'd actually happened. She brushed me off, said I was probably imagining it. And when I suggested I was actually *there* she went all weird on me. She didn't say anything, but the indifference, sometimes awkwardness in her face each time I recounted my dreams showed how uncomfortable they made her. I wasn't so open after that, though it didn't stop her reaching out when I'd had a bad one. She supported me the best way she knew how, though not always the way I needed.

So my solitary quest to figure out the meaning remained exactly that – solitary. Maybe I ought to listen to Max after all and stop with the crazy thoughts, but seriously, what the hell?

Why was I seeing the aeroplane dream again? Was it because he'd shown up, or did it mean something more? Add the fact I was sure he recognised me too, and I was back on the train, on an endless loop I couldn't get off, reeling with a dizziness I knew all too well.

I hated feeling out of control; I liked answers, and I'd be damned if I wasn't going to figure these ones out.

* * * * *

I STOPPED BY MY locker to grab the textbooks meant to assist me for the next forty minutes in my least favourite subject. I slammed the door shut before diving into the crowd. A sea of teenage faces stared back, and I swam through them like a salmon against the current. Their voices echoed in my ears, ricocheting against the rise of my inner screaming. I plucked the dangling earphones from my shirt and positioned them in my ears.

I'd almost reached the doors when I saw him walking toward me. Our eyes met, and I was transported back to the airport, making my skin heat. I yanked my gaze away and picked up my pace.

I ducked into the toilets so I could breathe without fear of seeing him. He might be good looking, but he was still a painful reminder of my insanity. I splashed my face with cold water and gasped. I felt like I'd run a marathon, and as my reflection gaped back at me – sunken dark eyes, whiter than usual face – I decided I might look better if I had.

Maths was a greater than usual effort. How could I concentrate on the banality of numbers when depressing images of the plane crash lingered in the forefront of my mind? All those lives, gone.

I slumped into the desk beside Sean. He was Max's twin, but aside from similar dark hair and soft brown skin, they were unique individuals. Sean was also my ex.

I opened my internet browser and brought up the news article from ten months earlier when flight S108, bound for L.A. from Sydney crashed into the ocean off the coast of Hawaii. The initial stories were filled with fear and speculation. Then details emerged as the wreckage was found, and all three hundred and twenty seven souls on board were confirmed dead.

I glanced up at Mr Blythe, droning on as he paced the front

of the class. I heard nothing but the numbers of those lost swirl around my mind.

I clicked on a more recent story from two months ago. Angry family members claiming there were still no answers as to why the plane had gone down. There was also a story about the pilot, Charles Sims, heralding his experience in the industry, and the high regard his fellow pilots had for him.

I closed the tab and let my gaze drift to the window. Cotton clouds floated in the otherwise clear blue sky.

Ouch! A searing pain shot through my foot. I flipped my head toward Sean, his eyes darting sideways letting me know I faced the wrong direction.

I looked to the front of the class where Mr Blythe stood with hands in the pockets of his vomit-coloured vest.

'Care to join us, Lucy? Or do you have something more entertaining going on up here?' he said in his monotone voice, tapping his finger three times on the side of his forehead.

'I, ah, sorry I–'

'Her cat died last night, Mr Blythe,' Sean said. I didn't have a cat.

Sean's eyes were full of gentleness and sympathy. One of the by-products of growing up in each other's pockets; an effortless familiarity. It's what I loved most about my friends – the ease. With Sean the ease had gone away for a while, and sometimes I felt I was trying to get it back.

Sean and I fell for each other for the same reason we went to this high school – because it was convenient and easy. He was also cute and made me laugh and happened to be one of my best friends. But none of that helped when, in my desire for someone to *hear* me, I told him about my dreams. A bit like his sister, he laughed me off, then looked me straight in the eye and said, 'You know how delusional that sounds?'

We never talked about it again. He'd said sorry, but I forced him to swallow the rest of his words. Our friendship was more important than trying to savour what was barely more than a childhood crush. Eventually the regret, hovering in the air between us, cleared, and our easy friendship came back into focus.

Funny how six months ago he couldn't handle my truth, yet today he oozed understanding without knowing the reason for my inattention. Still, it meant a lot to me, and I thanked him through blurry eyes and a small lift of my lips.

'Right, well, I've never let that excuse stop me from enjoying quadratic equations before,' Mr Blythe said and returned his attention to the numbers at the front of the room.

I somehow got through Maths, trudged out, shoulders high, straight for my free lesson in the library where no teacher could get in the way of my investigation. I found my favourite table near the rack of European history and ancient Egypt books, in the back corner where I could keep an eye on the room.

Quiet chatter trickled from the tables around me. Turning up my music I reached out to the only other place that might hold answers. I typed in my username, @LucidLucy, and scrolled the dream forum I'd frequented since my online search led me there years ago. My pursuit to find out all I could about my nightmares, their meaning, and about dreams in general, left me with a search history of pretty much every website on the topic, plus some.

I never found anyone else who dreamed repeatedly of real-life events. But I kept coming back, on the off chance I'd find someone who was like me. My dreams weren't like those of a lot of forum users, but it was still a place I felt less like a freak and more like a member of an extended family. I knew Granny Tess was both family *and* like me, but sometimes it was easier to ask strangers my questions, and sometimes I simply preferred to read their discussions from the outside.

I couldn't find anyone asking about my particular problem, so I started my own thread. 'Seeing someone in a dream before meeting them in real life.'

I knew my dreams contained accurate accounts of reality, especially the faces of those who died in the dreams. But I always believed that, unless they played major roles in the disasters I witnessed, they were imagined extras on 'the set' of my dream, white noise.

He was clearly not.

And as much as the fear of the unknown terrified me, the need to know the answers propelled me to learn more. I'd have to pluck up the courage and confront him about what he knew. What was his connection to the crash, and how the hell did he recognise me?

— 4 —

Lunch arrived, and the weight of the last couple of hours lifted at the prospect of a carefree forty minutes with my friends. Aside from Amber, who we'd only met a little over two years ago, I'd grown up with my friends being as dependable and constant as if they were siblings. And in a world of eternal shifting sand they were my mainstay.

But first I needed food, and I hurried to the canteen in the hope I'd get there before all the Vietnamese cold rolls were gone.

Damn it!

The queue snaked out the door. Why didn't I leave the library earlier? Now I had to trade some of the best part of my day for standing behind two pimply thirteen-year-old boys whose voices pitched higher than the gum trees outside.

The school was brimming with cumbersome, hormonal teenagers who wouldn't notice me if I passed out at the top of the stairs, which only made me love my friends more. There'd been six of us growing up, including Jake and me, and with less than two years in age between us we took it as a sign we were meant to do everything together. If one of us was climbing a tree, the other five weren't far away. Chicken pox and nits were shared equally, and lasagne and mud pies were made in bulk.

But life can be as precarious as our misshaped mud pies, and ours began to crumble to pieces six years ago when Cal's older brother, Richie, lost his battle with cancer. And the following year Jake headed off to high school without us, creating a distance almost as large as the one Richie left behind.

Things changed a lot since those carefree years climbing trees and living in each other's pockets. We always imagined we'd be together forever, but imaginations were wild and unpredictable, and forever was only for fairy tales.

I reached the front of the queue, and my day extended its punishment by revealing the canteen had sold out of cold rolls. I left with a consolation lunch of a BLT wrap, but at least I didn't land lukewarm fries.

I rounded the science building, and the old maple, with its mass of golden leaves carpeting the ground, beckoned me. Max and Sean's raucous laughter reached me moments before I saw them. Everyone had beaten me today; Amber and Cal sat beside one another, across from Sean and Max, and someone else. Who was that? My stomach dropped; that hair looked startlingly familiar.

I sucked in a breath.

You've got to be effing kidding me!

I stopped dead. My heart raced toward detonation. How could he? How could he be there with *my* friends, in *my* space? It was bad enough to have him appear at my school, but to infiltrate the one thing that was mine – argh. I scanned around for an escape. I couldn't do it. I couldn't talk to him. Would I be able to leave without drawing attention to my movement? Should I keep walking, and hope no one noticed me?

'Lucy!' Max waved.

Crap, crap, crap.

He turned in my direction, and I had no time to look away. His eyes were on me, and the shock I detected in them earlier returned, followed by the same memorable smile from my dream. This was almost dreamlike too – surreal, obscure, and a little bit hazy.

I pasted a painfully fake smile onto my face, forced my leaden feet into action, and made it to the seat beside Amber, once again face to face with someone whose presence in my regular, normal life freaked me out. I refrained from looking at him as I sat.

'Hey, Luce. Where you been?' I found Sean's eyes. Maybe if I held onto those I could use some of his strength.

Nerves gathered in my throat, and I swallowed, holding up a brown paper bag. 'Queue was long.'

Sean's eyes left mine, and I plummeted to earth, scrabbling for an anchor, a hook, anything. Cal banged his hand on the table, making me jump. Damn his permanent enthusiasm, as if my heart needed to pick up more speed.

'And this is Lucy Piper, or just Luce.'

I drew in a deep breath, and slid my gaze over the table toward the far too good-looking boy from my dream, to James Dean. His mouth sat in a straight line, but his eyes held the glimmer of a smile, as if he found enjoyment in this moment. His lean arms rested on the table between us, hands folded in front of him, sitting too comfortable for my liking, and what was with his floppy hair? So imperfect, it made it perfect. Oh boy.

'Luce meet Simsy, aka Tyler Sims. He's just moved to town.'

No kidding. Hang on. Did he say Sims?

Sean whacked Tyler on the back. 'He's joined the soccer team, so he already passed the first test, hey Cal?'

'Shit yeah. All the best guys play soccer.'

My head grew foggy, registering the name – the connection. 'Wait, what?' I clasped my hands tightly in my lap, waiting for answers to the rampant questions of the past two hours. Had it really only been that long?

'Yeah, I know, sorry, Luce,' Sean said. 'Another soccer nut, we're multiplying.'

'No. Not that.' I flicked my head to look directly at Tyler. 'Your name...' The words chafed my dry throat.

His eyes went wide and his mouth fell open. 'Just Tyler.' The smooth voice of earlier now cracked and coated in unease.

And right there was the answer. He didn't want anyone to know who he was: the pilot's son.

I cleared my throat and steadied myself on the seat. If anyone understood what it meant to hide your true self it was me. 'Right, sure. Nice to meet you.' My lips trembled, but I forced them upward, offering him the reassurance he needed.

'You too, Lucy,' he said, saying my name slowly, like it was a flawless piece of music on his lips. And then he grinned, eyes conveying a mountain of gratitude for not outing him.

'So you just moved here from Sydney?' Max asked.

'Yeah, yesterday. Unpacked the truck last night, ready for first lesson this morning.'

'You don't muck around, do ya?' Cal said.

'Not when it counts.'

'So what'd you move here for?' Amber asked. 'We came a couple years ago, Mum and Dad wanted a fresh start.'

'Yeah, sea-change for us too, without the sea of course.' He raised his eyebrows and spoke with mock disgust. Or maybe he really was annoyed we had no sea. I couldn't tell.

'But we have mountains and snow.' Amber hovered the spoon of yoghurt halfway to her mouth. 'And a lake.'

'So they say,' Tyler said with barely a hint of a smile in his eyes even though his lips turned up.

'You have any other family here?' Amber pressed her spoon against her lips.

'Dude, we don't normally interrogate the newcomers.' Cal wrapped an arm around Amber.

'You did me.' She shoved at him, sat up straighter and leaned her arm on the table staring across at Tyler. 'You should've seen their faces when they found me here on my first day, at *their* table. I was Goldilocks.' She jiggled her golden hair, her smile reaching the edges of her blue eyes. She nudged the air with her thumb. 'This lot, the four bears.'

I laughed at the memory of her ignorance to her intrusion, and my nervousness drifted away, making way for complacency, and I accidently caught sight of Tyler. His eyes met mine. My stomach lurched into my throat, my inhibitions returning in full force with an ever-present barrage of butterflies. His eyes pulled me in, and I darted mine away.

'But then she shared her peanut butter, chocolate cupcakes with us,' Max said.

A collective moan broke out around the table. Those cupcakes – too good.

'So...family?' Amber's soothing voice made the push come across as a gentle nudge, but I wanted to elbow her in the side. Leave the poor guy alone.

'No, we know no one, and no one knows us,' he answered, sounding briefly dispirited. 'Although I did run into someone earlier who looked familiar.' He surveyed me across the table, amusement in his eyes. 'Or should I say, she ran into me?'

Great, like I needed a reminder of my earlier humiliation. I wanted to smack that look off his face. I also wanted to hide under the table, or maybe climb the tree behind me.

Instead, as the conversation continued, I sat fixed to the seat, whilst those butterflies launched an attack on my insides, willing me to be sick. I tried to come up with an excuse to leave but couldn't find one. Nothing that wouldn't send off alarm bells with my friends who sometimes knew me more than I liked.

It was torture. Like trying to contain a rabid dog. So many conflicting emotions I needed to squash before I came across as some kind of psycho. There'd be absolutely no reason to look freaked out and shaken up. Nothing I felt would make any sense to these guys unless I told them why.

I managed to steal occasional looks at my mobile, creating a barrier around me. Nothing like a phone to deflect conversation.

'Are you all right?' Amber said quietly. 'You're extra quiet. Bad dream last night?' I'd never confided in her or Cal about what my dreams were made of, but still, she cared, and in that particular moment, it made an excellent distraction.

'Yeah,' I answered. A nightmare – sitting across from me.

'Need to share?' I always felt safe with Amber. She'd never connected my dreams with news events, and I usually removed certain details that might implicate me, but this was one dream I wasn't willing to divulge.

'Nah, that's okay. Thanks.' I slid my eyes away, and Amber left me alone with my thoughts – curse words included – as they screamed inside me.

My head ached from the effort of ignoring my inner ramblings about what he might be thinking. It was even harder to avoid looking in his direction. My eyes kept betraying me, fleeting to meet his. But it didn't matter how exquisite they were, constant, involuntary, out-of-focus glances across the table were not my idea of a peaceful lunchtime. Even worse was feeling his eyes on me while I distracted myself.

When the bell finally rang, I shot up faster than a SpaceX rocket, slamming my knee on the underside of the table as I tried to bolt.

'Shit.' I winced and slumped back on the bench.

'You okay?' Amber placed her hand on my back as I hunched over.

I gritted my teeth, avoiding all five sets of eyes as I stood again and threw my bag over my shoulder. 'Perfectly fine. Gotta get to class.'

I left them gathering their own gear and hurried up the path to Geography. Heavy footsteps quickened behind me, and I nearly jumped out of my skin when Tyler appeared and matched my pace.

'I wanted to catch you before you left.' He brushed his fingers through his hair and tucked his hands into his shoulder straps. 'I know you recognise me.' His eyes pleaded with mine, the desperation evident in the tremor and speed as he continued, 'Please don't say anything, no one can know.'

Was he talking about the plane crash? No, he said recognise, which I did. My pulse gathered momentum. Was he talking about the dream, about being like me?

I'd been living alone on a deserted island for so long that when the rescue boat sailed past I forgot how to shout. It stood before me but I was lost for words.

I shook my head, gave myself a virtual slap in the face and asked, 'You mean about the dreams?'

'What?' Tyler slowed then caught back up. 'No.' He shook his head. 'About my dad, the crash. You recognised my name, please don't tell anyone.'

The boat sailed straight past and I slammed back into the sand. I stumbled on a crack in the cement and steadied my feet if not my heart. 'Right, yeah, that's what I meant.' I turned away from him, my feet picking up speed. How humiliating.

Of course he hadn't recognised me. Even if he saw me in the dream he wouldn't remember it when he woke – I wasn't really there. In my eagerness, I'd jumped to the wrong conclusion, and once again embarrassed myself because of this Goddamn supposed gift.

But I couldn't let my anxiety stand in the way of his. I turned to Tyler. 'I won't say anything. I get it. Your secret's safe with me.'

He let out a breath. 'Thanks.'

I nodded and the large double doors ahead burst open. We jumped aside as half a dozen blue and white uniform-clad students spilled out. We manoeuvred around them and made our way inside.

Tyler glanced around the room, looked down at the timetable in his hand, and then up again, eyes wide. 'Jada. What're you doing here?'

A girl maybe a couple of years younger than Tyler, but with an identical shade of hair, dark brown with natural light streaks, rounded the corner from the library.

'Trying to work out where I'm meant to be,' she mumbled and shrugged a shoulder, staring at her own slip of paper.

'Want some help?' I asked, leaning to peer at the timetable. She angled it toward me, and I ran my finger over the days. 'G12E, Maths.' I stuck out my tongue and imitated a gag.

Her face remained lifeless, but Tyler laughed. 'Jada loves Maths.'

My face fell. 'Oh, sorry.' I brushed at the loose strands of hair around my ears.

'Lucy, this is my sister, Jada. Jada meet Lucy.'

She parted with a weak smile. 'Hi.' I couldn't tell if her lack of vitality was due to shyness, grief, or her personality.

'Nice to meet you.' I placed a foot on the bottom step of the stairs, resting my hand on the railing, and shifted my attention back to Tyler. 'Where you headed?'

'Geography. G9.' He slid the scrap of paper in his pocket and looked up the stairs. 'God, I'm so lost.'

I couldn't help smiling at his awkwardness. 'I can show you both.'

We trudged up the stairs, their presence sending my breath into uneven flurries. Thank goodness for the distracting clang of locker doors and taunting kids scurrying into classrooms.

I stopped at the top of the stairs and pointed down the corridor. 'You're that way, Jada. Turn right at the end, it's the first classroom on your left.'

Shoulders hunched and head down, she muttered a thank you and shuffled away. I led Tyler in the opposite direction.

'Here we are. Mr Beck's great. One of my favourites.' I stepped into the room, Tyler bumbling in behind me.

I slid into a seat at the back of the class. My bag fell heavily off my shoulders to the floor, and I pulled out my books, glancing back to the front of the class where Tyler chatted with the teacher. With a small nod, Mr Beck offered a sympathetic look and patted him on the upper arm.

Tyler walked toward the back of the room. I shifted my gaze and glimpsed the empty table beside me. Crap.

My poor chest endured another pounding from the heart I was beginning to hate. Anyone'd think I'd never seen a good-looking boy before. Traitor.

I dropped my eyes to my books and opened to a page, any page. The words blurred, my eyes unable to focus. They couldn't, not when everything had tuned into him. He eased past the desk next to mine, and I concentrated on keeping my head and eyes down, though still unfocused. The chair grated against the floor, and my spine shuddered. I jumped as his bag landed with a thud at his feet, and then, as though he meant to punish me for ignoring him, scraped that damn chair again as he sat himself down.

Shoulders lifted high, eyes focused straight ahead. Geography was my life; it meant nothing that he sat within arm's reach. *Yeah, right.*

My appearance showed little of my racing heart, with no one aware how desperately I needed to take a huge gulp of air. If it weren't for the heat on my neck I'd have let my hair down and created a thick black curtain to hide behind. I'd never been so conscious of anyone's presence before and grew acutely aware of every little move I made, the ringing in my ears, the jackhammer in my chest.

'Righteo, everyone.' I nearly fell off my seat at the boom of Mr Beck's voice. 'Let's continue where we left off last lesson, you'll get an opportunity to work on your assignments later.' Muffled utterances and groans filled the room. 'Lucy, I'll get you to explain to Tyler where we're at.' Jeez, could this day get any better?

Breathing in, I shifted to face Tyler. I avoided his eyes, instead looking past him to Jason and Zack, the jerks who'd driven Daniel Bonheur to suicide two years ago. They were the two biggest tools in school. My hatred for them boiled over. With a glare I repelled from the foul sight. Tyler glanced over his shoulder and swept back to me, a slight frown on his face, a question.

'Biggest jerks this side of the equator.'

He raised his eyebrows.

'Don't ask.' It wasn't a story I liked to repeat, especially when I hadn't been able to prevent the outcome.

I filled him in on the class details instead, what to expect, what to read up on. 'You do this class at your old school?'

'Yeah.' He tapped his thumb on the desk and shifted in his seat.

'You all right?'

'Huh? Yeah, sure.' He stilled his thumb, and his voice steadied. 'Just getting used to all the changes.'

My chest constricted at the obvious pain I sensed in him. 'Give it one game with Cal and Sean and you'll wonder what you ever missed from home.' I clapped a hand over my mouth. 'Crap, sorry.'

He lowered his eyes. 'See now that's why it's better if people don't know.'

'I'm sorry.' I screwed up my face.

He peered up at me from his hunched-over position. 'That's what I mean. I don't want you to be sorry. It's uncomfortable for everyone. Think you can do me a favour and pretend you don't know anything?'

I let out a mini huff and nodded. 'I'm good at pretending.' I returned to my work and focused on evening out my breath. *Get a grip.* He'd been here one day, I'd *known* him for less than two hours and already the struggle to control the pull felt as large as the Louvre.

But maybe if I understood why the dream had come back, or how in hell the details were as accurate as a security camera, I'd feel a fraction less freaked out by my lack of control around my dream apparition. I needed to see Granny Tess. Maybe she could help decipher the questions buzzing in my brain. But until then, yes, I could pretend.

—5—

M UM SLUMPED INTO HER chair at the table, makeup smeared
around her eyes, and wisps of hair fell from her once tightly
pulled back bun, evidence of an attempt to catch up on sleep after
her night shift.

Jake and Ollie galloped down the stairs, bustling shoulders as
they whirled into the room. Jake was almost a foot taller than our
younger brother. A lot skinnier too. Ollie still had that teen tubbi-
ness he'd lose once he eventually had a growth spurt. They jostled
for a seat, Ollie taking a swipe when Jake rubbed him on the head
like a dog.

'When you gettin' a haircut, Shaggy?'

'When you stop bein' a toss bag.'

Dad settled into his seat, placing the remote control beside
his fork. The TV hummed quietly from the other end of the room,
which he'd barely taken his eyes off because, of course, the news
was on.

I couldn't understand Dad's desire to read and watch the news,
or his persistent urge to ram it down our throat, as he so often did,
but maybe it ran in his blood. As a reporter for the Antil Springs
Newspaper, he was your regular Clark Kent, complete with suit,
tie, and black-framed glasses – although no heroics or cape, and
with a slightly broader frame.

Dad and I had identical black hair and pale skin, but when it came to the news we were like opposite ends of a magnet. Where he was drawn to the dramas around the world, I was equally repulsed by them.

Still, it was a struggle to ignore the flickering light behind Jake and Ollie's heads. I pushed the food around my plate; the peas rolled past the carrots and popped as I caught them under my fork. I felt as fragile as the peas, that in any moment, with barely a prod, I might burst too, explode even.

'Aren't you hungry, love?'

'What?' I jerked my head up. Mum slid a fork of chicken into her mouth. 'Uh, no not really. Hey, can I go to Granny Tess and Pop's for the weekend? I don't have any shifts, thought I could go hang with them for a bit.'

'They're already coming here for lunch on Saturday.'

'They are?' That'd save me a bus fare. I shrugged. 'Guess I'll just see them then.'

'You okay?' Mum asked slowly, her curiosity coated in disinterest as her eyes stayed fixed on the cutlery in her hands. I knew what she was thinking.

My dreams had once been the epicentre of our family; they'd demanded attention and vied to be heard. Mum had never been comfortable with that though, so we played a continual game of pretend. I pretended I no longer had them, and that she didn't know I still did, and we both pretended I was perfectly fine.

Mum glanced at me, waiting for an answer.

'Strange day at school. I'm fine.' I pronged some peas.

'Hey, Mum, can you take me into May on Friday night?' Ollie conveniently pulled her attention away. He was good at that, and I loved him for it. 'Eddy and Fletch wanna go to the movies, but they'll already be there so I need a ride.'

Mayfield was a fifteen-minute drive from Antil Springs. It lacked the beauty of Antil, but we couldn't knock it. It had all the things we didn't: a cinema, the hospital where Mum and Cal's mum, Marie, worked, and the rival soccer team.

'I'm on a late on Friday, I won't be heading there until later. Jake, honey, can you take him? Maybe you can take Sarah to the movies at the same time?'

'Ew, gross,' Ollie groaned. 'And have 'em smoochin' behind us in the back row, no thanks.'

'But if you need a lift,' Jake said with a grin, 'I'd be happy to help.'

A smile tugged at the corner of my lips.

'Dad, can you take me?' Ollie's voice pleaded.

Dad dragged his eyes away from the TV and joined in the teasing. 'How much's it worth to you?'

'I'll do the front lawns on Saturday?'

'You're on, kiddo.' He was easily swayed when distracted. His eyes flitted back to the TV and he lifted the remote to increase the volume.

'Dad, seriously?' I gripped the edge of the table.

'It'll only take a minute, I wanted to hear the latest on that young couple—'

'Tom.' Mum shot Dad the look that, combined with her tone, meant she didn't need to say any more.

Relief washed over me. I put my fork down and turned to her. 'Do you mind if I go to my room?'

'No, of course not.' Her worry was evident in the slight hesitation of her words.

Once upstairs, I sat on my bed and removed my blue Converse. My phone beeped from the top of the tallest paper mountain on the table. Grabbing it, I brought up a message from Max.

Max: *Forgot to ask at lunch if you were feeling better, did you see the boy again?? Remember where you saw him??*

Me: *Yeah, all good, pretty sure I stood behind him in the canteen last week*

Lies, always lies. I changed into my pyjamas and threw my clothes into the washing bag behind the door.

Max: *See told you, although it wouldn't be so bad to conjure up guys from our dreams hey??*

I smiled.

Me: *Depends on the kind of guys you're dreaming of*

I'd dreamed up plenty of unsavoury types and, come to think of it, I had no idea which type Tyler was in this scenario. I climbed into bed and waited for the impending reply.

Max: *Lol true. See you tomorrow, night hon x*
Me: *Night Max x*

I set the phone down and scanned the postcards tacked on my wardrobe, sent to me by Granny Tess and Pop from places they'd visited around the world, and above my bed, at my favourite piece of artwork. Granny Tess had painted it for me – an oil-painted canvas of the Canadian mountains covered in soft powdery snow. It beckoned me, called to me, showed me some of what lay beyond the edges of our small town – if I'd ever be brave enough to leave. But each night, my fantasy of a winter on the other side of the world got trampled with blood-splattered boots, when I'd close my eyelids and witness the horrors of the ugly world beyond the window panes of my room.

I flicked off my lamp and twitched with the impossibility of sleep. Over and over, my mind replayed the events of the day in sickening vibrancy. It was like being forced to watch reruns of a bad TV sitcom you didn't enjoy the first time.

I willed my eyes to close but couldn't quiet my thoughts as images of Canada, airports, and chiselled cheekbones remained. But it was the lady from two night's previous who I saw in my dream when I eventually nodded off. This time she reached onto the passenger seat and dug into her handbag for her water bottle. Her foot lifted off the accelerator, and the car swerved slightly to the left. As she straightened and lifted the bottle to her lips, the rock that'd previously brought her death sailed past her side window.

*****

MAX AND I STROLLED through the school to our table for morning break. The two-storey building loomed ahead, its dull orange brick a harsh contrast to the surprisingly beautiful day of blue skies and a scattering of cotton clouds. We were a winter town, but the mountains were selfish buggers and although it rarely snowed in town we expected more wintry grey than this perfection in the lead up to winter.

It sweetened the palate for what waited around the corner. My stomach lurched. And the moment Tyler came into view my feet hesitated. It didn't matter that I'd dreamed something else in the meantime. Seeing him made the plane accident slap me in the face all over again.

Max looped her arm in mine, easing the way forward. 'What's up, hon?'

'Huh, uh nothing.' I shook my head.

'Really? My guess'd be a nightmare.' She angled her head, knowing me too well. My shoulders sagged and she squeezed my arm. 'What was it this time? You can tell me.'

I knew I could tell her, and I desperately needed a listening ear. 'Plane crash, but can we not talk about it?' Not when we were five steps from Tyler.

She let go of my arm and we slid onto the bench. 'If you say so.'

'Say so, what?' Sean asked.

'Noth–'

'Luce had another dream. Doesn't want to talk about it.'

I rolled my eyes. 'And yet we are.'

Max laughed. 'I am, *we're* not.'

'Nice try.' I looked down, hyper aware of Tyler's presence at the table. I rubbed my hands over my pants before lifting my head. He studied me, and almost as if he knew my inner turmoil, lifted his lips in sympathy. *Shit. The dreams could be the least of my worries.*

'What about?' Sean ignored me and peered at Max, waiting for her to answer.

She shrugged. 'Can't say. But it did involve a flying metal object crashing to earth.'

Tyler's eyes widened, flickering in defeat. Damn it. I elbowed Max in the side. 'You're a shit sometimes.'

She wrapped her arms around me, and whispered in my ear, 'Sorry.' Then louder for everyone to hear. 'But you love me.'

'Unfortunately.' I tried to smile, but Tyler's flat expression unnerved me. I was the girl who couldn't keep her mouth shut, who couldn't pretend at all. Dream or no dream, I'd been talking about a plane accident.

Cal's eyebrows creased. 'You had a dream about a crashing spaceship? Why can't I have sick dreams like that?'

I didn't answer him.

I SETTLED INTO THE back corner table, determined to talk to Tyler before the lesson was over. I lined my pen up with the opened book on the desk, left side; no, right side. *Damn it, just leave it alone.* I twisted my fingers together in my lap, wishing I could wring the nerves out of me like a damp cloth. I'd been thinking about Tyler for most of the day, about what he must think of me snitching on him. I couldn't handle the guilt, even if it wasn't true. But the moment he walked into the room I froze. His eyes flitted to mine and then lowered to his phone, and all the words I planned to say clamped together in my throat.

He sauntered up the aisle, impossible to ignore with his lean figure and strong stride. His bag hung off one shoulder while he fidgeted with his phone. A set of bulky headphones sat over his head, and he slid them around his neck as he dropped into the chair at the table beside mine.

I cleared my throat and returned to my book, wiping the pages as if straightening them. My fingers brushed at the pen, sending it flying off the desk, and as it hit the floor, the chink echoed painfully behind my temple.

Crap. I sensed Tyler's movement from the corner of my eye and eased around in my chair to finally look at him, I could do this. He held the pen out for me but didn't say anything. His smile seeped with humour, as if the mere fact I'd dropped my pen was worth enjoying, or perhaps he found my discomfort amusing.

I plucked the pen from his grip. My apology could wait.

'Thanks,' I said almost inaudibly, before returning my eyes to the front of the room.

'*Il n'y a pas de quoi.*' He paused and clarified, 'You're welcome.' What was that? Spanish, French, Italian? They all sounded the same, but my stupid disloyal heart didn't care what language it was. Spoken so smoothly, it sounded like magic. It took every ounce of willpower to maintain an even breath, but then he leaned closer and spoke again. 'Why were you dreaming of a plane crash?'

I stiffened, knowing the moment of impact had arrived. 'I'm sorry. I know it looks like I said something, but I didn't tell her about you...about your dad.'

'I didn't think you had.'

My shoulders slumped. So I apologised for nothing, great.

He continued, 'But you did dream of a plane crash.'

Fight or flight, I tried to back out of the conversation. I didn't want him knowing what a freak I was right off the bat. 'Yeah, so?'

Lines etched along the length of his forehead. 'You don't think that's weird?'

I shrugged. 'I have dreams. Very lucid dreams.' I shifted in my seat, back straight, eyes on my book, taking on the perfect charade as if my heart hadn't just skipped a few beats.

'Oh, okay.'

I exhaled, and Mr Beck's boom from the front of the room conveniently grabbed my attention. Give me the weekend. A little time to let the events of the last two days sink in, to come to terms with Tyler jumping out of my head and into my life. Then maybe I might be able to have a conversation without freaking the hell out about what he knew, or didn't know, if anything.

I did have an overactive imagination, after all.

—6—

I WALTZED INTO WORK later that night wearing a grin like the makeup at a beauty contest – thick and flawless. I welcomed the distraction work always brought to my ceaseless thoughts, but Amber was rostered on with me and I needed to avoid the inevitable questions.

We worked for her mum, Laurie, who'd started up a catering business when they moved to Antil. I began working for her eighteen months ago when she was short a waitress for a wedding. It was a dream job – smile, pass out food, repeat. No one ever paid attention to lowly waitresses and that suited me perfectly fine. And the food at the end of the night – to die for.

But my brain activity had reached seismic proportions, and no amount of work could distract me from my thoughts. My foot caught on the strip between the kitchen and the hall, and I stumbled into the room where crowds of middle aged couples mingled in stiff celebration of someone's fortieth birthday. The tray of pulled pork sliders wobbled on my unsteady palm.

'Easy there.' A man in a black suit rested his hand on my back. I offered him a tight smile, a silent thanks for his help. Trying to act professional, I straightened my shoulders and proceeded to circle the room.

'Lucy, your smiles are just as important as my food,' Laurie said when I returned to the kitchen with one lousy slider remaining.

'Your smiles show confidence in your offerings. I can put as much love in my creations behind the scenes, but unless you give it when you hand it out, it'll only taste half as sweet.'

Amber rolled her eyes and lowered her empty tray onto the stainless steel bench.

'I saw that.' Laurie pointed her finger at her daughter, but the light in her eyes told me she was laughing as much as scolding.

'Sorry. My head's elsewhere.' I picked up a tray of fresh food, sweet scented miniature cupcakes, but Laurie stopped me before I left the room.

'It has been all night, I think. Do you need to go home?' She scanned the room. 'There's enough of us to manage for the rest of the night.'

I didn't want to go home early; it wasn't like that'd make my thoughts go away. But this work thing wasn't playing out as intended either. I lowered my tray and my head, I hated letting people down. 'I'll send Dad a message.'

Amber flung me a sympathetic look before Laurie shooed her from the room. I shot out a text to Dad, and kept busy cleaning while I waited for my ride.

'You have any leftovers yet?' I asked Laurie as she strolled out of the cool room.

She pushed a bag of buns along the bench. 'I don't know about sweets yet, but you can take these, they won't be used tonight. And I'll grab you the leftover pork.'

I loaded the bags of food into the back of the car and jumped into the front seat.

'Shelter first?' Dad asked eyeing off the bags.

'Yep.'

'Smells amazing. I wonder if they realise they're the luckiest homeless for miles.'

'Yeah, *so* lucky. I'll bet that's exactly what they think when they get Laurie's leftovers: "Gee, I'm so glad I've got nowhere to sleep tonight."'

Dad laughed and pulled onto the road. 'You know what I mean.'

The clock on the centre console clicked over to the hour, and my heart accelerated, bracing for what naturally came next. Dad reached over and dialled up the volume. Even though he didn't know they were the source of my nightmares, I wished he had an ounce of awareness for what the stories did to me. Sometimes it even felt like he did it on purpose. Like he was trying to harden me up to the realities of life, as if he were training me for a game of soccer. If only he knew I'd already had years of training, I was as fit as Ronaldo.

Without Mum to step in, and unable to reach into the back seat for my earphones in time, I had no choice but to accept the invasion. But what was new? My life was full of things beyond my control. The news began, and I gripped the sides of my seat. My eyes flickered closed as the cascade of words seeped through me.

'The identity of the deceased man discovered by two joggers in Sydney's North East yesterday morning is believed to be that of Aaron Jacobson, forty-eight year-old English professor and father from Melbourne.'

The news report went on to say the coroner had determined the cause of death to be cardiac arrest and did not suspect foul play. I exhaled, as horrible as it was to put a scale on death, this one I could handle...I hoped.

When I arrived at the shelter a few minutes later, Patty greeted me at the door. We stood eye to eye, but only because I stood one step lower than her. 'Lucy.' She ushered me into the room. 'I wasn't expecting you this early.' Her crinkled face scrunched even more at her endless smile.

'Quiet night so Laurie sent me home.' My smile formed

painlessly with her warmth rubbing off on me. It was easy to forget my troubles when the room housed a group of men who had nowhere to call home. All faces I recognised, all regulars. Stubbly, gap-toothed Henry grinned as I followed Patty to the kitchen. These people were amazing. I admired their resilience and strength in the face of so much hardship. If only I had as much. But it was difficult when the hardships were all in your head.

When I finally crawled into bed all I wanted was the black void of sleep, but thanks to my less than attentive father, it really was no surprise when death knocked on my door during the night.

THE MAN RAN WITH *determined speed, darkness encroaching on the quiet path. I pumped my arms, stretched my legs further, but he surpassed my normal pace and I struggled to keep up. His tall strides grew staggered and slowed.*

I spun around, my hair floundering behind me. He was alone. Crap. I sped along the path, gaining on him easily. His face contorted in pain, and he gripped at his shoulder, his knees buckling beneath him. I reached out for him, but couldn't stop his fall as he collapsed to the ground. I wasn't a visible participant in tonight's viewing, only a useless bystander.

Dread pummelled into my chest. No one would hear his cries of pain; no one would find him until the morning.

The desperation in his eyes as he reached the same lonely conclusion seared a hole of despair straight through my heart, and I crumpled onto the ground beside him.

Sweat coated the back of my neck. I sat and pushed my hair aside to allow some relief. Rubbing at my temple I let out a small whimper for the man who, in his final fleeting minutes, must've felt so alone. I reached blindly for my jet bracelet, sliding it onto my wrist, and grabbed at the pencil and book in my top drawer. Half awake, half asleep, I let my fingers glide over the page, the form of his face, ever so slowly, taking shape beneath the lead.

*****

'OH, LUCY, MY DARLING girl, look at you, gorgeous as always.' Granny Tess held her arms wide, taking me in as I reached the bottom of the stairs. 'You look tired though, dear. Are you getting enough sleep? You know they say a sixteen-year-old should sleep for at least ten hours.'

I wrapped my arms around her. 'I think it's actually a lot less than that. But don't worry, I'm getting enough.' It probably didn't help that I'd only woken thirty minutes earlier, and from a gut-wrenching nightmare.

I loved Granny Tess's ability to compliment and criticise at the same time; it was oddly endearing. Surprisingly, though, I never felt judged by her. She said what she saw, in a less than subtle way, but she loved me all the same.

Granny Tess's dyed red-orange hair, normally rolled in a bun, fell loosely down to the hollow in her back as she headed into the kitchen to help Mum with the tea and coffees. She never was the sort to conform to the ideal grandparent model. She still wanted to pretend she was twenty-five. With red hair instead of the usual purple blond, and long when society said short, she fought hard against the norm, and that was only her hair.

'Don't pay her any attention, Lucy Lou, she's just jealous.' Pop looked sideways at Granny Tess, a small smile on his round face. His eyes were alight with happiness, a constant whenever he was around any of his grandchildren. 'You look perfect.' He opened his arms, and I stepped into them.

After lunch I snatched the first opportunity to speak with Granny Tess. Mum had disappeared into the kitchen, Dad was on the phone for work, and Pop went to watch Ollie play a computer game.

'I need to talk to you.' I grabbed her arm and, forgetting for a moment she was nearly seventy-five years old, dragged her out through the sliding door into the enclosed outdoor pergola. The weather had shifted during the night, and rain tapped endlessly like pebbles against the glass surrounding the small room. The chill of cool winds seeping through cracks in the bricks made me shiver. We lowered ourselves onto the tattered green outdoor sofa, the musty scent growing from our bodies pressing into the cushions.

'What is it, dear? Something's bothering you.' Understatement of the century. She frowned, pressed her lips together, and waited.

I folded my hands in my lap. 'What would you say if I told you I dreamed of someone before I met them in real life?' I gulped. Always the moment of truth when I laid myself bare.

Granny Tess smiled, the edges of her eyes laced with years and years of wrinkles, or as she would call them, laugh lines. She caught hold of my fingers and squeezed. 'I would say tell me more.'

I sucked in a lungful of air and released the avalanche of tension I'd been holding onto for the last two days. I told her about the plane crash, about Tyler, and not being entirely sure if he recognised me or not, even though saying it out loud sounded like the most absurd idea in the history of forever. I exhaled. My heart had climbed a mountain, but now that the words were out, the throbbing lessened to a steady beat.

'I don't know all the answers, but this is what I think. You're connecting with other people's souls in your dreams, and that's how you see what you do. So let's say you've gathered the memory of the last moments before those people were killed. If the last moment for the pilot was saying goodbye to his son, then it's fair to say you're seeing the truth, his truth.'

'And now he's moved to Antil.'

'Precisely. And I would guess you're still dreaming it because you would desperately like to help those people on the plane.'

'I want to help all the people I see die. But I can't, it's too late.'

'Mmm.' Granny Tess retreated into deep thought, her brows inching closer, fingers pressing the pleats on her pale pink pants. She fixed her eyes on me, still faraway, but here as well. 'I think you're like me, or how I once was at least. See, the thing is, most people are so concerned with their own anxieties that that's what they dream of, but you, Lucy, are such a deeply passionate person who cares so much for everyone else, that you dream of their problems as though they were your own.'

Yeah, sometimes the weight of it felt too much, but not caring would be as foreign to me as walking the streets of Rome.

Granny Tess's chest rose and fell painstakingly slow. 'I'm going to tell you something, but you have to promise not to freak out.'

'After what I just told you, not a chance.'

She glanced over her shoulder into the house, her thick red hair swishing over her face. Dad sat at the table with Pop, the remains of lunch still in the centre of the table. He viewed us briefly with a tight smile, a 'what're you two doing' question in his eyes. He looked away and Granny Tess nodded once. To what, him? Me?

She patted her knee. 'Good. So you already know I used to dream like you, although most of the people I dreamed of hadn't died–'

'But if those people weren't dead, how could you dream it? You just said it was their dead souls connecting with mine.'

'See, I told you I didn't know all the answers.' She chuckled. 'Really I don't. I don't think anyone does. I think we're all fumbling our way through this...I've been so worried about getting this wrong, Lucy.' She looked down at her hands folded perfectly in her lap.

'It's okay, I can handle it.' My pulse quickened. Could I?

She dragged in a breath before continuing. 'When I was fourteen, and my father was on his death bed, I found out he was like us.'

I whirled back in the seat, the shock rippling through me. There were more? I always thought it was only me and Granny Tess. Without evidence to prove otherwise, it had been easy to believe. 'Your dad was a dreamer?'

'Well I suspect, because of what he said. "Dream well, Tessa, change the world." I'd already been dreaming for a couple of years, so in some ways I knew what he was talking about. But change the world? In my dreams? For years after he died I felt like I failed to live up to his expectations. Then one day I did change the world. For one person at least.'

What the hell did that mean? I held my breath, the wind whispering faintly against the glass doors. I lifted a cushion onto my lap, snuggling into its meagre warmth.

Granny Tess spoke so softly I could barely hear her. 'There was this girl at school who wore big thick glasses, and she hated it because kids used to tease her – grade twelve, would you believe, and kids still teasing about something like that. Anyhow, I dreamed she didn't need them anymore, and I went to school the following day and her eyes were fixed.' Granny Tess's smile widened, pride evident in her eyes.

'No way.' I shook my head. I always wondered if it were possible; maybe that was why I always hoped so hard. But holy cow, I never expected that.

'I know. Once I figured out what I was doing I couldn't wait to do more. It was only small stuff, but huge to the people I helped.

Sometimes I helped the homeless find a bed for the night. And I remember overhearing my uncle, he was a farmer, telling someone how much they needed rain. I made it rain.'

'Why don't you dream anymore? What changed?'

'I don't really know, they simply went away.' She peered absently out into the fading light through the window behind me as if remembering something long gone.

'Just like that?' I couldn't imagine my life without my dreams. As much as I hated them, they felt as fixed and sure as if they were another organ in my body. Sure, I'd love them gone, but how does the saying go...if you can't beat 'em join 'em. Yeah, my life was made up of unavoidable resignation.

'More or less. I grew up, stopped caring so much and they were gone.' She shifted her gaze back to me.

'Stopped caring?'

'Yes. It's exhausting, isn't it? That's why you dream in the first place, because you care.'

'Not enough to save someone's life.' Sharing my irritation, the wind rose to a roar, whistling through the gutters and trees.

Granny Tess heaved out her own anguish. 'No, maybe not. I tried once.'

'You did?'

'Yes.' Sadness always made people look old, and right now with the lines etched on her forehead, the cracks pushing from the edges of her lips, and the distant stare in her eyes, Granny Tess looked old. 'But there comes a time when even we must accept our limits.'

'So why do I dream at all? What's the point if it changes nothing?' I slumped back in the chair.

'I don't know. But maybe this boy is the reason. Maybe you can help him. Or maybe he can help you? You said yourself you weren't sure if he recognised you. What if he did, wouldn't that mean something wonderful?'

'Yeah, but when I mentioned the dreams he brushed it off.'

'Have you ever sidestepped around something that makes you uncomfortable? Scared even?' Only nearly every day. Could he be equally worried about being found out?

TELLING GRANNY TESS DIDN'T help me understand as much as I'd hoped, but her insight did settle the nerves rumbling through me from the last two days, but by Sunday, knowing I'd be seeing Tyler again the next day, the tension returned.

The rain insisted on hanging around, but I didn't care, I needed a run. I laced up my shoes, stuck in my earphones and bolted out the door.

Outside, with the wind in my hair and music in my ears, it allowed me time to process. My nose caught the full brunt of the frigid air rushing past me, and the rain pierced my face with an intensely satisfying bite. Feeling pain, real pain, reminded me I was alive, and *that* had always been more favourable than the alternative.

I ran past Tyler's house. The 'For Sale' sign was gone and a large black pot with a spiky purple plant now sat beside the front door. Despite the recent rain and new owners, the dying lawn had yet to come back to life.

I gritted my teeth, a flood of turmoil returning, and charged up the hill, turning up the music. An old one, The Cat Empire's 'One Four Five' blared in my ears. My muscles burned as I pushed myself and increased my speed. I left the road for my dirt track, the once crunchy, brown leaves now soft and slippery, adding a spring as my feet hit the ground.

I made it to the top of the hill, out into the clearing where the rain continued to fall, and my lip quivered from the cold that inched through my body, but I felt nothing except peace. Right until the harrowing thoughts from the past few days invaded my mind. But if all I got was a moment, then that's what I'd take. The starving didn't scoff at a crumb of bread in the hope they'd soon see a loaf – not if all they'd known was a crumb.

I gathered my crumb and started back down the hill as the assaulting wind and rain pummelled down. But it took a lot more than a fierce deluge to hold me back. Determination drove me on. This week would be different. I knew what was coming. And regardless of what Tyler did or didn't know, if there was a way I could help, even if I had to share my crumb, then that's what I'd do.

—7—

MONDAY ARRIVED AND I psyched myself all morning for Geography. I could do this.

Shoulders back, I walked into class, my smile tucked in my pocket for when Tyler walked in the door. I could do approachable.

I slipped into my seat and waited. Students filed into the room, and half of them must've recently had P.E. because the stench of a Rexona factory wafted in behind them. I pressed my hands between my jiggling knees, eyes flitting to the door.

Mr Beck began the lesson, the drone of his voice trailed into the background. I scanned the room, maybe I missed his entrance.

I examined the backs of the heads. After only a few meetings with Tyler I'd easily recognise him from behind. I closed my eyes. He wasn't there. My heart sank to the same depth as the wave washing me in relief. I exhaled with the slump of my shoulders.

Damn it. I was braced and ready for lift off. Now I'd need to diffuse all my inflated air, but at least I could breathe again.

At the end of the lesson I headed off to break, with the added bonus of being able to enjoy it with my crew in relative peace.

'You guys all set for the weekend?' Cal said, landing his broad frame onto the bench.

Sean slid in beside me. 'Mate, you kidding? Course we are.'

It was a dumb question. We'd been hanging out for it for weeks, as usual. Cal's parents owned a holiday house by the lake, a half hour's drive north of Antil. The trip was a yearly tradition for Richie's birthday, and this year it came at the beginning of two weeks of school holidays.

'Dad's fixed the boat so it's all set to go, said we shouldn't have any trouble with it for now.'

'Sick. Fingers crossed it's a bit drier by then too.' Sean took a large bite of his chocolate donut, reminding me of my own hunger.

I pulled out some kind of muesli slice from my bag as a leaf from the overhanging maple tree fluttered onto my shoulder. I put the slice on the table and picked up the browning leaf, twirling the stem between my thumb and forefinger. I loved our maple. We never had a short supply of gum trees around our school and town – they meant home – but there was something magical about this tree. Something provoked a sense of wonder every time I sat beneath its shelter. I looked at it in awe, the same way half the school admired the German exchange student, simply for being foreign, for being native of somewhere exotic and fanciful.

Sometimes I imagined I'd been transported to the tree's homeland in Canada, no longer at school, but out travelling the world. Oh, who was I kidding, the thought terrified me. Like the bed sheets in the school sick room, you could never be sure what you'd get. Home, on the other hand, was like a quilted blanket – warm and familiar. Although not always perfect, and even if there were stains, at least they were yours. I recognised the stains from home, found comfort in them even. I'd just have to snuggle up in my blanket and *pretend* to be in Canada, it'd have to be enough.

'Hey Luce, you mind if Tyler joins us on the weekend?' I flicked my head up. *Say what?* Cal waited expectantly on the other side of the table, his forearm resting on the wooden slats.

I wasn't sure I wanted to answer that question. I glanced over at Amber, and then Max and Sean on either side of me, equally curious looks on their faces. I frowned. 'Why you asking me?'

''Cause you're the only one who hasn't answered.' Right. I guess they said yes, then. As usual, I was caught daydreaming and left with little choice in my response. Say no and I'd look like a jerk, because even if I was a little guarded around Tyler, what reason would I have to say no?

I hated that there'd be no escaping him while at the lake, but then I could never escape my dreams anyway so that'd be no different. And what would it mean for him? To get a break from the grief that surrounded him, even if momentarily. Maybe my first opportunity to make a difference just presented itself.

I shrugged. 'Sure.' I tore open my muesli bar and halfway through my mouthful, as if it were the most normal thing in the world, Tyler showed up and sat directly across from me. I nearly choked, and tears sprang to my eyes as I tried to contain the urge to cough my food out everywhere.

Cal patted Tyler on the back. 'Hey dude, you're here. Luce said you weren't at school today.'

'She did?' He glanced my way as I rapidly finished chewing. 'I wonder what made her think that.'

I swallowed, praying the pieces would go down. 'I...uh...didn't see you in class. Sorry, I...assumed.' Everyone turned and stared at me. My cheeks warmed and I wanted to slide under the table, or even better, board a plane and fly to London.

'Don't be sorry.' He didn't take his eyes off me. 'I'm just surprised you noticed.'

I scrunched my face. It wasn't like I'd been ignoring him. 'Yes, well...' I didn't know what to say and broke off a piece of the slice, popping it in my mouth, immediately regretting my decision. I was far too tense to chew. The table grew quiet, all eyes on us, flitting from Tyler to me.

'I got held up at home,' he said. I recognised the sad lift of his lips, that half smile you feign when you feel anything like smiling. God, how many times had I used one of those?

Conversation shifted and frivolity clamoured around the table again. My mind drifted away, but with all his enthusiasm I couldn't ignore Cal bragging about coaxing his teacher into an extension.

'Ms Lincoln ended up giving me that extension on my English essay. She *had* to take pity on the school's best soccer player for all the extra practice he's doing.' He puffed out his chest, but Cal didn't need to inflate anything, his presence alone was enough.

Amber's brows bunched together. 'She does know it's natural born talent and no extra practice was necessary, doesn't she?' She patted Cal on the knee.

'Yeah, nah, kept that detail to myself. But ya see, that's what happens when you're the best player: everyone knows it and you reap the rewards.' He hit his hand on the table, affirming his achievement.

Max rolled her eyes. 'You're such a charmer.'

'Why, thank you.' Cal displayed his usual all-consuming smile, where his eyes thinned to almost nothing and a white grin filled half his face.

With my elbow on the table, I rested my head in my palm, looking sideways to Cal before biting into my muesli bar. 'How do you manage to care *and* not give a crap all at the same time?'

He shrugged. 'It's not easy.'

'That's okay, you might be the best player' – Sean nudged Tyler with his elbow, a grin plastered across his face – 'but I'd rather be the best looker on the team any day. At least I get the attention of the girls instead of the teachers.'

'You sure your looks are getting the girl's attention, Sean? If they are they mustn't know where you live.' Max raised her perfectly shaped eyebrows at her brother, not even bothering to hide her amusement.

'Aaah, she got you there, dude.' Cal's shoulders shook with enjoyment. 'I on the other hand...' He wrapped an arm around Amber's waist, pulled her close, and planted a kiss on her cheek.

'You really think you can take that one as well? Which one of us did Luce choose, huh?' Sean said, glancing across the table, shoulders back, laughter in his dark eyes.

'Keep me out of this.' I held my hands out in defence.

'Yeah, and it must've been your incredibly good looks that kept her around,' Cal said, tilting his head to the side as if I hadn't spoken. 'Oh, hang on?' He scrunched his brow, mocking.

I started to laugh, but as I looked over at Sean and saw the flinch at having his still-painful bruise prodded, a surge of regret landed in my guts. Not regret that we were over, regret that Sean wished we weren't.

'All right, Cal. No need to torture us with reminders of our sordid affair,' I said, trying for a touch of humour.

'Is that what you're calling it now?' Amber surveyed me, and I focused on the thin scar above her left eyebrow to control the heat in my skin.

'No, I was just hoping to shut Cal up.' I elbowed him in the side, dreading it may've done the opposite. Stupid mouth. 'Besides, it was never a competition.'

'I know.' He cast a tender look at Amber, then trying not to laugh said, 'Sordid, hey?' Crap, I wouldn't live that one down.

I gulped a swig of water. How the hell did I land myself in this mud? Being reminded of my rotten lapse in judgement was bad on any day, but with Tyler as witness? Kill me now.

'I like the word sordid,' Amber said. I groaned and lowered my head onto the cold table top. She ignored the chuckles and continued, 'All the thoughts that one little word has conjured up make you two seem so much more interesting all of a sudden.'

I raised my head. 'Keep those thoughts to yourself. Nothing sordid happened. Imagine away, it won't change anything.'

'Except now everyone thinks we're sordid.' Sean winked and huffed out a laugh.

Shaking my head, I ripped off a piece of crust and threw it across the table at him. 'How did this conversation start?'

'Soccer, good looks, and a sordid affair,' Amber answered cheerily as always.

'So...' I chanced a look at Tyler, amusement in his eyes, arms folded over his chest. 'Do you have more siblings or only Jada?'

He smiled; he knew exactly what I was doing.

'Just her.'

'What do your Mum and Dad do, Tyler?' Amber must've thought my question granted her permission to interrogate further.

Tyler's easy posture stiffened, a fleeting expression of pain hovered over his face. 'They're actually not working at the moment,' he said, trailing off. Panic surged through me. I needed to say something before Amber tried to dig further. Tyler needed that dirt.

'So what do you do?' I jumped in, my voice not quite up to speed, choking on the words and attention. The relief in his eyes gave me the kick I needed to finish my sentence. 'In your spare time, that is?'

He closed his eyes, mouth curling up in a chuckle. 'Surf. Fat lot of good that'll do in a place like this.' Had anyone else noticed the pain behind those words?

'It'll actually do you a lotta good come winter and we get you on a board,' Cal said.

'You reckon?'

'For sure, dude. You'll be beatin' us down the hill in no time.'

'Beating you, you mean,' I said, smiling at Cal.

'All right, beating me. You won't beat Luce. No one can.'

'Is that a challenge?' Tyler studied me, the idea of it dancing behind his eyes. The thought made my pulse quicken.

I held his stare. 'Only if you like to lose.'

'Not particularly.'

'Looks like you've met your match, Luce.' Cal bumped his shoulder against mine.

'We'll see.' I reached into my bag for nothing except a reason to act unaffected by Tyler's expression of admiration and the traitorous and nasty butterflies that'd returned.

*****

EVERYONE HAD LONG GONE to bed. Intermittent bursts of bright light from the neighbour's sensor light being set off by a stray cat irritated me more than usual and prevented me from sleeping. That, and my mind slipping back to thoughts of Tyler, along with the tug of feelings his looks had elicited. Could it be any more confusing, being around someone who I was both terrified of and attracted to? I gave up, threw off my quilt and tiptoed downstairs to scrounge up something to eat.

I found some left-over chicken wings, a piece of garlic bread, and a row of chocolate – that'd do, considering I wasn't even hungry.

I curled up on the couch and switched on the TV with the hopes that any late night re-runs might block out my personal horror screenings.

Australia's Next Top Supermodel – *uh, no thanks.*

Escape to the Country – *already there.* The escape part sounded good, but no.

X-Files – better. I placed the remote beside me, content with my choice for now.

Mulder lay in a hospital bed with Scully standing beside him.

'...there's only my hope that you'll be able to see past this delusion.'

'You have to be willing to see,' Mulder said.

'I wish it were that simple.'

'Scully, you have to believe me; nobody else on this whole damn planet does or ever will.' Mulder's voice was laced in desperation as he looked up at her. *'You're my one in five billion.'*

They stared at each other dramatically, and then it went to an ad break. I flicked the channel to find something else and got smacked right in the face with pictures of a train wreck – I'd switched over to the news. The remote dropped from my hand and I sat in panic-induced shock.

Words scrolled along the bottom of the screen below the images of a fatal accident that killed a mother and child earlier in the day.

'No...' I puffed out a hollow protest.

I didn't want to see this one. Acrid revulsion coated the walls of my mouth as I gathered the images together.

The remains of a small white car. The train derailed and sitting perilously with its front two carriages lying off the tracks. An orange SUV truck sat guiltily to the side with only a dented front bar as evidence of its involvement.

'...and a man has been charged with drink driving. He's being held without bail...'

I closed my eyes and a small whimper escaped. I'd already been dealt some crappy cards this week, and now I'd been given an even worse hand to play tonight. I'd seen enough. I switched back to the X-files, stood with bitter annoyance for my lack of control, and paced the room. Why had I turned it on to begin with? So stupid. I whacked my palm against my forehead, as if it could somehow jar the images from my mind. If only. I switched off the TV, threw the remote back on the couch, and stormed from the room.

I crept out the back door and stomped across the grass to the fence, spun around and crossed the yard again. The damp earth seeped through my socks, sending a shiver across my skin, but I wasn't about to climb into bed when I knew what worse fate that would spew up. Wet feet were nothing in comparison to a darkness filled with death.

But how long could I really last? Mum would throw a fit if she caught me out here refusing to go to bed. It'd never work either, never had – sleep always won.

My irritation quivered, and I ripped my socks off and marched to my room. I welcomed the warmth, but not the dread. It settled in like a dull ache upon my chest as I laid my head on the pillow, but my eyelids were heavier than the fear, and sleep finally arrived.

I STOOD OUTSIDE THE *front of an aging, sand-coloured, weatherboard house in desperate need of a paint job. The blinds were still down, smothering the sounds of early morning activity behind them. It reminded me of our mornings at home, rushing around preparing to leave for the day.*

A car sat to the left of the house on a gravel driveway – a little, white Pulsar, with a child's booster seat in the back. The one I'd seen earlier when my eyes betrayed me, and I'd had a glimpse into the tragedy about to unfold.

The door to the house opened abruptly and today's victims appeared. The mother and child. She was young, they both were. I stumbled back, the shock ramming into me. I'm not sure what I expected, but it wasn't this. The mother appeared about twenty, no older than twenty-two, but either way not much older than me. She had long beach-blonde dreadlocks pulled into a low ponytail. She wore black slack pants and a white shirt with a pale blue logo above the left breast pocket. She held her son's hand, not for pleasure, but rather out of a need for him to hurry along. Too little for school; child care, perhaps. He carried a small, brightly coloured dinosaur backpack on his shoulders, and his undone shoelaces flopped as he scurried along. Tears welled in his eyes as they rushed down the stairs from the front porch, climbed into the car, and reversed out the driveway.

I was in the car with them then, my body propelled by the driving force of the story.

Dreadlock Lady's fingers tapped impatiently on the steering wheel. Her agitation filled the space, and I clenched my teeth as anxiety charged through my bones. We rounded a corner as the boom gates to the train track lowered.

'Damn.' She smacked the steering wheel and brought the car to a stop. We were the only ones there, peak hour hadn't surfaced yet.

My body returned outside the car, with a better vantage to see everything.

The still morning illuminated the crispness in the air, and the garbled chirp of the birds rose above the rumble of an oncoming train not too far behind me. Dreadlock Lady looked in her rear-view mirror at her son. As though resigned to the unwelcome delay in her morning, she began to sing. The tune sounded familiar, but she'd changed the words.

'There was a mum who had a boy and Benji was his name-o.' She grinned, a reflection of the chuckles coming from the back seat. The tiny voice of the boy joined hers. 'B-E-N-J-I. B-E-N-J-I...'

The roar of a speeding car pierced the early dawn, the increasing vibration as out of place as laughter at a funeral. I glanced over my shoulder. A large orange SUV sped down the road – too big, too fast, and too drunk. No way in hell he'd be able to stop after he rounded the corner.

'B-E-N-J-I, And Benji was his name-o.'

A tear slid down my cheek, my legs trembled. The little boy's soft curls bounced as he giggled and sang. Please don't let them die.

The dream shoved me back, and I jumped with the force, naturally *attempting to distance myself from the blow as the SUV careened toward us, toward them. Brakes screeched to a lock, and orange collided with white as the solid SUV crunched into the back of the car.*

Oh, God, no.

The impact propelled the bodies forward and slammed them backward as the car lurched onto the tracks.

'No!' I shrieked, lunging forward.

Dreadlocks flung around the lady's face as she turned to take in the oncoming train. Screeching train tracks muffled the sound of her scream.

My legs buckled, crumpling in a heap on the cold bitumen. My hands pawed at the rough surface under my fingertips, dragging myself closer, drawing blood. But nothing, not my blood, not her hands splaying in front of her face, or the raging desperation in my heart, could stop the freight train from barrelling into the car, wrapping the frame around the engine and carrying it down the track.

My body jerked awake, and my scream fractured the still quiet moments of the night. Tears stung my eyes, and I closed them tightly, focusing on the rise and fall of my chest and slowing my racing heart. The drum of my pulse timed the seconds before Mum appeared in my doorway.

'Was that you?' she whispered, her voice clogged with sleep.

'Yeah sorry. I watched *The X-Files* last night.'

'Oh, okay. You good now?'

'Mmm.' I gripped the blankets under my chin and eased my eyes open. Darkness greeted me, morning barely inching in at the edges of my window. The clock beside me read 5:25, I wouldn't be going back to sleep. Sinking into my pillow, I let the tears fall.

—8—

A LL MORNING MY ATTENTION remained on the little boy and his mum, Dreadlock Lady. My body on autopilot, I shuffled through school to Geography and slouched in the chair with a groan. I chose a seat by the window and instantly regretted getting out of bed, when Tyler arrived and sat at the table behind me. And I thought I could feel his breath on my neck last week. Thankfully I'd left my hair down today.

But the weight of two lives resting on my shoulders kept my mind too preoccupied to think of his eyes staring at the back of me. All double lesson I played with the jet bracelet around my wrist and pictured the mother and child; I even accidently drew their faces a few times. It was always hard to draw such young and beautiful faces. Faces that no longer were. The ache in my heart grew heavy at the thought of lives gone at such a young age, at the child who would never grow old.

I didn't know them and yet the loss seemed too heavy. I had to remind myself that what was done was done, and my imagination, my dreams, had only created a version of reality. I made up the likability of them, the cuteness of the boy, their age. I didn't know the details; I didn't want them. But if I could stop dreaming up nice people I might be able to find it a bit more agreeable.

Unfortunately, I'd imagined an amazing mum who tried her best, who dreamed of the future for her and her child. Heartbreakingly, my dream signalled the end of hers and, hand on my heart, I wished I could take it back.

If only she'd been like half the population and hit the snooze button, rolled over and fallen back to sleep, she'd still be alive. Now, all her seconds were gone; all for the sake of a few minutes.

Morning break came straight after Geography, and although I would've preferred to walk in quiet contemplation, Tyler strode beside me. His silence tangled uncomfortably with mine, until at last we reached the protection of our noisy friends.

We sat across from each other, and he flashed the tiniest hint of a smile. Could he see my pain like I saw his?

I shifted my attention to Amber as she rummaged in the floral backpack on her lap. 'What are you looking for?'

Her eyebrows rose, and a 'you'll see' twinkle shone in her eyes. She dumped a water bottle, a tattered novel, workbooks, a bag of carrot sticks, and finally a container on the table. 'Salted caramel or cherry?' She removed three cakes from the container. 'Sorry, this was all the leftovers I could steal today, I'll share with Cal.'

Max held up a hand. 'None for me.' A true gymnast, always conscious of what she ate.

'Tyler?' Amber held up each of the flavours. 'I hope you like cupcakes.'

'I have a feeling I'm gonna like these. Either's fine. Whatever's left.'

Cal laughed. 'Don't say that, dude. There won't *be* anything left.'

Amber held up a knife – you know 'cause everyone carries a knife in their bag. She cut the cakes in half and slid them into the centre of the table. Tyler chose the caramel and before Sean could steal the other half, Amber passed it over to me with a smile. She knew me far too well. I held up the cake and nodded my thanks.

I savoured the taste of Laurie's little pieces of perfection, drifting away from the chatter. A cool breeze blew my hair around my face and images of the little boy's bouncy curls and his mum's dreadlocks crept into my vision, followed by the crumpling of the car beneath the train.

'Luce?'

Sean's voice startled me. I sucked in a breath. 'Huh?'

'I was asking if we're good to catch a lift with you on Friday. Jake taking you?'

I shook my head, trying to dislodge the stills from my head and concentrate on the conversation. 'Yeah, sure.'

'Spill.' Max raised her brow.

'What?'

'You're daydreaming, and we all know what that means. What was it?'

I loved that she cared, but when you can only share half-truths is it even worth it? It'd be different if I could be like, 'You know that mum and kid who died in the train wreck yesterday. Yeah, that's what it was, I was there'.

Um, no.

I'd learned *I was there* crossed over the fuzzy lines of what my friends could accept about me and my dreams. And with Tyler here, I really couldn't say that. But with all eyes on me waiting for an answer, what remained was the choice to lie or dull down the details.

'Train accident, two dead,' I said matter-of-factly.

'Ew.' Max scrunched up her face and swallowed a large gulp of water.

'You mean that mother and her kid in Wollongong?' Tyler asked. I jerked my head in his direction, surprised at the question.

'Um, no, just a dream I had.' I picked off a piece of the cake.

'Of the same thing?' he pressed.

No way would I make that mistake again. I laughed it off and brushed my hand in the air. 'Nah, only a dream. But, gee, talk about being in the wrong place at the wrong time.'

'Can say that again,' Cal said.

Max popped her water bottle on the table. 'Isn't that how most people die? Freak accidents?'

'Guess so. But don't you think sometimes they'd be avoidable, like if she slowed down instead of rushing to beat the clock.'

'Says the girl who runs for fun,' Amber said.

Tyler propped his elbow on the table. 'How do you know she was rushing?'

Damn it, why was he so observant? 'I...I don't. I just think that's how a lot of people die, carelessness, speed.'

'What, and if she slowed down she wouldn't have been in the way of the train?'

'Exactly.'

'But you could argue if she was faster, she also wouldn't have been in the way.'

I pursed my lips. He was right. Speed up her morning by five minutes and she would've been well out of the way, but she was already rushing and that hadn't worked. If she could've changed anything to prevent their deaths, she'd have needed to slow down.

'True.' I cast my eyes down. 'But I still think they should've slowed down.'

I hoped he wouldn't argue more. It wasn't as if the alternatives hadn't already been careening around in my head since I woke. Especially the how. It had to be one simple change from the morning, which had to exclude her alarm because it was likely set to the same time every morning. The little boy's tear-filled eyes came to mind, his sniffles as she rushed him out the door. If he'd pleaded to have his laces tied, or simply held on for a longer hug over breakfast, it would've given them at least one more minute. That's all they needed.

Max's elbow landed in my side.

I glanced up, giving my mind whiplash as I propelled my thoughts back to the here and now.

'Tyler was talking to you.'

Crap.

'You'll get used to it, mate.' Sean chuckled, and I scrunched my face in a sarcastic *thanks* smile.

'Sorry, what were you saying?'

Tyler frowned, but the slight concern under his scrutiny helped ease the thundering in my chest. The bell sounded and his focus shifted. We clamoured out of the bench seats and gathered our bags, the bustle muffling any answer Tyler might've been about to give.

Cal and Sean shepherded him away, and I made my way to the library, my relief and curiosity battling it out with every stride.

I DREAMED AGAIN OF the train crash that night. It wasn't unusual for me to see the stories over and over again. Sometimes they stayed the same, but other more favourable times I managed to change small details. And those what-ifs meant I slept soundly for a night or two. At least until I saw, read or heard a news story and it all started again.

But those few nights of deep, impenetrable blackness were my Bahamas vacation.

Before sleeping, I sketched their faces again, better than I'd done earlier, and without distraction, with the time and effort they deserved. My pencil circled back and forth for each frizzy dreadlock, pushing firmer into the paper to capture her painted nails. And her son, those blue, blue eyes tempting me to pick up a coloured pencil. A stray tear dropped onto the page, and I wiped my eyes so I wouldn't further damage the paper. Why did young people have to be taken so soon?

I carried the injustice into my sleep and back to the dream. This time the little boy did what I'd contemplated earlier. He tugged on his mum's hand, spoke three simple words that made her pause, look into his eyes, and tie his laces. Instead of reaching the track before the SUV, she arrived afterward – after the drunk driver barrelled through the boom gate into the train. It was still horrifying to see unfold, but I rarely expected anything pretty when I closed my eyes.

When I woke, I leaped out of bed and fired up my laptop. After what Granny Tess said on the weekend, about being able to change the ending, I couldn't help crossing my fingers and holding my breath as I waited for the images to appear in front of me. Could it really be possible?

A small cry escaped my lips even before I knew what I was seeing. Nothing had changed. They were still dead – I fixed nothing. I slammed my fist onto the table, the agony twisting in my guts and gathering behind my eyelids.

The plunge back to reality hit hard. My Bahamas vacation just got crapped on big time.

*****

On Wednesday, I spent morning break in the art room, earphones in, avoiding what I expected would be a repeat of the day before. The way Tyler looked at me like he knew what was going on. As if it were remotely possible he had any idea what my night had been like.

I had a double free lesson straight after break and headed for the library. Meg Mac's 'Every Lie' played in my ears. I turned up the volume and settled into my favourite back corner table.

I lifted out my laptop and books, spreading them wide, making myself both comfortable and unsociable. I signed into the dream forum, @LucidLucy. Surely after five days someone would've responded to my question. They had. Three times.

@nightwalker suggested I was manifesting my dreams into my real life. So, when I saw Tyler I decided his must've been the face I'd seen in my dream. *Um, no.*

@lostatsea said the same thing as Max, that I'd likely seen him subconsciously first.

And @dreamtripper wanted whatever I was on.

A shadow crept in front of me, and I lifted my head. Tyler stood on the other side of the table, hands in his pockets, shifting uncomfortably. His lips moved. With my long hair over my ears he had no idea I couldn't hear a single word. I pressed my lips together, fighting hard not to laugh. I enjoyed the charade for a moment longer, before I tilted my head to the side and unplugged the sound from one ear.

'Sorry,' I said, raising my eyebrows. 'Can you repeat that, I didn't hear you?'

He rolled his eyes. 'I just asked if anyone was sitting here.'

'Uh...' I fumbled. 'No, but–'

'Great, you won't mind if I join you then?' He threw his bag on the table.

'That might be going a bit far,' I mumbled, peering back at the laptop screen – fat lotta good those guys were – and closed the tab.

Tyler cracked a smile as he dragged out a chair. 'How'd you go with your art homework? Caught up yet?' His voice held a slight mocking tone.

I frowned. I couldn't tell if he was having a go at me or not. His expression told me he knew more than he was letting on, like my friends had outed me. Brilliant.

I ignored his question.

'I didn't realise we shared a free,' I said, grudgingly dragging some of my books back.

'Neither did I until now.' He reached into his backpack and heaved a large text book onto the table, followed by his laptop.

'But you haven't been here all week.' I would've noticed if he had.

'You're very observant.'

I huffed through my teeth. 'It's a small library.'

His smile slipped away. '*And* you've been avoiding me like the plague.'

I opened my mouth to argue, but his eyes dared me to lie, to pretend I hadn't been wary of him all week. He'd already seen straight through me. 'Well,' I said with a straight face, 'you can never be too careful.'

Tyler coughed out a laugh and his rumble teased out my own giggle.

'Ssh!' Ms Oliver's scathing glare speared us from the other end of the room. I covered my mouth and tried to suppress the giddiness gathering all the way to my toes.

I lowered my gaze to the screen and popped my earphones back in. Tyler placed his own over his head, and we settled into a bumbling but pleasant working rhythm. Pages turning, mouses rolling, eyes meeting. We lasted without speaking for nearly the entire first lesson until I pushed back my laptop to heft a text book in front of me and sent one of Tyler's careening to the floor. I felt the thump in my chest as it landed on the carpet, not daring to turn in case I was impaled by more daggers from Ms Oliver.

I ripped out my earphones. 'Sorry,' I mouthed to Tyler.

He retrieved the book and shook his head. 'It's fine.' Then pointed to my earphones. 'What ya listening to?'

I looked down. 'Uh...Meg Mac.'

'Nice.' He shifted in his seat.

I nodded to the headphones hooked around his neck. 'You?'

'Arctic Monkeys.'

I grabbed my phone and scrolled down my Spotify list. 'Think I've got one of theirs on a playlist.'

He slouched in his chair. 'Let me guess, the one everyone likes? Is it 'Do I Wanna Know'?'

'Does that make it bad?'

'No way. It's just the one most people like.'

I pursed my lips. 'Glad I could be predictable.'

Tyler flicked his eyes down to his laptop and mumbled, 'You're anything but that.'

What does that mean? I straightened in my seat, about to ask.

'Do you often dream of real life events?' He said it so casually it took me a few seconds to comprehend, but when I did the question landed right in the centre of my guts.

Taken aback by the blow, my instincts took over. 'I don't.'

Tyler's eyebrows rose. He held up a finger, then another. 'Plane crash the night after we talked about my dad's crash. Train accident the night after an actual one.'

My pulse beat like a drum. 'Wouldn't those things give most people nightmares?'

'Yeah, maybe, but I was just curious if it was normal for *you?*'

I half laughed, half whelped. It was so much my normal I barely knew a life without them. But to admit that to an almost stranger felt far beyond any kind of normal. I sat on my hands to stop them shaking.

'Sometimes.'

'*Désolé* – sorry – we don't have to talk about it.'

But I did want to talk about it. He was the first person, aside from Granny Tess, who'd shown any interest. Everyone else told me to stop because it made them uncomfortable, but he offered an out after sensing *my* uneasiness. But it wasn't my dreams that made me so nervous, it was him.

'No, it's all right. It's nothing exciting.' Unless you were into crashes, drownings, blood, guts, and death.

He ran a hand through his hair, brushing the tangle from his eyes. 'Does your mind dull it down then? You see the boring parts too?'

I let out a small burst of laughter even though there was nothing funny about it. 'No, not at all.' I shook my head. 'All I see is death. In all its spectacular gore.'

He scrunched his face. A perfect depiction of how I felt about my dreams.

'Are your dreams ever so horrible, you'd die to wake up?' If he was like me he'd pick up on the double meaning.

He regarded me, his eyes projecting warmth. 'No, my dreams are amazing.' His expression took on a hazy longing, and boy, would I love some of those kinds of nights. 'I'd die just to stay in them a little longer.'

'Lucky you.' I didn't mean to sound so sarcastic, and perhaps slightly bitter, but the hope I'd clung to that he might be anything like me had crumpled into a heap. It landed alongside the hope from last week that he'd seen me in the dream. I guess that's why I never hoped. All it did was lift me too high for the fall not to hurt. I blinked from the sting.

But it wasn't about me – one thing my dreams reminded me of constantly. It never was.

My eyes flicked to the book in front of him, the words indecipherable. 'What language is that?'

Tyler's head bobbed up and down – me, book, me. 'Mandarin.'

I frowned. 'Mandarin?'

'Chinese.'

'Yeah, I know. I didn't think they taught that here?'

'They don't. I take it externally.' He leaned his elbow on the table. His relaxed posture and the change in conversation drew me in. 'Why?'

'Because they don't teach it here,' he said slowly, with a glimmer of a smile.

I huffed out a small laugh. 'Yes, but why do you bother? Why not do one of the ones in the curriculum?'

'I do. I also learn French.'

'Ah, that explains things. You like languages?'

He shrugged. 'I guess.'

'You guess? Why do you do it then?

His smile disappeared. 'My dad always wanted us to learn more than one language. He said the world would be more open to me, and me to it, if we could talk to one another.'

The mention of his dad was sobering, but he wouldn't want me dwelling on it. I ignored the fleeting pain in his eyes, pretended it meant nothing that he'd lost his dad and I didn't possess a shred of sympathy for his loss. 'You planning on travelling a lot, then?'

'I'm outta here the moment that final bell rings next year.' He paused. 'What about you?'

I dropped my eyes to the book in front of me. 'European Art.' I brushed over the crisp pages beneath my fingertips.

'No, I meant the travelling. Do you want to travel when you finish school?'

'Oh...uh...' I shifted in my seat and pushed a strand of hair behind my ear. 'No...not really an interest of mine.' Actually, my interest was so big it almost scared me, and the thought of leaving Antil...even more. But I wasn't about to tell him that.

'Really? I can imagine you travelling.'

I laughed nervously. *I couldn't.* 'How? What does that even look like?'

He chuckled a little, a slight glow in his eyes. 'I dunno, I can just imagine it.'

I wished I knew exactly what he imagined, but I was satisfied that whatever image I conjured up for him helped to erase the sad memories of his dad, even for a moment. Our words drifted away and allowed for silence to surround us again, both comfortable and uncomfortable. I lowered my gaze back to my book.

—9—

FRIDAY AFTERNOON ROLLED AROUND and as everyone jostled up to our lunch table we were full of excitement. A gust of air, surprisingly warm for that time of year, whipped my hair across my face as I sat down.

'How's this weather?' Cal's bronze hair flicked over his eyes from the restless wind, but he smiled, because despite the breeze picking up, the sun showed signs of a perfect weekend for skiing on the lake.

My gaze wandered past Sean's head, the direction I'd see Tyler come from. He was the only one not here yet. It amazed me how quickly I'd grown used to his presence, and how much I liked it. And if the way my pulse quickened from the anticipation of his arrival was any indication, perhaps even more than that. On Thursday Tyler and I had shared a free again, and then another double on Friday morning. Our nervous energy had still zapped like a storm in the tropics, but I was getting used to the current. I suspected Tyler was too, because when we sat at the back corner table in the library at the end of the longest week in the history of ever, we didn't drown it out with our music.

I caught Sean's cheeky sideways grin. Damn it, he knew who I was looking for.

'I think he likes you too,' he said with a gentleness in his eyes that offered his acceptance, and I knew how hard that'd be for him.

I opened my mouth to deny it. My liking Tyler or his liking me, I wasn't sure. My heart fluttered. I barely believed myself anymore, these guys would see straight through the lie. I closed my mouth.

'Yeah, I noticed that too.' Cal leaned his arm on the table.

Amber and Max only nodded, but the sly grin in their eyes spoke volumes. I wanted to bury myself in my shame of not being able to hide it better.

I glanced along the path. God, I hoped he wouldn't show up now, not with my cheeks flaming red hot.

'Don't worry,' Cal said. 'He's not coming. Gone home.'

'Already? We've still got geography.' And another free at the end of the day that I was stupidly looking forward to.

'Said his mum needed him to do a job before he went away.' Sean shrugged.

'But hey,' Cal said. 'Who's this old lady you helped? I thought the homeless shelter was mostly men?'

Huh? 'What are you talking about?'

'Something Simsy said.' He held up a hand. 'Now don't get mad, you know we love you, but we might've been dissing you for not showing up for break on Wednesday.'

Taken aback at his honesty, my face went taut. 'Thanks. I had work to do.' I didn't.

Cal ignored me and continued, 'We may have told Tyler it was a lie.' They *did* out me.

'You guys are supposed to have my back.' I glared at my friends. Amber elbowed Cal in the ribs. Max placed her palms on the table.

'We said nothing,' she protested.

'It was on the way to class.' Right before he showed up in the library. 'I said something about you going into your own little world, but to just ignore it. Sean said it came across as standoffish but you're actually a nice person.'

I shot a glare right between Sean's guilty eyes. 'Am I meant to thank you for that?'

'Only if you want to?' He grinned hard, teasing.

'But Simsy stuck up for you. Said he knew that already. Something about you helping an old lady when no one else did.'

My vision blurred, an intense pulsing slammed through my body.

'When did you catch up with Tyler?' Max asked, pouting like a toddler.

I blinked back the shock. I needed to find words, but they too were stunned into silence. I coughed, jarring myself into enough sense to at least speak. I needed to find a lie – fast.

'I didn't. I...uh, he must've seen me at the shops on the weekend. I helped an old lady who'd dropped her bags.'

Amber cupped her hands together. 'Aww. You're so sweet. What would the world do without you?'

My lips turned up a fraction, and I thanked her silently for the compliment.

'Why didn't you tell me you went out on the weekend? We could've met up.' Max put a hand on her hip, making her shoulders appear wider than they already were.

A small breeze burst from behind and caught my hair, giving me a moment to lean forward, collect it off my face, and compose myself before continuing the most bizarre lie I'd ever concocted. 'It was super brief, wouldn't have been worth it, promise.'

And it was in my dream.

He'd seen me.

I waded through the rest of the afternoon in a stunned blur.

He'd seen me and never said anything, even pushed it aside when I'd asked him about the dream on the first day. Had we been dancing around the truth every time we talked about the dreams?

I know *I'd* made a few subtle suggestions. Had he?

*****

AFTER SCHOOL I STOOD in my room; frustrated, excited, and scared. I'd thrown multiple piles of clothes on my bed, more spilled out of the wardrobe. I gritted my teeth and threw my head back.

'Argh.'

What the hell would I say when I saw him? And what would I wear? I glanced at my alarm clock. *Crap.* No time to waste. I slid into my skinny jeans and tossed my white Picasso cubic sketch t-shirt over my head. I tied the laces of my pale-blue cons, grabbing up the dark-grey pair and throwing them in my bag.

'Mum, do you know where my jacket is?' I called down the stairs.

I carelessly folded a hoodie, a couple of t-shirts, more pants, and my PJs, cramming them into the bag propped open on my bed. *Oh my God, he'd be seeing me in my pyjamas.* Why hadn't I thought of that until now? My legs wobbled, and I placed a hand over my stomach to calm the thwack of butterfly wings.

'Can I come in?' Without waiting for an answer Mum strode over to my wardrobe, the acrid scent of sterile bandages and disinfectant trailing behind her, the smell normally as calming as lavender, but now put me on edge. If Mum had any idea what was going through my head she'd pass out.

After a quick rummage she held up my almost black denim jacket. 'This the one?'

'Yep, thanks.' I grabbed it and stuffed it into my bag, groaned, pulled it back out and slid it on.

'Is everything all right?' Her forehead furrowed, and I concentrated on keeping my breath steady, normal.

'Perfectly fine.' I pressed my lips into a smile.

She leaned against the doorway. 'You're looking forward to the weekend, aren't you?'

'Yeah, I...uh...I've been busy with school so I'm not feeling very prepared.'

'Okay, and that's all?'

I nodded. 'Yep.' I looked her in the eye briefly and then continued to breeze around the room, gathering the bits I'd need for the weekend. Our silence hung heavily, but she didn't need to speak for me to know her thoughts. She'd noticed my jitters, and only one thing had ever caused those. My imperfection had been a constant struggle for her, but my dreams weren't like a bad headache or the flu, and as much as she wished she could nurse them away, she couldn't.

'This is for two days?' She eyed the oversized bag with a grin. My face mirrored hers when I smiled, dark eyes creased at the corners and high cheeks that lifted for the occasion.

'Yep.' I laughed when I struggled to close the bag. Mum stepped over to hold the sides together as I yanked the zipper closed.

Mum pulled me in for a hug, her worry making her squeeze longer and tighter than normal. 'Have fun.' She kissed the side of my head and left the room.

I knocked on Jake's door as I headed out. 'Ready when you are,' I called.

JAKE PULLED THE VAN in by the back entrance of the lake house. Max jumped out excitedly, Sean right behind her, but I struggled with more trepidation than excitement. My attraction to Tyler, my recent discovery, and the fear at what that meant kept my backside firm in the seat. Knots twisted, nausea churning my insides. Closing my eyes I gulped. *I can do this.* I stepped from the car into the quiet empty afternoon, my feet crunching on the sandy gravel driveway.

We'd spent so many weekends here while growing up it

always felt like coming home. The limestone house with oversized wooden columns stood in graceful silence, the gumtrees rising proudly beside it. A handful of honey eaters danced under their shade, foraging in the brush. Sucking in the crisp scent of gum and country air put me instantly at ease, despite my inner turbulence.

'You sure you've packed enough?' Jake said, lifting our bags out the back.

'You know what, I don't think we did.' Max poked out her tongue, hoisted up her bag, and headed inside as Marie opened the big double doors. Billy Bob, their black and white cocker spaniel, grabbed the opportunity to escape. He dashed around her short legs, but was too old to go far. No one bothered to call him back.

'Lucy, Max, Sean, Jake, come in, come in.' Marie held her arms wide and ushered us into the gorgeous living area; exposed wood, with hues of cream and rich chocolate, and floor to ceiling windows that captured the view of the lake. 'Pop your bags over here. Yes, that's fine, Max. Everyone's out the front. Can I get you kids a drink?' Her platinum hair bounced on her shoulders with the pleasure of our arrival. 'Jake, are you staying for a drink?'

'No, can't sorry, basketball tonight, I need to head straight back, but I'll be back tomorrow night for the party. Mum says hi.' He passed her a container of Mum's famous shortbread biscuits. 'Here, she sent these.'

Jake left and Marie hurried back to the kitchen, off to the side of the massive open plan area, while I dropped my bags next to the sideboard and admired the perfectly placed photos of Cal and his family. I paused on the one with him and his brother. Richie had his arm slung over Cal's shoulder, embracing him in a one-sided hug Cal was shrugging away from. If it weren't for his face being all teeth, the angst might've been believable. A warm smile faltered on my lips as it often did when I remembered them all those years ago.

I followed the others out onto the deck and soaked up the wide view of the entire waterfront. Sweeping grass sloped down onto the sandy embankment of the lake and an expanse of crystal still waters beyond. The pink clouds still held some warmth from the day but were a reminder the sun would soon be leaving us. A long jetty ran from the right side of the shore out to a gazebo over the water, and on the other side of the jetty, *Vivianne – the lady of the lake,* bobbed peacefully on the water. She showed her age, but it would be a sad day when Cal's dad replaced his much-loved speed boat. She was like family.

I shifted my attention toward the sound of Cal and Tyler coming out of the boat shed with Cal's dad at the other end of the landing. Tyler wore tan jeans with a maroon and white-chequered flanny rolled up to his elbows and opened over a grey t-shirt. He looked so composed, making me lose all of mine. His hair billowed over his forehead, the afternoon sun reflecting bronze streaks amongst the brown. With his steady gait and easy chatter with Cal, an unrestrained grin spread over his face. He held an armful of logs, exposing the muscles in his forearms. I hitched my breath and the lurching in my stomach started up again.

'Hey, you're all here,' Cal called up to us as he dropped his pile by the fire pit. 'Who's ready for a party?'

I wished I could trade some of my hyper-nervousness for his calm, vibrant energy.

Sean and Max trampled down the steps.

I moved a little slower, my shaky legs barely keeping me upright. It'd only been hours since we'd seen each other, yet a chorus of excited greetings rang out as everyone anticipated the weekend ahead.

'Hi kids,' Harry said, stacking the wood into a neat pile. Cal's dad brimmed with a more subtle energy than his son's, always less pronounced, but easily as charming.

'Hey.' Tyler kicked at the dirt and spoke with such uncertainty, it almost didn't sound like him. The unfamiliar apprehension in his eyes surprised me, but it served him right after what he'd been keeping from me. So what if I'd been partly to blame.

'Hi.' My voice quivered despite wanting to act unruffled at seeing him again. As if. Who was I kidding? I hesitated to smile, but as his lips turned up and the doubt in his eyes softened, so did my defences. Crap, this weekend might be more challenging than I thought if I couldn't stay unaffected by his smile. I had a million questions, but the heat from the flames was increasing. Distractions – I needed distractions. And time to figure out what to say to him. I should've spent less time deciding what clothes to pack and more on how to broach the tiny matter that we'd seen each other in our friggin' dreams.

'Need us to do anything, Cal? Where's Amber?' I asked.

'She's in the house somewhere. Uh, nope.' He tipped his head and pointed behind us. We spun round as Amber, with her camera strung around her neck, skipped out of the house and pointed the lens in our direction.

'Hey lovelies,' she called and waved from the veranda. We waved back and the flash displayed an enthusiastic hello to match.

'Get yourselves a drink, get comfortable, you know, the usual,' Cal continued, still smiling at Amber's interruption. 'I'm just gonna get some more wood, then I'll join you all.' He trudged back to the shed, Tyler and Sean trailing behind.

Max looped her arm in mine and we strolled back up to the house. 'C'mon, hon, let's go get you an ice pack.'

I groaned and elbowed her in the side, and her mischievous laughter rang out over the expanse of the lake. She wouldn't be laughing if she knew all the reasons I was a trembling mess. With the impending exchange between me and Tyler, I certainly wasn't.

—10—

M Y HANDS FOUND THE distraction I needed by helping Marie carry drinks to the outside fridge, but my eyes still found opportunities to steal glimpses of the boys. Ridiculous. This attraction had appeared out of nowhere, and now I couldn't make it go away. And if I was going to have any chance at a rational discussion about what sharing the same dream might mean I needed to push those thoughts aside.

I loaded up another armful of drinks and ignored the chorus of excitement when the guys barrelled through the doors into the bedrooms. Something about going in for a quick dip. It had been a mild day and only the faintest bit of warmth remained as the sun began to sink below the horizon, but it was entirely like Cal to wring out every bit of daylight even with the temperature dropping by the second.

I carried the drinks outside, smiling at the laughter that drifted from inside. The doors burst open and the three guys whizzed past me and jumped off the deck. I gaped at a bare-chested Tyler, and stood achingly still as they sprinted down the grassy slope and dived straight into the lake.

Their whoops and hollers echoed off the shimmering water.

'You comin' in, Luce?' Cal yelled.

Hell no. It was the middle of April – freezing. My eyes darted to Tyler throwing a wave of water over Sean's head. Okay, maybe I was more worried about the heat than the cold. But no one needed to know that. 'You guys are nuts.'

'C'mon, Luce,' Max said, slipping through the door with Amber skipping up behind her.

'You're going in? It's freezing.' How would I get out of it now?

'Where's your adventure?' She winked. 'Tyler's in there.'

'You think I haven't noticed.' I waved my hand in the air. 'Go on, I'll be right behind you.' That would bide me some time.

The girls ran to the water's edge and squealed the moment they dipped their toes in. I turned my back on them. Yeah, the cold would drive them out before I'd have to join them.

I spotted the salad and chopping board on the kitchen bench and busied myself with a job Marie could handle perfectly well on her own. Especially considering we were ordering pizza for dinner. It was roughly fifty metres from the house to the water, but I easily heard their screams and laughter, followed by the endless cries for me to join them. I clenched my jaw. Damn it, why hadn't I just gone in?

Silence descended, followed by a barrage of yells. I stood on tippy toe to see through the window; Sean sprinted up the grass toward the house.

My stomach leaped into my throat. *Crap*. I gripped the kitchen bench.

'Sean!' Marie shrieked seconds before his dripping wet body ran into the house. He stopped abruptly, panting, and clutched the door frame.

'Come on, Luce, you're missing all the fun.' He jogged on the spot and wrapped his arms around himself.

'I'm not missing a thing. I can hear you all from here. And look at you.' I pointed to him. 'It's freezing.'

'Only out here. And since when did that stop you?' He was right, but I was damned if I'd admit it to him.

'Since today,' I said, not budging.

Sean grunted and turned to leave, at the exact moment Cal shoved in from behind him, and ran straight into the house dripping profusely onto everything.

'Quick, Sean, help.'

'Calvin, you're soaked.' Marie stepped in front of Cal, waving her arms, Billy Bob yapping at her feet. 'Get out!' But Cal's grin was stronger than her shrieks and she backed into the sink. He turned his sneer on me.

I widened my stance, anchoring me to the spot. 'Don't you dare.'

My reaction time was a second too slow. I saw the intention in his eyes and spun to dart around the other end of the kitchen bench, but Sean, now brave enough to ignore Marie's shrieks, had his sodden hand on my arm, his grip tight. I screamed when Cal wrapped his arms around me, and his wet skin and shorts soaked straight through to my clothes.

'I'm gonna kill you two!' I squirmed as they dragged me outside.

Cal threw me over his shoulder.

I pummelled my fists into his back in pathetic desperation. I writhed and yelled for him to stop, but my efforts were useless.

'You're gonna regret this!' Someone tried to remove my shoes.

I heard a pained cry as I kicked something hard. 'I hope that was your head, Sean.' He deserved any blood that came from it too.

Roars of laughter sailed up from the water, getting louder as we bumped down the lawn. At least someone was enjoying this.

With a grunt, Cal launched me into the air.

I flew, my limbs limp like a ragdoll, unable to change my course. The water swallowed me, and I sank deeper than I expected, taking a huge gulp of water as I went under. I surfaced in a fit of coughs and the chill of the water stunned the breath right out of me.

Cal waded into the water laughing, but he was an idiot if he thought it was smart to be near me after that stunt.

'You jerk!' I yelled, and he laughed harder. I wiped my hair off my face and stumbled forward, the sludge oozing around my sock-covered feet. My hands clenched at my sides, and I gritted my teeth. The heat within me rose, warmed me, and I welcomed the anger. 'You're so gonna pay for that.'

The water rushed at me as Cal stepped closer, a big cheeky grin on his face; I refused to let it get to me. 'You wouldn't know payback if it hit you in the face.'

I frowned. 'Really?'

He stared me down, the light in his eyes daring me. My lips twitched. Damn it, he was good. He might not think I had it in me, but if he got to dunk me fully clothed into an extremely cold lake, I owed it to myself to show him some of his own. I lifted my hands to the surface of the water and propelled them forward directing a missile of water straight into his face.

I caught him off guard and grabbed the opportunity to lunge at him. Placing my hands on his head, I pushed my body up and dunked him under the water. I immediately swam into deeper water where, finally, I laughed.

I pulled off my socks. 'And Sean?' I threw the wet ball across the water into his face. 'Those are for you.'

He spat out the water they'd served him. 'Gross.'

'Max, help me with this, will you?' I shrugged out of my jacket and she pulled it away. 'Catch.' I tossed it to Cal, who threw it to the shore. I thought about going down to my underwear, it couldn't be any worse than a bikini, but I chickened out. If it weren't for Tyler being here I may've done it, but his presence meant I wore an extra coating of self-consciousness.

The mood of everyone else lifted with mine, and the air filled with the sounds of laughter. The cool water rolled over me and it grew surprisingly pleasant. I floated on my back, enjoying the peace that came with being out on the lake. The voices softened as I drifted further away and surrendered to the calm.

'Beautiful, isn't it?' I turned my head toward Tyler's gentle voice. He floated beside me, not close enough to bump me but enough to hear him clearly above the ripples of lapping water. *This is it, now or never, the moment of truth.*

'Sure is.' I returned to admiring the changing sky; the darkening blue behind clouds that reflected the last of the sun's light, transforming them into a delicate but bright pink.

'I've never seen pink clouds like this before.'

I looked over at him. 'Really? How is that possible?'

'I grew up in the city. Too many buildings and lights, I guess.'

'You live close to the city centre?'

'Nah, not really. But obviously close enough not to see these. Or maybe I just never noticed them.'

'I've never been to Sydney.'

Tyler treaded water and faced me. 'How's it possible to live in Australia and never go to Sydney?'

'Not sure.' I laughed. 'But why would you when you've got all this?' I swept my arm to take in the mountains on the other side of the lake. *Just say it.*

'Fair point.'

'Do you miss it?' I inwardly groaned. *Just rip the friggin' Band-Aid off already.*

'What, the city?'

'Yeah.'

'The waves I do, but it's not so bad here.'

I drew in a breath. *One, two...* 'You saw me.'

As soon as the words were out I wanted to take them back. I'd fired the bullet without thinking of the consequences. What if he closed up? I kicked harder, moved my hands faster, as if I needed to stop them from reaching out and clutching at the words flying across the water.

Tyler questioned me with his eyes.

My chest tightened uncomfortably as I waited for him to say something, anything.

He didn't. Instead, he bobbed in the water two metres away, staring at me intently.

I was back at the airport, gazing into those deep dark eyes.

A splash of water struck my face, and Sean burst up from under the surface beside us. 'What're you two doin' all the way out here? The crocs'll have a feast.'

'Shame there aren't any crocs then, hey.'

'Shame for who?' He crumpled his nose and swam away laughing.

Tyler's eyes zeroed in on me. 'I did.'

The air left me, and the vice around my chest squeezed harder.

'Why didn't you say something?'

'Why didn't you?'

I opened my mouth – because I'd been too scared, because all signs pointed to it only being me. I closed it again.

'Exactly. I kept dropping hints, but I didn't want to be the first one to say something...even if I did know you recognised me.'

Hang on, what? How?

'Hey, you lot, time to head in,' Max called from the bank. 'Pizza's nearly here.'

I shifted my attention to everyone swimming to shore and a chorus of 'Awesome' and 'I'm starved', leaving Tyler and I alone in the water.

'I guess we should go in,' Tyler said reluctantly and curled his lips.

No way, I wanted answers. We'd finally landed at the destination we'd been avoiding for days, and I wasn't leaving till I'd checked out the sights.

I narrowed my eyes. 'Don't do that.'

'What? Look at you?' He said it with a straight face but a tease flickered from his eye.

'Aargh, don't side step, how the hell did you know I recognised you? What else do you know?'

'Nothing.' He avoided my eye.

'Now you're being difficult.' I kicked away from him, tired of this standoff. Pizza sounded good.

He swam to me, and I stopped kicking, began hoping.

'Lucy, wait, I'm sorry. I'm not sure what you want me to say. Yes, I saw you in a dream, and yes I know you saw me too. If you want me to tell you why we were in each other's dream, then I'm afraid that's something I have no explanation for. I've got nothing.' He wiped his wet hair from his eyes and held my look, his eyes softening the sharp lines of his jaw.

'Are you like me? Do you dream like me?' I whispered the words then held my breath.

His look of sympathy gave me the answer before he spoke. 'No.'

I liked Tyler, and wanting him to be like me would be inflicting pain on a friend. Still, the rock, hard disappointment, settled in my stomach, and tears bristled behind my eyes. I slowed my feet and let the weight swallow me for a second, disappearing under the water.

I surfaced with a gasp, brushing my dark hair away from my face. A flock of birds soared across the sky. I concentrated on the dark shapes, clear even against the deep evening blue, before moving my attention back to the question and concern in Tyler's eyes. 'How did you know? I mean, how did you know I saw you too?'

'I didn't at the time, before I moved here that is. But when you bumped into me, when you looked up at me, nothing could be clearer. It was written all over your face.' He smiled. 'And then when you couldn't get far enough away from me, well...it left no doubt.'

'Why didn't you want to stay away from me? I mean, this is scary as hell.'

'Because it was you.' He spoke with a hushed tenderness, and I caught my breath. What did he mean by that?

'We couldn't get you in the water, now we can't get you out?' Cal's voice boomed. He stood twenty metres away on the shore, his hands cupped around his mouth, silhouetted by a backdrop of the golden glow of the house. 'You get first shower, Luce, it's only fair, hey? But you gotta hurry.' His wide grin was his attempt at a truce.

'More than fair I'd say,' I shouted. 'Might take me a while to get up the bank in these clothes though.'

'That's your own fault, should've joined us when you had the chance.'

We swam to shore, and the soft mud of the lake bed squelched through my toes. I pulled my hair behind me and squeezed out the excess water.

'Are you all right?' Tyler paused and flicked his head, droplets of water arcing over him. He ran his hands through his hair, dark eyes piercing in the growing moonlight.

'Depends. Are you talking about the clothes or the fact I've just discovered we have some mutual supernatural power?' I smirked.

'The clothes,' he said. 'But I think we should talk more about this super power you think we have.'

'Super *natural*.'

'Nah, just super.'

I really wanted to stay and talk more, but my body had other ideas. My teeth chattered and sopping wet clothes stuck to my skin, inducing an all-body shake. Cal called again.

'Come on, let's get up to the house, you need to change,' Tyler said, raising an arm to wrap around my shoulders. He hesitated and dropped his hand. 'Uh, sorry.'

I grinned. 'It's all right. I won't bite.'

We walked toward the amber light and noise from the house. 'It's not your teeth I'm worried about. It's those daggers you keep using on me.'

—11—

How could Tyler act so calm? I'd spent over a week in near apocalyptic frenzy over seeing him, and he sat there like a Buddhist monk, not a care in the world. His easy posture on the other side of the fire pit was clearly visible through the copper flames, and our shared glances warmed me as much as the heat from the glow between us.

My feet were tucked under me, and I clutched a blanket around my shoulders, savouring the scent of smoke and burnt marshmallows. Cal's parents retreated inside, leaving the six of us staring quietly into the firelight.

The neighbours were too far away to be heard, and traffic had stopped hours ago. The only sounds came from the wildlife in the trees above and the spit and crackle of the fire. It was almost serene.

Almost.

It might've been perfect had it not been for the thundering turmoil spinning out of control inside my head. I tried to shut it out, but my mute button was broken. The flames and darkness were like a lullaby encouraging my thoughts to wander. How much longer would I need to sit in agony before we got the chance to talk?

In my frustration I impaled another marshmallow and poked it toward the coals.

A shadow appeared over me, and I turned as Tyler sat beside me.

'I need one of those,' he said, reaching into the bag of marshmallows and plonking one into his mouth. He lowered his head and whispered near my ear. 'Actually, I just wanted an excuse to come sit beside you.'

I was immensely grateful for the darkness. 'To talk about super powers?'

'That might have to wait. It's too quiet out here.' Ah yes. Any conversation around the stillness of the fire was open for all to hear. He must have sensed my disappointment and leaned in again to give me a single word of hope. 'Tomorrow?'

'Tomorrow.' I pulled the blanket under my chin.

'Who wants to play *fact or fallacy?*' Amber said to a chorus of groans. 'Oh come on, guys, you know you want to – just one round?' Her eyes pleaded, and Cal relented.

'I'm a lost cause when you look at me like that,' he said.

'I know.'

Cal poked at the fire. 'Fine. *Fact or fallacy*...I hate playing soccer in the rain.'

I laughed hard to a yelled chorus of 'Fallacy!'

'Too easy,' Sean said. 'You couldn't pretend to hate soccer if you tried.'

'Do another one.' Amber tapped his knee.

He gave in. 'All right. *Fact or fallacy*, I once killed a magpie.'

'Fallacy. There's absolutely no way you'd do that,' Amber said.

'I dunno.' Sean bunched his eyes together. 'Cal's looking pretty guilty. I say fact.'

'Me too,' Max said and the rest of us followed suit; the guilt on his face plainly obvious. He sat quiet, eyes cast downward, and Amber waited for him to refute what now appeared to be fact.

She gasped and placed a hand over her heart. 'No. When, how?'

Cal slunk his shoulders. 'It was an accident. With a slingshot I made camping last year. I'm sorry, I didn't mean to...well, I didn't think I'd get it.'

'I thought you'd at least say you did it when you were a kid! How could you?' Amber pouted. 'Sometimes I wonder about you, Cal Brooks.'

'You wanted to play,' Max said.

'I know, I know, doesn't mean I'm going to like what I hear.'

'If it makes you feel better, I felt really, really bad.'

'It does, I didn't think you were that heartless.' She placed a hand on Cal's leg. 'Okay. Dare I ask who's next? Lucy?'

'No way, I got nothing. You guys know me too well.'

'*Je ne* – I don't,' Tyler said, and the gentleness of his words, as if he wanted to know me, tingled the skin on my arms beneath the blanket.

I was barely able to stutter my response. 'Maybe later.'

Tyler lowered his eyes and the edge of his lips rose.

Sean moved quickly to my defence. 'All right, I'll go. *Fact or fallacy*...when I was younger I almost ran away to join the circus.'

'Define almost,' Cal said.

'Bags packed.'

'No way,' Cal said. 'Fallacy for sure.' And everyone except me agreed with him.

'Fact,' I piped up, and all eyes zoned in on me. 'I remember it.'

'Really? It's true?' Max said, and Sean nodded slowly.

'Ah, so there are some things you two don't know about each other.' Cal waggled a finger at the two of them.

My eyes met Sean's. 'It was right after your dad left. You wanted to run away, like he had. I was going to come too if I remember rightly.'

'Yeah, you were.' He waved his stick in the air as he told the story. 'You wanted to be a tightrope walker, and I was gonna learn the trapeze.' He sputtered out a laugh and I joined him.

We had it all planned out – as much as you do when you're ten. The circus was coming to town in a week; it was the only detail we needed.

'I can't believe I knew nothing about this.' Max put one hand on her hip and swivelled to face me.

'Me either, I would've joined you.' Cal laughed. 'So why're you both still here, what stopped you?' he said mockingly.

Sean's face fell. We exchanged looks, before he said in a soft voice, 'Richie.'

If it were possible for a falling pin to make a sound on the soft earth at our feet, we would've heard it.

Richie died the day after we made plans to escape with the circus and, until now, those plans were forgotten like the little packed bag behind my bedroom door.

A tear fell onto my cheek, and I quickly brushed it away. I wasn't the only one with renewed grief at remembering our friend, and Cal's brother. A hush enclosed around us. It had been a shared loss and it would always be a shared grief.

Tyler shifted uncomfortably on the bench alongside me. Did he know the details or the gravity of the moment he'd found himself in?

'*Fact or fallacy...*' He gently broke the silence, and our tense shoulders relaxed as we moved our attention toward him. My heart fluttered when his eyes locked with mine, nervously anticipating what he might reveal. He paused as if undecided, if he should continue.

'I'm secretly terrified about skiing tomorrow. Everyone thinks I'll be a natural because I can surf, but I have a feeling I'm gonna be humiliated.' He let out a big breath.

I covered my mouth to stop a laugh, but when Cal snorted and Tyler's lips turned up, I didn't suppress it any longer. It wasn't something particularly funny, but off the back of the sombre mention of Richie, it was our undoing. Our unrestrained merriment echoed across the lake, and it didn't take long for the kookaburras in the nearby trees to join us in the cackle.

THE BEDS WERE ALL prepped when we headed inside for the night. It didn't matter how old we got, or that the occupants had changed over the years, we still acted like six-year-olds as we dragged the mattresses out to the lounge room when we stayed at Cal's. It was a small part of our childhoods we weren't prepared to give up yet.

I changed into my spotted fleecy pyjamas before joining everyone in the lounge room. I stopped short at the edge of Sean's bed. The only way to reach mine was to climb over the already occupied mattresses covering every available surface of the floor. Obstacle course style, I leaped and balanced from one bed to the next. I was doing well as I dodged Sean's head and Tyler's legs, but then I misjudged my footing, fell, and wedged myself between two of the beds. I was unflatteringly stuck, with not one of my friends ignoring the opportunity to laugh at my expense. I tried to laugh myself, but with the mattresses pressed into my rib cage I couldn't move. Cal's feet were on one side of my head and Tyler was, just my luck, on the other. He lay on his side smiling, his head inches from mine.

'I feel I need to ask you again if you're all right,' he said.

'Perfectly fine.' I forced out a smile and tried to hide the embarrassment that flared inside me. 'All this padding to land on helped.' I patted the mattress beside me.

'This falling thing of yours, is it a new habit?' His grin radiated over my skin.

'It's not so much a habit, as a misfortune, I think, but yeah, it seems to be a more recent happening.'

His brown hair flopped over his creased forehead and rested right above his full eyebrows. And on his chin, right below his well-formed mouth, a tiny, dot-like dimple twitched when he spoke.

'Need help to get up?' His question dragged my focus back to his eyes. How long had I been staring?

'Oh, um, I think I'm all right.' I tried to bring my arms behind me so I could leverage myself up, but there was no space on either side of me and I felt like a beached dolphin as I flapped my arms and legs about. We both laughed, and Tyler knelt to give me a lift. I placed my hands into his offered ones and the tingling coursing through my body exploded. His eyes were full of a heat I'd not seen before now. It rushed to my fingers where our skin touched.

I was light-headed as I stood and, without noticing until I felt their cold emptiness, my hands were no longer in his. I dropped my eyes and turned, more carefully this time, and hobbled to my own bed.

I flopped onto my mattress, letting my head sink into the soft pillow.

Max appeared in my face, whisper-shouting in a barely contained voice. 'Geeze Louise.'

'What?' The dim light made it easier to avoid her gawk.

'Talk about flirtension.' Her voice rose slightly and I desperately hoped it wouldn't travel across the room as easily as the boy's deep voices.

'Keep your voice down.' My glare did little to hide the smile on my lips.

She pointed her finger at me. 'You've got it bad.'

'I don't.' I spoke as if I barely believed the words myself, so quiet I may as well have mouthed them.

'Don't even try to deny it.' Her eyes shone with humour.

'What're you two talking about over there?' Cal's voice rose into the air. 'Have you forgotten our rule out here? No whispering.'

'It's girl stuff, Cal.' Max turned to me, letting me know I wouldn't be let off as easily. She mouthed the word 'tomorrow'.

Yes, tomorrow.

A short while later the soft sounds of steady breathing told me someone had drifted off. Other than that, the room lay quiet, uncomfortably so. Tyler lay only a couple of metres away, and I was conscious of every movement I made, as if at any moment I would set off an alarm. The moon shone through the mass of windows, lending me a hazy blue light and illuminating the hands of the ticking clock – just after midnight.

'Happy birthday, Richie.' I spoke softly, not thinking anyone could hear me.

Cal sounded close to sleep. 'Mmm. Happy birthday, big brother.'

I closed my eyes and rolled over onto the side I'd avoided so far, the one that faced Tyler. I tried to relax, tried to ignore the image on the other side of my closed eyelids, but it was impossible. The urge to open them was too great, and my control proved as weak as Samson without his hair. I opened my eyes slowly. The view was even nicer than I'd imagined. Tyler lay but two beds away, Cal and Amber's feet between us. He wore the same intense expression I'd first seen at the airport. He was still, and I lay motionless. What was it about the way he looked at me that made my insides do somersaults? His eyes bored right into my soul, and I wondered what he'd see if I allowed him a view. I felt exposed and vulnerable to an unrecognisable force. Without giving permission, and with no awareness of the moment between the time before and the time after, I relinquished my control to the force that raged between us.

Exhaustion took hold, and my eyelids closed.

—12—

*T*HE TREMENDOUS DISPLAY OF *red, brown, and gold leaves rippled in the breeze. A soft golden haze permeated around and through every-thing. My breathing slowed. Mesmerised, I started toward the tree, realis-ing in that moment, I was all alone.*

I turned slowly, freely taking it all in, school like I'd never seen it before. Not another soul in sight. No annoyingly loud girls nearby, or arrogant teachers strolling past. Bliss. It was strangely peaceful, and I sighed as the tranquillity settled over me. I circled back toward the tree and this time found I wasn't alone after all.

Tyler sat beneath the tree, his back against the trunk, one leg crossed over the other. His hands were folded in his lap and, like everything else in this dream, he was perfect.

He had the smallest glimmer of a smile in his eyes. 'Hi.'

'Uh, hi. What're you doing here?' I sat on the bench facing him and leaned my back against the table edge.

'I could say the same to you, but then you've dreamed of me before so why not again?' And there it was again, the smirk-like grin, proving his unmistakable enjoyment.

The truth in his words didn't make this any less strange though. 'Seriously, this is crazy.' I inspected our surroundings and crossed my legs. 'Insane.'

'I know, right, but how cool is it.' His face beamed with infectious amusement.

'Very.' I smiled.

Tyler threw his legs in the air and leaped from his spot on the grass. His eyes stayed glued to me as he strode to the table, my heart picking up speed with every step. He held out his hand. 'Wanna have some fun?'

'Fun? Have you looked around us?'

'Actually, no I haven't,' he said, sarcastically glancing around us as if for the first time. 'I've had my eye on other things.'

I rolled my eyes as a warm flush crept up my neck. 'Good one.'

'Okay then, back to fun. We're at school, no one's here – and no one's coming either.'

'What did you have in mind?'

'Well, what've you always wanted to do at school that you couldn't? Now's your chance.'

'I've never really thought about doing anything but my work.'

He shook his head like I'd insulted the fabrication of spontaneity. 'I've got an idea.'

'All right then, master of all things fun, I'm game.' He still had his hand out, I took hold and he hauled me up off the table.

'You don't wanna know what it is first?'

'Nope, surprise me.'

We ran inside one of the building blocks, and Tyler led me into a bathroom, because the toilet block was always where the fun was, right? My face scrunched when he pushed his denim sleeves up to his elbows and bent to dismantle one of the soap dispensers, pulling out the inner pouch, two-thirds full of pale blue soap. He passed it to me with a smile, and my eagerness to know his plan grew. Once he had the other two almost full bladders out of their dispensers we pushed open the door into the foyer and climbed the stairs.

At the top of the landing Tyler stopped to put the soap down, removed his shoes, and rolled up the bottoms of his faded-black jeans.

'Okay, now I have to know,' I said, unable to bear it anymore.

'Nope, you said surprise, I'm not saying a word.' His now adorable smirk had returned. 'Take yours off too.'

I bent to unlace my yellow Cons and cocked my eye up at him. 'Should I be nervous?'

'Maybe, depends.' He beamed, a gorgeously full-faced, couldn't be happier with himself grin. My insides flipped. 'Do you trust me?'

I tapped a finger on my cheek. 'Good question...trust is something you have to earn. What've you done to earn it?'

'I'm not sure I've done anything to earn it, but I don't think I've done anything to warrant being untrustworthy, have I? Trustworthy until proven otherwise?'

'All right then, I trust you...for now.' I finished taking my shoes off and stood until my eyes were level with the dimple on his chin. It was my turn to smirk.

We ran bare feet down the stairs to the home economics room, where Tyler rummaged through the piles of fabric in the boxes against the back wall like a dog finding a bone.

'Voilà,' he said, lifting out a bundle of thick, white wadding.

'What's that for? We doing some quilting?'

'No.' He paused. 'Not unless that's what you wanna do.'

'Not today.' I bounced with anticipation, desperate to know what he was up to.

Back upstairs in the completely empty hallway, I marvelled at how different it felt with no one in it. No tinny sound of banging metal from the locker doors, or the resounding yells of hundreds of annoying teens. No strong smells of sweaty bodies or rancid school bag stench.

'What are you thinking?'

I blinked and shook my head. 'Just how different it is without everyone here.'

'You like it?'

'Love it.'

'Good, now come over here so I can attach this.'

I nervously stepped toward him, and he placed a thick piece of wadding on my backside. My pulse raced at the thought of the location of his hand.

'Here, hold this,' he said, and I snapped out of my daze.

Tyler broke off a long piece of tape with his teeth and leaned to wrap his arms around me, hovering alarmingly close to the thud in my chest. Oh God, give me some of that corridor noise back.

He removed his arms and attached a large wad of padding to his own butt, causing a spurt of laughter I tried to contain with my hand.

'What? Too much?'

'Depends. Were you going for the Kim Kardashian look?'

'No, but it suits me, right?' He bent and deliberately arched his enormous butt in the air as he grabbed the soap pouches off the floor. Using the scissors we borrowed from the home ec room, he cut the bladders and poured the insides over the linoleum corridor. When all three soap packets were empty, and the hall looked like a unicorn had puked all over it, he grabbed hold of my hand. We both grinned boldly, puppies in a park waiting for the fun to start.

'Ready?'

'Yep.' I gripped his hand in apprehension and we moved forward, the sludgy soap coating our feet like velvet as we slid up the hallway.

My legs widened, and I clutched Tyler's hand tighter, causing his legs to wobble with mine. It was like trying to balance on a pool of jelly. We'd ungracefully slid ten metres, level with the blue door of Mr Blythe's Maths' room, when my left leg slid out from under me, taking my other leg with it. I let out a squeal and yanked Tyler down with me, our butts landing with a dull thud on the lino. Our laughter echoed along the corridor, Tyler's deep cackle fusing with my raucous giggle as we lay in the slimy mess.

'Oh God, it's so slippery.' I pressed a hand on the ground to sit up and slipped straight back onto my side.

Tyler wobbled to a precarious stance. 'Here, hold on.' He held out his *sudsy hands but my slick fingers slid straight out of his grasp.*

'Sorry, I think you're on your own.' He grinned down at me and then launched himself along the floor as if he stood on a skateboard, legs apart, one foot behind the other.

I fell two more times – thankful for the padding on my backside – before I stood on two feet again. Then I was off, with arms flapping at my sides to maintain some semblance of balance. I glided toward Tyler, already at the end of the hallway, but with no way to stop myself I slammed straight into him, sending us to the ground in one big messy pile.

Skating on foot turned into skidding on our knees and eventually my favourite of all, penguin style, on our stomachs. Our laughter didn't ease until we were completely exhausted, bruised, and covered completely in unicorn puke.

Tyler grasped my hand as we headed outside, where we sat, backs against the rough tree trunk, and rested our worn bodies. Our hands were interlaced, because dream me was free of all reserve – the shackles had fallen off long ago.

'Do you think we can do this again?' I asked.

'What, slide down the hallways?' He raised the side of his mouth. 'Only in our dreams, I'm afraid. Unless you like detention.'

'No thanks, and no, have another dream like this?'

'It's been fun, hasn't it?'

Savouring the moment I rested my head on the tree. 'Mmm, one of the best.'

'Well, I'm glad I could be here for it.' His body shifted so he sat facing me. 'It's been nice to get to know you, Lucy Piper.'

Tyler looked down when he spoke and he reached over to clasp my other hand in his. His fingers were soft, as if the salt from the sea he'd frequented had smoothed away all imperfections. I brushed my thumb along the back of his knuckles, and his eyes lifted. 'Ma petite rêveuse.'

My pulse quickened even though I had no idea what he said. 'French again?'

'Oui.'

'*And it means what exactly?*' *I slanted my face to meet his eyes.*

'Tu es ma petite rêveuse – *my little dreamer.*' *The words danced from his lips, and the warmth from his thumb radiated through me, making my heart skip a beat, moments before I realised what was coming. Tyler dipped his head until our noses almost met. He paused, his eyes drawing me in, the rush of my pulse nearly drowning me. My sporadic heartbeat grew deafening between my ears and then it was gone.*

WHEN I WOKE, MY pulse still beating an irregular pattern, the burn of my face was a sure sign of its brilliant red. Thankfully the moon had shifted, and the only thing surrounding me was blackened guilt. I shifted my head on my pillow. Tyler's eyes remained closed, and I couldn't help using the cloak of darkness to take an uninhibited peek at those lips. Oh God, what was I doing? I closed my eyes briefly. It wasn't like they were the same lips. I needed to get myself together. I tugged at my covers, hiding beneath their protection, before I rolled over, closed my eyes, and went back to sleep.

Hours later, strange voices and yellow-tinged morning light surrounded me, and for a millisecond I'd forgotten where I was. My eyes darted open, grasping at the memory of why I wasn't in my own bed. The unfamiliar smells helped and then Max's sleepy voice from beside me firmly anchored me to reality.

'Morning, hon. Sleep well?' She stretched and curled back under her blanket.

'Yeah, you?' The recollection of last night's dream hit me like a deluge. My smile stretched absentmindedly across my hidden face while images replayed of Tyler holding my hand as we slid down the hallways and the almost kiss under the tree. The heat in my cheeks returned, and my smile disappeared, uneasiness settling over me like a lead blanket. I was relieved when Max shut her eyes again – she'd have seen it all over my face.

'Mmm,' she mumbled, stifling a yawn.

Marie had piled the food high and wide on the large oak table; bacon and eggs and banana pancakes with everything to go with it – maple syrup, cream, strawberries, you name it. A large plate of citrus and poppy seed muffins sat beside a bowl of freshly cut fruit. I loved how much Marie adored this. Pottering in the kitchen for hours on end didn't tire her; she thrived on it.

The raw scent of freshly ground coffee and hot bread drifted through the living room mingling with the crisp air that blew in from the lake, and we clamoured around the table, eager to dig in. The delicious commotion, and especially Tyler's presence on the other side of the table, was anything but an intense and abrupt way to begin the day.

Cal poured orange juice for everyone, and before I even had a chance to think it, Marie stood behind me with a cup of coffee.

She patted my shoulder and placed the mug on the table. 'Here you go, love. Would anyone else like a coffee?'

None of my friends were a 'where's-the-drip' kind of coffee person like me, but it never stopped her from asking.

'Yes please, Mrs Brooks.'

I jerked my head up to see Tyler smiling reservedly at Marie.

'Only if you stop calling me Mrs Brooks, it sounds much too old,' she said with a big grin. 'Would you like any sugar?'

'Yeah, one thanks.' Exactly how I liked it.

I couldn't help noticing how different he appeared today, especially those lips, and his hands, the same gentle ones that'd held mine last night. I pulled my eyes away, embarrassed by my undisguised appraisal of him. I had to remember I wasn't looking at the person from last night – *I* wasn't the person from last night.

It had all been a dream. I couldn't decide what was worse: the fact I dreamed him in the first place, the remorse for what I'd imagined, or the sadness that something so real and meaningful didn't essentially happen.

I reached for a strawberry and my eyes fluttered up to meet Tyler's, heated and butterfly-inducing. His cheeks rose in a knowing grin, as if he was privy to my thoughts, which only compounded my embarrassment tenfold. I distracted myself by piling loads of the deliciousness onto my plate and swivelled on the oak chair to chat to Max.

—13—

With pencils beside me and art book on my lap, I sat curled up on the couch while everyone else ventured out into the sunlight after breakfast. Music blasted in my ears, the outside world shut out yet again. I hadn't intended on another day of avoidance, but after last night's dream, the need to be alone, to escape the knowing glances of a certain person, were too big to ignore.

Almost of its own volition, my hand glided across the paper, the pencil's grey tip shading the shadow of a curl over the child's forehead, a different angle of the child who'd been killed in the train accident. Regret churned in my stomach, drawing him the only medication to ease the pain.

I squeezed my eyes tightly closed, pushing back the sadness inching over me. Sensing company, I tilted my head up and opened my eyes to Tyler. The pencil fell from my fingers.

I sucked in a big breath and pulled my buds out. My heart thundered and my chest grew heavy, struggling to slow the rhythm. 'You scared the bejesus out of me.'

Tyler slumped onto the couch beside me. 'Sorry. Daydreaming again?'

'No, just concentrating.' My heart rate slowed to normal. 'What do you mean again? Don't *you* start having a go at me like everyone else.'

He had that all knowing smile on his face again. 'No, I only mean you've been somewhere else all morning. Don't worry, I have too.' He leaned in and whispered in my ear. '*Ma petite rêveuse.*'

A bolt of electricity hurled me away from him. 'What the hell?' The slight amusement in his eyes became more visible from the distance I'd created between us. 'That was real?'

'Not real, but I was there as much as you were.'

I shook my head to startle the part of my brain capable of grasping what his words meant. 'Oh my God. My dreams are supposed to be private. The fact you've been in here...' I pointed to my head where a dizzying pulse thumped with brutal force.

'I'm sorry, but you know the same goes for me. You've also been in mine.' He lifted a finger to his own head. 'Do you really feel that bad about last night? I had a great time.'

'It's not that I didn't have fun...' I hesitated, the almost kiss replaying in my mind, and I placed my fingers across my lips.

'But you wouldn't have let me almost kiss you if you knew it was really me?' His voice faltered, but his eyes were fixed in determination.

'No.' My cheeks warmed. 'I mean, we only just met.'

'So did Romeo and Juliet.'

I rolled my eyes. 'We're not Romeo and Juliet, and besides, that's fiction. Anyway, doesn't matter either way. I have no control over what takes place in my mind, so anything that may've happened last night didn't really happen.'

I slumped back in the chair, grabbed a cushion and hugged it to my chest.

'If you say so.' Tyler glanced out the window with the hint of a smile still on his lips. He didn't agree at all. 'You know some people say Romeo and Juliet was based on truth, plus we met months ago.'

'Months ago?'

'Yeah, at the airport, in the dream.'

'Doesn't count, I don't recall being introduced to you.'

'Counts to me. I've seen you in my dream almost every night since then, and each day I woke hoping I'd get to bump into you. So when it finally happened...I kinda felt like I knew you.'

I swallowed. '*Every day?*'

'For the last ten months. You?'

'Once, the night before I met you. Oh, and the first time, when I first dreamed of it. Tyler, this is absurd.'

'I know, and frickin' amazing, right? But last night's dream isn't so different to the first time, is it?'

'Seriously? We created last night's dream. The first one I came into because it'd already happened.' Although that part had never been confirmed. The plane crash had been on the news, but the airport? 'It did, didn't it?'

'Yeah, it did,' he answered slowly, Tyler shifted in his seat, his eyes cast downward. He lifted his face, sorrow in his eyes. 'It was the last time I saw my dad alive.'

What was I supposed to say to that? He wanted me to pretend I didn't know the sad side of his life, but how could I now? 'I'm sorry.'

He shook his head, eyes glistening. 'It's not your fault, just one of those things. I'm used to it now, well...no I'm not, not at all.'

The air hung thick and uncomfortable, and I averted my eyes from his. I gripped the cushion on my lap, resisting the urge to reach out and touch him, to offer a condolence I had no right to give.

What I could give him was the last moments of his dad's life. 'I...I heard him, you know...on the plane.'

Tyler's head jerked up, his eyebrows crumpled together. 'What do you mean?'

I swallowed the lump forming in my throat and fiddled with the tasselled corners of the cushion as I failed to come up with the right words. No one had ever been able to comfortably accept the dream part of my life before, so how do you tell someone you'd heard their dead father in the moments before they died? Would he call the loony bin straight away, or wait until we'd eaten the birthday cake? Then again, Tyler had shared my dream on more than one occasion, so he had to have possessed his own level of insanity, which would make him the safest person to confide in. I filled my lungs, gruellingly walked to the edge of the cliff and took the plunge.

'You know how I dream of things that've happened in real life?' He nodded, waiting. 'Well, my dream didn't end when you drove away that day...It ended when the plane ploughed into the sea. I was on it.'

Tyler frowned, questions written in the lines on his face. His eyes widened and he reeled back in his seat, silently gaping as he processed my words, the recognition erasing some of his creases. He rubbed the back of his neck and eventually found his voice. 'Holy crap.' I huffed out a nervous laugh. 'For real? You sure it was the same plane?' Of course he'd doubt, everyone did. But I didn't fear his questions, trusting they merely paved the way to his belief. I smiled.

'Yeah, I'm pretty sure. I don't usually dream anything random. I remember seeing it on the news last year. Flight S108 from Sydney to L.A., carrying three hundred and twelve passengers–'

'And fifteen crew,' Tyler finished. 'All killed, including my dad – the pilot.'

I reached over and placed my hand over his, and we sat silently for a while.

'What did he say?' Tyler whispered.

'It was only his voice over the speakers. He told us to brace for impact.'

'Was it horrible? I mean, it was...everyone died, but before that?'

The hope in his words pinched around my heart. I thought about lying, pretending for his sake that we barely had time to fathom what was coming. But I could no longer wear a mask with Tyler any more than I could walk away from the couch we shared.

'Yes.' I squeezed my eyes closed. 'Terrifying. Sorry.'

'No, I thought so. Doesn't change anything.' Except now he'd lost hope.

'Why do you think we saw each other at the airport? It makes no sense why I dreamed of that to begin with, I'd normally skip straight to the bad part.'

'Your guess is as good as mine.' His brow lifted and he shrugged as if it was no big deal, but no big deal would be waiting an extra two minutes in the ski lift queue, or missing out on the last white chocolate ice cream in the freezer.

'What if it means something, like there's some reason behind it which explains why we can do what we did last night?'

'You like to know all the answers, don't you?' His mouth turned up in a grin.

'You have no idea.'

'I'm beginning to. But if they're out there, how do we find them?'

'Same way we find the pot at the end of the rainbow,' I muttered, fearing the itch from the plaguing question wouldn't fade as smoothly as the coloured sky on a grey day.

Tyler shared with me the story of his family. Of how close he'd been to his dad and how his father would be gone for days at a time but pack the others full whilst he was home.

'He used to take me fishing up the coast,' he said. 'No boat. We'd climb out onto the rocks and spend half the day standing in the sun while the waves crashed around us. It didn't matter if we caught anything or not, that wasn't the point.'

His dad spent so much time away from his family and yet they were his everything. Tyler said his mum and dad were nauseating to watch.

'They were still so in love with each other after twenty years of marriage, it was sickening.' He let out a small chuckle, as if bringing the image to mind. 'Dad always said Mum made him a wise man, she was the brightest star of them all and he'd always find his way home to her.' He pressed his mouth into a tight line and stared off into the distance.

'What was it he said to you that day at the airport?' I asked quietly, worried the reminder might upset him.

'He said, "Look after my girls while I'm gone". He said it every time he left. I haven't let him down yet.' Tyler spoke with a heaviness, drawing on the importance of his dad's words, which held more gravity than any time he'd said them before. 'After Dad died, Mum didn't leave her room for two whole weeks. She only came out to use the toilet. We took all her meals to her and even then she didn't eat most of them. She acted as though she was the only person who lost someone. I was angry with her for a while. Angry that she couldn't keep going for us, she should be the one caring for us, she was our mum. I think I resented her for months after that. It took me a while, but then I realised, anything more than going to the toilet for her was like climbing a mountain with half a lung, and carrying us was simply too much.' Tyler ran his hands over his thighs.

'That must've been tough.'

'Yeah, 'cause I ended up doing all the carrying. Still think I am sometimes. Jada nearly dropped out of school after Dad died.'

'Really?'

He gave a short nod, pursing his lips. 'She couldn't handle the attention that came with losing someone so publicly. It took some convincing, but I managed to get the teachers on side. I used to take work to and from school every day so she didn't fail completely.'

It hurt to witness his pain. The scars might be nearly a year old, but they were still healing. Who'd cared for Tyler through all this? He seemed to have held all the pieces together for his family, but who held him together?

'Mum came round eventually. And she returned to being the mum we needed, I could tell she found it hard though. And that's why we're here.' He lifted his arms and let them fall back into his lap.

Apparently it had always been a dream of theirs, his mum and dad's, to leave the city and escape to the mountains.

'Dad loved to snow ski when he was younger and he always promised to teach me when we moved here. I wasn't always keen on the idea; leaving friends and the city and the sea. But now I wish, more than anything, that we'd done it sooner. Now here we are, one month away from winter, and no one to teach us how to ski.' He laughed at that.

'I can. Actually, I don't ski so well, but I can snowboard, which is way better anyway, especially if you're a skater.'

'You sure you're that good?'

'What do you mean?'

'Well, after last night's efforts in the hallway–'

I slammed the cushion into his chest.

'Hey, snowboarding isn't half as difficult as that was.' I smiled as I recalled the soap-laden corridors from our dream. 'But first, we have to teach you to water ski.'

—14—

T HROUGHOUT THE DAY, THE sun teased us with suggestions of more warmth. It never delivered but the cooler temperatures didn't stop us from diving into the lake and appreciating what little we'd been given. Then Harry started up the boat and we all had a ski before it was Tyler's turn.

Cal and Sean jumped in the boat, while Max, Amber, and I sat on the shore, watching Tyler's anticipated humiliation. We failed in our struggle not to laugh at his attempts to balance on the skis. It took three flops to get him up and now they were well and truly out of view.

I lay on the grass with the girls, the barest hint of *Vivienne* roaring in the distance. The crisp breeze sent a shiver over my wet skin. I sat and pulled my knees up, wrapping my arms around myself, gazing out on the water as my thoughts wandered to the revelations from the past few hours.

'So, what's going on with you and Tyler?' Max turned her head toward me and Amber stilled to listen. I wasn't surprised at the question; I'd been expecting it all morning. But now, with both sets of eyes cornering me, I felt like a caged animal. Startled and in full view.

The clouds drifted across the azure horizon beyond the lake.

'I saw you last night, and we all noticed the two of you inside, *alone*, earlier. You've got a big thing for him, haven't you?'

'No.'

She raised her eyebrows.

'Maybe...all right, yes.' I screwed up my lips to cover the smile breaking out.

'I knew it.' Max threw her head back and raised herself onto her elbows, her hair cascading behind her onto the grass. Her smile crept all the way into her dark brown eyes. Amber jiggled her knees up and down and squealed.

'What did you two talk about in there?' Max asked. 'How do you go from barely speaking, to this, in a couple of days?'

'I dunno,' I said casually, except I did. 'Just getting to know each other, I guess. He's...I don't know, there's something about him that makes him really easy to talk to.'

'His good looks?' Max said, and Amber laughed.

'No, Max, not that.' But my mouth lifted in its own agreement.

The rumble of the boat grew louder as it approached the shore with Tyler behind it – still upright. The boat pulled into the sandy embankment, and Cal and Sean jumped out.

'How'd you go?' Amber called as she stood.

'Simsy's a natural.' Cal slapped Tyler's wetsuit-clad back. 'Well, after we got him up anyway.'

'I wouldn't say natural. That entails effortless grace, which I did not have.' Tyler's lopsided grin found mine as they walked to shore. Instant warmth settled over my skin.

'But no humiliation either,' Sean said.

'Really?' Tyler said, flitting his eyes between us girls. 'You didn't hear the laughter coming from the shore then.' We tried to feign shame, but our returning laughter made us appear anything but.

OUR FEET DANGLED OVER the end of the jetty, the water lapping at our toes, Tyler's bare legs making it hard to think of any rational words to say now we were alone again. He wore a black t-shirt with bright yellow boardies, the most colour he'd worn since I met him.

A honey eater flew past us and I followed it, casting my eyes into the distance at the squat trees lining the far side of the lake. Distant laughter echoed over the water from the girls in the boat while Sean and Cal skied double.

'What happened to Richie?' Tyler scratched at the wood beneath us. 'I mean, I know he died, Cal told me that much when he invited me here, but he didn't say anything else.'

I flicked a piece of floating bark with my foot. 'Brain cancer.'

'That sucks.'

I let out a sigh. Reminders did that; tightened in my chest and struggled their way out in big surges. 'Nearly six years ago now, still feels like yesterday though.'

We sat in silence, our feet creating ripples in the water.

'So, do you think we can do it again?' Tyler broke the stillness surrounding us.

'Do what?' I asked, glancing up at him.

'Dream together again, you know, like last night.'

'Dunno. I mean, I've got no idea how we did it the first time, let alone how to do it again. I usually don't have any control over my dreams, do you?'

'Me? Not at all. I've had the same dream every day for the last ten months – you – and believe me, if I could've had some control, jazzed it up a bit, I would've.'

'What? Getting a bit bored with this?' I said sarcastically, drawing a circle in the air around my face.

'Are you serious? That was the best part of the dream.' He beamed. 'That, and seeing my dad again each night, but if I could've walked over and talked to you I'd have done it. If I could've told my dad I loved him one more time, I'd have done that too.'

'Oh crap, I'm sorry, I didn't mean to make a joke about it.'

'No, it's okay.' My hands gripped the wooden planks beneath us, and Tyler's little finger moved to brush mine. My breathing wavered. 'I can still remember that day so well, and not because I've replayed it in my sleep so many times. It was the last time I saw my dad alive, but something has always struck me as odd.'

'Oh?' Tingles of excitement glided from my fingers to my stomach, where tiny pastel-coloured butterflies fluttered.

'Yeah, you obviously weren't there in reality, and the first night after Dad died, and the dreams started, I didn't see you. I remember because of the old lady. She fell and it was me who went to help her. Then one night you appeared, and well, you didn't leave.'

'What are you thinking?'

'I'm not sure, but I'm wondering if maybe when you dreamed it, it was the same time you showed up in mine.'

'You know, you could be right.' I jumped up. 'It makes perfect sense.' I ran back up the jetty.

'Where're you going?' Tyler called.

'Just getting something, be right back.'

I rummaged in my bag, found what I needed, then hurried back outside, grabbing a couple of cupcakes off the table on my way.

'Here.' I passed him one of the cakes and landed with a thud back on the wooden slats of the jetty. 'Peanut butter, chocolate.'

'*Merci.*' He took a big bite, his eyes flickering closed for a second. 'Oh my God, these are amazing.'

'I know, right. I reckon Laurie, that's Amber's mum, would win *MasterChef* with these.'

'I'm surprised you're not twice your size with these to contend with.' His eyes grazed the length of me, my white see-through shirt hung loosely over my black bikini and board shorts which suddenly felt too short. His appraisal was brief, but enough to see the attraction behind his eyes.

'I might be one day.' I laughed but sobered when his smile fell away at a glimpse of the worn and faded book in my lap.

I placed my cupcake on the splintered wood and opened the book near the front, to the page where his face peered up at us.

'Why've you got a picture of me in a book?' he asked, his normally high cheeks rising even higher with his cheeky grin. His eyes danced with amusement and I had to look away.

'I drew it,' I said tentatively. 'I draw most of the people I dream. I've never shown these to anyone before.'

He placed a hand over the book, brushing against my fingers. 'You don't have to show me if you don't want to.'

'Actually, I think I do,' I said sedately, but without hesitation. 'That's a first.'

'Well, I'm honoured.'

'You should be.' I joked with a half-smile on my lips and cautiously passed the open book to him. 'This is nearly a year's worth...promise you won't laugh.'

Instead of promising he turned serious, and with a trembling voice asked, 'Do you have anything from the plane crash?'

'Yeah, but only the man sitting across from me and the lady beside me. They're on the next page.' He flipped to the gentleman's face, and hers.

He jerked his eyes up in surprise. 'This is the lady from the airport. She was on the plane?' His voice cracked and eyes glazed, but the few brutal words scribbled at the bottom of the page showed exactly how much more there was to be upset over.

Plane crash – 327 dead – June 12ᵗʰ – seat 41H – visible.

'What's "visible" mean?' he asked.

'Sometimes people don't see me in a dream, I just observe. Other times, like this dream, I'm there as much a part of the incident as if

I were really living it.'

'That's intense.'

'That's one word for it.' I could think of a few more – unfair, scary, grim.

'When did you have the dream?' He turned back a page to see the date I'd scribbled on the top of my sketch of him. 'The fourteenth?' He pointed to the date.

'Yeah, looks like.'

'So you dreamed of it two days after it happened? Is that what normally happens?'

I laughed, a dry humourless chuckle. 'I don't think there are any rules to how and why I see what I do.'

He continued to flip through my extensive and personal collection of death, pausing every so often to read a line or take a closer look at a sketch. My heart raced at what he must be thinking.

Tyler peered up at me. 'This is...these drawings are incredible. Are these all people from your dreams?'

'Mm-hm.' The thin rustle of the turning pages as he absorbed dream after dream felt like a cheese grater peeling away at my skin. I rubbed my hands over my arms.

'You don't know any of them?'

'No, they're all people I've never seen before,' I answered. 'Well, I've seen them in my dreams, but that's it. Sometimes more than once, but mostly it's different people each time.'

'They're so realistic, how do you do it?' He curled a corner under his thumb and forefinger.

'I don't know. I seem to recall faces easily and I can draw, I guess that's the key.' I shrugged.

'Yeah, I can see that.'

My fingers fidgeted in my lap. No one had ever peered so deeply into my soul before, and this book was the very heart of it.

'Hey.' Tyler rested his hand on mine, calming me with the understanding in his eyes. 'You okay? Do you want me to stop?'

'No, no I don't. I've actually never wanted to show this to anybody more in my life. I've always kept it so well hidden. What is it about you that makes me wanna fess up?'

'I'm not sure, but you've got the same effect on me.' He held my gaze for a few more tense moments, then removed his hand from mine and returned to the book.

'Want to tell me about this lady, this dream?' He held up a page from last week – Dreadlock Lady. 'She looks interesting.'

'She was the mother in the train crossing accident,' I said, the gravity of the recent loss lodging in my throat.

'Where were you in this dream?'

'Watching from outside the car. Useless.' My nerves made me speak faster than normal. 'It's so damn frustrating. I know I'm dreaming, I usually know what's about to happen, because I've seen it on the news or something, but I'm powerless to do anything about it. All these people are dying, and I'm just standing there watching.'

'I guess it's a good thing you don't dream them again and again like me then,' Tyler said, lightening the mood.

'Actually, I do dream about them again, but it's usually a bit different. It's like I go away and come up with an alternate ending.'

'What was hers?'

'She slowed down. Tied her little boy's shoelaces. They made it to the tracks thirty seconds later and the man in the Ute died instead.'

Tyler's brow furrowed, shadowing his dark eyes. 'So you don't always dream of a happy ending then.'

'Sometimes there isn't one. Some things just are. And sometimes there's no alternative at all.'

'When your time's up, your time's up.'

'Exactly. Suicides are sometimes like that. Thankfully most suicides don't make the news so I don't see many, but there was one at our school a couple years ago. A boy in our year. His name was Daniel, Daniel Bonheur.'

'That's unfortunate.'

'I know, it was so cruel, but that wasn't the worst of it. His family were beyond poor. He carried his books around in a plastic shopping bag and his clothes had holes in them. It only gave the bullies more ammunition. Each day I'd hear "Hey Bonheur, you happy to see me?!" And "Daniel, you've got a Bonheur!" Or "Bonheur's here, watch your back". You name the insult, we'd all heard it.'

'Did you do anything about it?'

'What do you do? Change his last name? No one was going to stop even if I said something. Jason and Zach were the worst; the dickheads in our Geography class. Unfortunately, they're really popular, and most people don't stand up to them, but I wish every day I'd tried a bit harder. The best I could do was be nice to Daniel when I could, offer a smile, say hi to him, the things no one else seemed to do. Now, I feel sick whenever I see those guys, knowing what they played a part in.'

'So what happened?'

'He killed himself. Grade nine, age fourteen. Overdose. I dreamed of him afterward. I don't know his family, but when I dreamed of him I got the feeling he received more insults at home than he did at school. It's strange how the weak ones always attract it. His mum was cruel and his dad was even weaker than Daniel. The house was filthy, but Daniel stood there and washed the dishes before going to bed, as if that'd make a difference. His parents didn't notice until the following morning. He'd been in his room having a seizure, foaming at the mouth and no one knew.' My eyes moistened at the memory. 'I watched him die over and over for a week until I reached the conclusion that there was simply no other ending for him. It makes me sick even thinking about it. That having a short crappy life was it for him.'

'Yeah, that's rough. It's a wonder you can function each day, seeing those things every night.'

'I know, and it's not like I can use it as an excuse for handing in my assignments late either. "Sorry had a bad dream",' I huffed. 'That's why last night was so good. I never dream the good stuff.'

'You do now,' he said, twitching his thick eyebrows up and down.

I laughed at his devious expression. 'You actually think it's possible to do it again?'

'I don't know, but it's happened twice already, why not again? So where should we meet tonight?' Tyler said, so sure of himself. He rested back on his palms and swung his legs, kicking water into the air.

'I don't think it works like that.'

'Why not? School was an obvious choice for our minds to take us. But what if we consciously chose somewhere? Somewhere we both know and agree on.'

'All right, what about right here?' I asked, pointing out at the lake.

'Here.' Tyler's eyes lit up, full of the same eagerness swirling within my stomach.

—15—

T HE FOG HAD LIFTED, my view no longer tainted by the grey
cloud of mourning that surrounded me. To finally see a horizon of happiness when, for so long, it had been murky with gloom,
was like a breath of fresh air for lungs that only knew ash.

My dreams were like a vice, unyielding, crushing around my
skull. Sharing them with Tyler released some of the tightness,
some of the pain. Trusting him with my dreams had been the best
decision I'd made in a long time, but I guess that's the thing with
trust – it creeps up on you like the spring appears after winter. One
day you see buds on the trees and before you know it the branches
are in full bloom again, providing a shelter you didn't know you
needed.

The sun hovered low over the lake, signalling the end of another
day, and Richie's birthday celebrations began like they did most
years, with Marie flitting about in the kitchen, preparing for the
big birthday feast. The aroma from the pork crackle in the oven
made my taste buds moisten in anticipation. It was Richie's favourite – we had it every year.

When Jake arrived, we gorged ourselves on dinner and an
amazing melt-in-the-mouth chocolate mousse cake. An hour later,
having eaten way too much, we pushed our chairs back, nauseated
by the food and dirty plates still piled on the table and shuffled into
the lounge room.

Everyone dispersed onto the couch and mattresses on the floor. I slouched into a bean bag underneath the TV, my bare feet stretched out in front of me. Billy Bob sat curled in my lap, tail gently wagging as I stroked his back. Music played in the background, something we didn't pick, something classical.

Tyler lowered himself onto the mattress beside me and leaned his back against the TV cabinet. So much for being relaxed. A trembling undercurrent vibrated under my skin. Like a metal detector, my body reacted to his close proximity.

He moved closer, his mouth inches from my ear. 'This night is taking forever,' he whispered.

I pressed my lips together, suppressing a smile as I rubbed behind Billy Bob's ears.

Cal jumped over the back of the couch and held up a beer. 'We're havin' Richie's first legal beer for him.' He lifted the bottle to his lips and threw his head back. He hissed, like you do when you're not used to drinking alcohol, and a barrage of laughs rang out. Wiping the back of his hand over his mouth, he passed the bottle to Sean.

The bottle landed in my hand, and I took a swig, gagging and coughing heavily. Good lord, who willingly drank that stuff?

When we'd finished our ritual, the effects of our few mouthfuls and a day in the sun mellowed our rowdiness. Sean lay in the corner of the couch, hand behind his head, his other scrolling over his phone.

'What's happening, Sean?' His brow creased and I stretched my arm out, pointing toward the double doors that led toward home. 'Out there.'

He looked back at his phone. 'The usual. Cats, sunsets, oh, and there's a pretty big party on at Jason James' place tonight – "hashtag JJsParty" is clogging my feed. I think half the school's heading there.'

'Not us.' I smiled, resting my head on the beanbag. I couldn't think of much worse places to spend a Saturday night than with a bunch of oblivious drunk sixteen-year-olds. I also despised Jason, so no thanks.

'Nah, this is the place to be, I reckon.' Sean sent a small grin over to me, knowing I felt exactly the same.

'Not very often the sixteen-year-olds get invited to an eighteenth,' Cal piped up.

'True, right. And Jason might throw the big parties, but this is where it's at, bro. Skiing all day, being waited on by your mum, and of course, all you lot, smelly feet and all.' Sean spread his arms out taking us all in, and I lifted my bare feet and wiggled them in the air.

'Were you a party boy back in Sydney?' Cal asked Tyler.

'Nah, not really. I'd rather be in bed dreaming than go to the sorts of parties the lads at my school went to.'

I spluttered out a cough, my eyes watering. Tyler patted me on the back. 'You good?'

With a hand on my chest, I darted my eyes sideways. 'Just the beer.'

His mouth remained serious but the laughter in his eyes was unmistakable. 'You sure...' He leaned closer and lowered his voice. '*Ma petite rêveuse?*'

It had been a massive day, physically and emotionally, in more ways than one. I expected to fall straight to sleep once my eyes closed, but I buzzed with more enthusiasm than an eight-year-old on Christmas Eve and couldn't for the life of me sleep.

I'd never planned a dream. Often I could expect to dream of something in particular, because I'd see it on the news, but I'd never collaborated with my mind before it had happened. I never thought it possible, still didn't, but this idea of Tyler's stirred my pulse into giddy excitement.

I tossed from side to side in the hopes of finding that all elusive position, the key to the other world. It never came and, after what felt like fifty years, when I was sure everyone had long fallen asleep, I gave up. I rose, wrapped the quilt around my shoulders, and headed outside with it trailing on the floor behind me like a queen. Tyler groaned as I stepped over him, nudging him with my foot to wake him. I slid the door open and moved into the cold black of night. I climbed onto one of the sun lounges I'd used earlier when the air had been much warmer, and we could see to the other side of the lake. Now, in the wee hours of the morning it was hard to imagine, if not for the soft sound of lapping water, a lake there at all.

'You know we wouldn't need the blankets if we were dreaming.' Tyler shuffled outside behind me, his sleeping bag draped around him. He pushed a lounge against mine and sat beside me.

'That's not entirely true. I usually feel all the elements in my dreams. Anyway, in order for one to dream, one must first sleep.' I offered him a tired smile.

'I would've waited for you.'

'I know, but I couldn't stand lying there any longer, and I didn't want to miss any fun you might've had without me.'

'It's only fun if you're there.' He shifted closer to me so the length of our blanketed bodies touched. 'I'm glad you woke me though. Dreaming's fun, but being with you for real is even better, even if we are freezing our arses off.'

I wasn't anymore. With his body so close to mine, warmth radiated through me like a furnace. Still, we pulled our blankets tight against our chins, and I bent my head to rest on his shoulder.

He lowered his onto mine, and we lay silently, looking up into the twinkling canvas above.

'My dad loved to star-gaze. They weren't so easy to see in the city, but whenever we went camping they were like this, perfectly clear.' Tyler pointed to a single star in the sky. 'See that one there.'

I lined up my head with his arm. 'Yeah?'

'Me too.' He laughed.

I pulled back. 'What? Wait, that's it? Nothing profound? No words of wisdom to share?'

'No, sorry, something my dad never passed onto me, the ability to recall so much useless information.'

'It's not useless.'

Tyler's brows lifted. 'Not unless I want to work for NASA.'

'Not true. He didn't work for NASA, yet it was obviously beneficial to him as a person otherwise you wouldn't remember it. Can't we just enjoy things for the simple pleasure of enjoying them? Not everything has to have a purpose.'

'You can't talk.' He nudged me with his elbow. 'When was the last time you just enjoyed your dreams without wanting to know what it all meant?'

I turned onto my side, bringing the blanket back up over my shoulder. 'Never. But that's because there is meaning behind them. If I could have sweet, meaningless dreams every night, like everyone else, I'd choose that any day.'

'Maybe one day you will, but then you might wish for the excitement of what you've got now.'

I shook my head, determined. 'Nope, not gonna happen, tried it.'

'Really?' Tyler shifted to face me, resting his head on his hand.

'Yeah, few years back. Mum was desperate to make the dreams go away, so we went to the doctor, who decided I had stress-induced nightmares, and prescribed some old person's drug. Horrible tablets.' I remembered my hesitation. I wasn't convinced taking something artificial to stop something as natural as a dream was the right move, but being young and easily influenced, I downed my first pill. That was three years ago.

'What happened?'

'To begin with, nothing. They took the dreams away.' I could still recall those nights. So deep and dark and empty. 'But then my days changed too. I began getting headaches, blurry vision, and was dizzy all the time.' Understatement of the year. The looks I got as I wavered, unsteady, when the stairs disappeared below my feet and rooms tilted, were testament to that.

'So you went off them?' Tyler asked.

'Yeah. I didn't miss my dreams, or the excitement of them, far from it. It was the longest break I'd had from my nightmares, but I began to doubt if it was worth the sacrifice.' Could I give up a semi-normal life for the sake of a good night's sleep?

'Obviously you decided it wasn't.'

'Mmm. Though some days, I'm not so sure.'

'Like the day you met me?'

'Yeah, the day I met you.' We laughed at the joke, but the truth was I *had* doubted my choice the day he showed up.

'I can't even imagine not meeting you, you know,' he said seriously, breaking me from my thoughts of that fated day.

'We still would've met though, just not in our dream first.'

'True, and then you mightn't have been so resistant to me sharing the library table.'

'Dunno.' I grinned in the darkness. 'I'm pretty territorial.'

Tyler's shoulders shook, then stilled. 'You know I feel really guilty for thinking it, but I'm so glad we moved here.'

'Why do you feel guilty?' I squeezed my eyes closed. Me and my big mouth. "Cause of your dad.'

'The only reason we moved here is because he died.'

'But you know there's nothing you could've done about it, nothing that could've prevented it, so there's no reason why you can't enjoy where you find yourself now. Grief is bad enough without adding guilt to the mix.'

'Actually I think guilt and grief go hand in hand, but you're right. And I am enjoying where I've found myself right now,' he said, gazing down the length of us and back up with the smirk I'd come to love. The awareness reignited my furnace. Could he feel the heat too?

'Damn this chair's uncomfortable.' Tyler shuffled on his lounge.

I leaned on my elbow. 'Are you lying on the frame?'

Tyler laughed. 'We needed to keep warm.' We still did. The chill in the air had dropped to near freezing.

Laughing, I edged back. Tyler heaved himself onto my lounge and threw his sleeping bag over us – the combined blankets and sparks between us multiplying the warmth by ten. My heart beat annoyingly fast, but I'd never been calmer. Was fate such a thing? Right then I'd have placed my bet on yes. We lay with our fingers laced together, and Tyler's other arm held me near. My head fitted into his shoulder, and his warm breath on my head acted like a sleeping balm. I finally allowed the pull of slumber to enfold around me and closed my eyes.

—16—

THICK BLADES OF GRASS tickled between my toes. The house loomed in front of me, its walls of glass reaching to the sky. A sky which, only moments ago, had been black with night, now transformed into a vivid cobalt blue.

I turned toward the lake. Tyler stood on the jetty with a massive grin, the happiness stretching over his cheeks all the way to his eyes. I squealed, hopped a step, and ran down the hill.

'We did it!' I called, and he opened his arms for me.

'We have superpowers.' His eyes lit up and he lifted and spun me around. Our laughter filled the air.

'Feel like a swim?' he asked.

'Hell yeah, what else are we gonna do in this most perfect of places on this gloriously sun-filled night?' It neared the end of April and yet it felt strangely normal to be here under the full heat of the sun.

With the absence of my normal level of fear, but still some trepidation, I peeled away my clothes, trying not to watch as Tyler did the same.

Strange how my mind could turn the night into day, but not my underwear into a bikini.

'Okay, just pretend I'm wearing a bikini,' I said, suddenly self-conscious.

Tyler swallowed as his eyes cast my way. 'I can try,' he said. 'Although I'm not sure of the difference, it's probably the same skin ratio as your bikini anyway.' I raised my eyebrows. 'What? You thought I didn't notice?' My bikini was almost as skimpy, and of course if I'd checked him out earlier I *shouldn't be surprised he'd done the same.*

'Fine, pretend I'm in a wetsuit.' I removed the last of my clothes and tried desperately to avoid Tyler's eyes.

'Not possible.'

'All right, can we just get in the water then? Race you.' I ran down the jetty, barely keeping the lead as Tyler gained on me. By the time I reached the end he was alongside me, and we both leaped into the air, landing in the perfectly silky water, sending a tide of waves in every direction.

We floated on our backs, like we had the night before in reality, this time staring up at a bright summer blue sky with the tiniest flecks of white clouds.

Tyler reached his arm over the top of the water and grabbed my hand, pulling me to him. I pulled back and as the tension raced through our bodies we lost our ability to float. Letting go of our hands we faced each other and treaded water.

'Lucy,' Tyler said softly.

'Mm?' My heartbeat grew faster at the intensity in his eyes.

'I want to kiss you.' He paused, and I swallowed. 'I know this is just a dream, but it feels so damn real and I want to kiss you. Last time you didn't know it was really me, and you said you wouldn't have done it if you did.' I opened my mouth to tell him I'd changed my mind, but he kept talking. 'So before I do, I wanted to make sure you were okay with it.'

A lump caught in my throat, but I managed to croak out the words, 'I'm okay with it.'

The water rushed around me as Tyler's body closed in, and then his lips were on mine, warm and tender. My eyes closed involuntarily, and his wet hands were on my cheeks bringing me nearer as our lips moved together. We swayed in the water, our feet and legs dancing below us as we kicked to stay afloat. My body dissolved, and it was quite likely I'd die if I woke right then.

I wrapped my arms around his neck as Tyler lowered his hands to rest on my waist. We parted slowly, and I opened my eyes to peer into his.

It was a perfect moment, too perfect perhaps, but an ingrained benefit of experiencing it through the filtered lens of a dream.

'What're you thinking?' Tyler asked still holding onto me.

'That this feels like a dream.' We shared a tender smile. 'You?'

'Happy. I've wanted to do that since the first moment I saw you.'

'What? Since I pummelled into you like a train wreck?'

'Maybe not right away.' He tilted his head up as if remembering the collision. 'But when I recognised you – yes, I would've kissed you right there and then if I didn't think you'd punch me in the face for it. But then you ran away anyway.'

'Do you blame me?'

'No.'

We held hands and moved to float on our backs again. We were silent; all the words we needed to say drifted away unsaid. But silence had a way of saying other things – comfort, unity, trust – and the gentle chirp of the birds reminded us of how idyllic those unsaid words were.

The clouds hovered above us, where the dragons and sheep gradually morphed into dolphins and palm trees, and then they were gone.

THE FAMILIAR SOUND OF Maggies in the trees, singing their morning gargle, stirred me from sleep. My toes were icicles, and it took me a few seconds to grasp that I was outside and they were poking out from the bottom of the blankets. I jerked them in and heard Tyler's intake of breath as my toes touched his feet.

'Morning,' he whispered into my neck. His arm draped over my side exactly as it had when we fell asleep. His hand caressed my stomach.

I widened my eyes at the touch, and then curled myself into him, savouring this moment of closeness. I'd never slept in the same bed with anyone, not since my younger days with Max, when we slept with one head up each end of the bed, but that was unparalleled to this situation with Tyler.

How had this happened so fast? Only two days before I'd been dreading the weekend and being so close to him, but now the thought of not being near him made my stomach twist in knots.

A hazy mist filled the air, and the horizon held an orange glow as the sun tenderly eased its greeting on us. I rolled over so I could look at Tyler. He beamed adoringly down at me.

Moments ago we'd been kissing in our dream, and as the new day dawned on us so did the memory, bringing with it a shyness I hadn't known the night before. Heat rose in my cheeks, my embarrassment gathering into quiet chuckles and mingling with Tyler's deep tremor. I buried my face into his chest and pulled the covers over my head, exposing my toes once again. Still giggling, I closed my eyes and inhaled his subtle scent: wood fire with a hint of spice.

'Did you sleep all right?' Tyler asked softly.

'Yeah, you?'

'One of the best sleeps I've had in a long time.' I tilted my head back and peered at him. His eyes shone bright, and he sighed so heavily it dripped with satisfaction. 'No seriously, best sleep ever. No hot sweats from waking from my dream like I normally do... you're good for me.' My cheeks grew warm.

'Well, I hate to tell you this, but it can't continue.' His smile fell away and worry etched across his forehead. 'The sleeping together part that is. What would we tell my parents?' I laughed, and he tickled my sides evoking a huge whoop from me.

'Don't say things like that; it's plain cruel to someone who's been waiting a long time for this.'

'This?' I raised my eyebrows teasingly, although I had a fair idea of what he might mean by 'this'. Still it wouldn't hurt to hear it.

'You...I've dreamed of you almost every night for the last year, and that was before I even met you. Now, well...'

This was too much for my just-woken-up mind to comprehend. I was falling hard; we both were. We'd become one big flaming asteroid headed straight for impact, and I feared no one would be able to stop us from ripping a great big hole in the earth.

'What else do you dream of?' I asked. 'As in aspire, desire, hope for?'

'Wow, that's deep for this time of the day.'

'Just trying to get to know the person I've shared far more intimate things with.'

'You don't regret it, do you? Now you're awake?' he asked, the hope in his voice palpable.

Without my dream to protect me, vulnerability settled over me, and the light of day allowed me to see his face more clearly than in the night just gone. I liked the rawness of reality, and at the same time savoured the memory of the perfect dream.

'No,' I said, and white fog escaped through his lips as he exhaled.

'Good.' He paused. 'I dream of seeing the world. I need to learn more languages, though 'cause I kinda agree with Dad, I don't think you can travel without seeing the people too. I don't know how I'll make money, but that's a minor detail,' he said with a chuckle.

I laughed with him but stiffened. I had a similar dream, one restricted by more than finances. He noticed my trepidation.

'What is it?'

'Nothing. It's a good dream.'

'But you don't get it, do you, not being interested in travel 'n' all?'

'It's not that I'm not interested, I'm terrified of it. So any thoughts I might have will stay as that, as thoughts, dreams.'

'What a load of bollocks. I've never heard anything so ridiculous.'

'Thanks,' I said sarcastically.

'Sorry, but it's true. You can't say you dream of something and then give up on it before giving the poor thing a chance.'

'I can in my case. You try seeing the things I do, then ask yourself if you wanna be exposed to more heartache, more death, more pain.' My palms grew sweaty and I was no longer cold.

'Is that how you really feel?'

'It's how I really feel. My death tally is staggering, I'm not sure my pencil could keep up.'

'You know that might be kind of cool.'

'What, to see more death? *So* cool.' Did he realise how thoughtless he was being?

'No, I mean to draw people around the world. With the skills you've got, you could draw a whole book full.'

'I've already got four.' I set my jaw, but the stillness of Tyler beside me and the gentle brushstroke of his thumb on my arm calmed me.

'Okay,' he said, before the casual edge to his voice returned. 'Sounds like I'm on the lookout for another travelling partner then.'

'That you are.' I hoped that might be the end of it. As rational as it was to me, I couldn't explain something as irrational as Hodophobia – I'd looked it up. An intense fear at the thought of travelling. The furthest I'd ever been in my life was the south coast of Australia. I was ten when we'd driven the Melbourne end of the Great Ocean Road. Ten, before the dreams started, before fear of the uncontrollable set in.

'All right then. Tell me one thing.' Tyler reached over and moved the hair from my eyes, tucking it behind my ear. 'Where would you go? If you weren't afraid, what would you want to see?'

'That's easy,' I said guided by the safe lure of his words. 'Canada.'

'Canada.' He smiled dreamily, as if conjuring the images to mind. 'Why Canada?'

The snow. Ours is nothing compared to what's over there, or so I've been told. I want to feel the thick fresh powder under my board, do trails I don't know like the back of my hand.'

'So not the people then?' He snickered at our complete opposite take on that aspect of travelling.

'No, not the people.' I swivelled and faced him. 'Unless they're painted or sculpted ones. I'd love to go to Paris too, I want to spend three days in the Louvre.'

'But the Louvre has crowds of people.'

My mouth gaped open. 'You've been?'

He smiled down at me and nodded. 'For a few hours, it was packed. Could barely get close enough to the Mona Lisa to see her.'

'I'm so jealous right now. But only a few hours?'

'We had two and a half days in Paris on our way to England a couple years ago, that's not a lotta time to fit everything in. And no, not enough time for the Louvre.'

I groaned and rested my forehead against his chest.

We lay together for a little longer before we collected our blankets, headed back indoors, and slid silently into our cold and empty beds.

The weekend ended as abruptly as it began. We loaded our bags back into Jake's van and, although I'd been in Tyler's arms only a few hours earlier, our goodbye was no more than the trading of phone numbers and a silent stare across the driveway.

I'd travelled this route many times before, but as Jake drove along the bumpy road towards home, it felt like I was entering new territory. It was terrain I hadn't wanted to venture into; but like I'd resisted snowboarding to begin with, once I felt the absolute joy of gliding down the mountain I didn't want it to end.

I had just as fiercely resisted Tyler, a fear of the unknown, but I'd learned he was like the snow; soft and gentle, with the power to incite a daily longing for its return. He made me feel things I never thought possible.

I felt adored, but most of all, believed; and with that came the ability to breathe again.

—17—

I SAT IN MY dimly lit room in front of my laptop, determined to find some answers. I bit into my apple and tapped at the keys, logging in as @LucidLucy.

The night before, I'd been on the phone with Tyler for over an hour before bed, yet when I closed my eyes – nothing. I woke to my phone vibrating from my bedside table and Tyler's eager voice down the line. 'Anything?'

'Nope.' I'd normally have been happy about that.

I spent the afternoon at work, helping Laurie at an office function in Mayfield, and all day the question had stuck to me like her scone dough – why? Why could Tyler and I share dreams at the lake house, but not since we'd been home?

I scrolled through the list of questions on the forum, but as usual, nothing matched. I started to write a new thread before spotting a notification waiting for me in the top right corner of the screen. A spike of adrenalin shot through me as I clicked on the little bell icon, my heart rate accelerating at finally having a response to last week's question.

@Star_Crossed: @LucidLucy *it sounds to me like you've met someone who could become a very important person in your life, your soul mate. This could be friendship level or something more, that's not important. What matters is that you're open to the changes a connection with their soul will awaken in yours, and allow your soul to transcend to a higher level of consciousness. Think of seeing them before meeting them as a sample, a teaser trailer for the latest blockbuster. Did you feel anything in the dream? If you did, then imagine what it's going to feel like now you get to sit and enjoy the full show. My best advice is to savour every magnificent morsel.*

A shiver slid over my skin. What an answer. Never in a million years did I expect something like that. It sounded too perfect but also too right. It might've been a super soppy answer and a little bit too spiritual, but hey, when the shoe fits. I picked up the phone. I had to read it to Tyler.

When he didn't answer I typed a message for him to call when he got the chance. His mum had been pretty clingy since we'd returned from the lake two days ago; we still hadn't seen each other again.

I jiggled my ankles and scrolled through my phone – Granny Tess.

'Lucy, darling.'

I told her everything, and although she sounded pleased and happy for me, her voice tinged with something more, sadness? She wouldn't be upset or worried about my dreams. It had to be something else.

'Is everything okay, Granny Tess? You don't sound well.'

'I'm sorry, dear, I am interested truly, it's only something's come up. A bit of a shock really.'

Fear contracted in my stomach. I gulped. 'What is it?'

Her sigh filtered down the line before she spoke. 'A friend of ours died last night in a house fire.'

I placed a hand over my chest. 'I'm so sorry. Are you all right?'

'Not really. She was from the church, loveliest old lady, made the best éclairs.'

I slapped my palm across my mouth to stifle my laugh. 'Granny Tess.'

'Oh dear, I didn't mean it quite like that. Obviously that's a loss in itself, but Beverly will be missed terribly too.'

'Well, you don't need to be on the phone to me then. I just wanted to share the latest.'

'And I'm glad you did, dear.'

The moment I pressed the red *end* button I wanted to hurl my phone across the room. 'Damn it.' I squeezed my eyes closed, fending off the nauseating blend of emotions. Worry for Granny Tess, grief for their friend and the family that'd recently lost a loved one, and regret for what lay ahead when I closed my eyes.

I glanced out my window, disappointed to see how dark it had become since I'd been in my room. I'd kill for a run, but that wouldn't be happening without any daylight.

I yanked my sneakers on. I'd have to settle for a few laps of the backyard.

I squeezed my eyelids closed, but it only intensified the sting. I opened them to the smoke and could barely see through my tears and the thick cloud in front of me. I inhaled a mouthful of congested air, and huge, racking coughs escaped my mouth. I was going to choke to death before I even made it through my dream.

The endless shrill of the smoke alarm penetrated through me, and my legs wavered as they moved forward. I tried desperately to escape the heat of the fire that gained on me from behind. My breaths came short and fast. Placing my forearm over my mouth and nose, I concentrated on sucking in the filtered air through my thick jumper.

I stood beside a tall side dresser, covered in a white lace runner and crowded with unmatched photo frames. An elderly woman strode toward me from another room, her ankle-length floral nightie flowing around her as she sped through the house. She didn't stop as she dashed past me, toward the fire. What the hell!

She rummaged in a drawer, fumbled, and eventually pulled something out. Smoke crept into every corner of the room, searching out its next victim, engulfing her. She stumbled to her knees, and the item in her hand landed with a clink on the floor. My heart raced in fear as she crawled to retrieve it. I knew I was safe, assured in my knowledge I would wake with clean air and a life, but it was little help for the lady about to slip into the longest sleep of her life. Her weak arms faltered, and she fell forward, her face etched in pain as it hit tiles. She didn't move. I stared at her, hoping for the flinch of a finger, anything. Nothing.

I screamed. 'You need to move. You're going to die.' But my pleas went unheard. All attempts to save her would be in vain. My being here was completely and utterly useless.

Dread crept over me as our death loomed.

I did the only thing I could and lay down beside her. I brushed the hair from her eyes – eyes wide with the aching agony of fear. Even though she couldn't see or feel me, I carefully lifted her aged hand in mine and yearned for her to sense some of the comfort she so desperately needed.

'It'll be over soon. I'm sorry.'

Her eyelids closed, but the heat from the roaring flames grew unbearable, and her eyes shot open in anguish. Flames grabbed at her nightie, groped for her hair, seared her flesh. I held onto her as she writhed in pain, her screams matching the wail of the smoke alarm.

Raging fire engulfed us, scorched my skin. I arched my back, desperate for an escape from the inferno. From death.

But all I could do was wait – wait to die, so my mind could bring me back to life.

I COULDN'T WAIT TO get out and run off my dream. Straight after breakfast I tore out the door and crossed the front lawn. I picked up pace, my ponytail whacking the top of my back, my pulse keeping time with the music in my ears, and soon enough the thud of my feet on bitumen joined the beat of Aurora's 'Warrior'.

I hesitated as I passed Tyler's place. It was too early to knock on his door. I pushed onwards up the hill and entered the track where the thicket of trees left the road.

My phone vibrated from my armband. Tyler.

'Hey,' I said, panting.

'What're you doing? You sound out of breath.'

'I am.' I rested a hand on my waist. 'I'm running.'

'Where are you?'

'I've just run past your place, actually. That's my route. I'm up the top of the road in the trees.'

'What? You mean to say the hot girl running past my place has been you?'

'You lookin' at hot girls?' I teased.

'Only the one,' he said and I could almost see the smile down the line. 'You called last night.'

'Yeah, I wanted to talk to you.' I tried not to sound as pathetic as I felt. One weekend with him and now I needed to tell him everything.

'Sorry, Mum needed me. I can talk now. Want me to join you?'

Did I ever.

'Sure.'

'Putting my sneakers on.'

My smile widened, and music returned to my ears the moment I ended the call. I jogged on the spot and shifted to calf stretches to keep my heart rate up, despite the fact Tyler's imminent arrival meant the thing raced at full speed on its own. I was barely out of town, but I could still make out the rising mountains on the horizon. Their distance made them appear dull and murky, but I appreciated their magnificence and admired the view none the less. The music seeped through me, my calves burned as I stretched, making me wince.

'Guess who?' Warm hands covered my eyes, and Tyler's simmering breath danced on my neck.

I plucked out my earphones, giving him my first smile of the day.

'Morning,' he said, in a deep early-morning voice, only slightly breathless from the short sprint from his house. But it wasn't his voice that made my legs wobble, it was the adoration in his eyes.

I cast my gaze to his feet, navy blue sneakers, and those bare legs again. 'Think you can keep up?'

He scoffed and rolled his eyes before taking off ahead of me.

'Hey,' I called. It didn't take long to catch up to him, and I quickly matched his pace. Tyler glanced over his shoulder, causing a tug of unbridled happiness to my lips. I never went running with anyone...ever. It was strange, but also unexpectedly exhilarating.

With only room for one body on the track ahead, I took the lead as the path narrowed. Wet soil, from the overnight rain, squished under our feet, and ripples of anticipation flowed through me at yet another sign that winter was fast approaching. We ran through the trees until we reached the clearing on the other side where my cow friends munched on thick grass in the paddocks.

'Wow, we're in the middle of nowhere out here,' Tyler said.

'That's why I come here. Beautiful, isn't it.'

'Sure is.'

A cow mooed in the distance, and the wind whispered through the grass, tempting us closer.

I climbed through the fence, and Tyler followed.

'Check this out.' I grabbed his hand and led him up the small hill closer to the cows. His eyes flickered to our entwined hands, then to the view of the town below, that moments ago had been hidden behind the bush.

'How often do you come up here?'

'Every couple of days, if I can.'

He rubbed the backs of his thighs. 'That's a lot of running.'

'Not really, it's only a couple of Ks each way. I don't do it as much in the winter, not if I can be up there instead.' I nodded to the mountains.

We sat in the damp grass, my nervousness heightened to a heart-pounding level at being around Tyler again. I twisted the bracelet around my wrist, instantly back on the tiled floor beside Beverly.

'Tell me about it.'

I squinted at him. 'Huh?'

'The bracelet.' He pointed to my wrist, the focus of my distraction. 'Whenever you fiddle with it, you go somewhere else.'

'Oh, it's my mourning bracelet.' I surveyed my hand and twirled the beads between my fingers. 'Mourning as in grieving. I bought it after Richie died. I was so afraid I'd forget him I bought it as a bit of a memorial type thing. They're not smooth, but the jet beads reminded me of little balls – Richie played basketball with Jake.'

'What's jet, a gemstone?'

'Sort of, it's a kind of coal or something. Queen Victoria wore it after her husband died. She wore mourning clothes for the rest of her life and all her jewellery was made of it 'cause it was black.'

'So, she mourned him till the end of her life? Now that's love.'

'Or madness. Most people thought madness, but it started a trend and brought jet into fashion. Well, back then anyway, pretty sure it's well into unfashionable now, but I like it.'

'Richie meant a lot to you all, didn't he?'

I nodded.

'You still wear it for him?'

'Yes and no. It'll always be for Richie, but now I wear it to mourn others too.'

'People from your dreams?'

'Mmm.'

'Did you have one last night?' Tyler crossed his legs, as if getting ready for story time. It'd been awhile since that had happened.

I nodded. 'After you didn't answer your phone I called my Granny Tess, and she told me about her friend who was killed in a house fire. That's why I dreamed it.'

Tyler closed his eyes before looking into mine, concern etched in the small creases. 'You died too?'

My shoulders sagged. 'Yeah, burning is a horrible way to go.'

'Shit.'

'Right? Sometimes I wonder if that's what I'm for?'

'What do you mean?'

'Comfort. Course, she couldn't hear me when I spoke, or feel my hand in hers, but I like to think perhaps she could and it gave her some comfort.'

'The touch of an angel.'

'Ha, that's a nice way of thinking about it. More like a kiss of death. I'm your real-life Brad Pitt from *Meet Joe Black*.' Tyler's blank stare made me laugh. 'You haven't seen that movie?'

'Um, nope.'

'We'll have to change that.'

'Will we?' His eyes lit up playfully before he glanced back to my hand. 'So this is your way of mourning the lady from your dream?' He twisted the jet beads between his fingers, and the whisper of his skin against mine sent tingles up my arm.

'Stupid. isn't it.'

'Not at all. I think it shows how much you care.'

Above the tall gum trees heading down to town, a thick covering of grey clouds slowly extinguished the pale blue sky. The trees bucked and swayed from the increasing winds.

'I just feel, like, by wearing this it's acknowledging that I was there, that I was with them. Part of me would love nothing more than to forget the dreams as soon as I wake up, but that'll never happen, so this is my way of reminding myself, and perhaps them if they're out there, that someone mourns their loss. I might not be the person they loved, but I still matter, right?'

'Of course you do. You matter a lot.' He brushed his thumb over the palm of my hand. I felt his words through the gesture and comfort at being able to tell him the intimate details of something so extremely personal to me.

His dark eyes were like a stormy sea. I stared into their depths, the door to his soul, and became acutely aware that I was at risk of falling far into the rabbit hole. But unlike Alice, I never wanted to leave. The thought terrified me as much as the movie.

'Blue.' I let the word fall from my lips.

'What?'

'Your eyes. They're blue. I thought they were brown before I met you,' I said shyly.

'You thought about my eyes before you met me?' He sat straighter, his mouth turning up, pride evident in his eyes.

'Yes, I did.' I smiled, before turning away and staring out at the mountains. Dark clouds swirled above the tips. 'I wish I knew what she was going back for.'

'Who?'

'The lady in my dream.' A gust of wind blew wisps of my fraying hair around my face, and I tucked the threads behind my ears.

Tyler frowned. 'Why's that important? She's dead.' He whacked his forehead. 'Sorry.'

'No, I get it. It's useless, but this is how I deal with it. I save their lives.' I rolled my eyes and nodded. 'I know, they're already dead, but I can't help it.'

Tyler offered a flat smile. Recognition beamed behind his eyes, like he understood. Maybe that's why he continued to dream of his dad, his mind's way of trying to bring him back. 'So how would you have saved her life?'

'I don't know. That's why I wish I knew what she ran back into the smoke for.'

'How do you know there was something?' Tyler rubbed the side of his face.

'Because she dropped it. I heard it fall out of her hand – it wasn't big, whatever it was. Almost sounded like a coin or something.'

'Maybe a key?' Tyler suggested.

'That'd make sense.' I pressed my fist into the damp ground. 'Damn it, it's so frustrating sometimes. To think if it was a key, that that was all that stood between her and life. Or it could've been something else. Think I'll look it up at home, see if there's anything I'm missing.'

Tyler laid his hand over my fist. 'You can't save her.'

I blinked, wishing away the hot tears building behind my lids. 'I know.'

'Wouldn't it be better to focus on what's here instead, on people you can actually help?' Tyler plucked up a blade of grass. 'I mean... maybe that'd help take your mind off what you can't control.'

'Maybe.' I bunched my knees and clasped my hands around my shins. The wind picked up, the chill increasing.

Tyler's hair shot up with a burst of wind, but it didn't deter him from taking in the splendour of my hill and mountains. He placed his hands behind him and leaned back with a sigh.

We stared out at the sweeping one-hundred-and-eighty degree view of hills and mountains. The peace and magnitude of it stretched from the soaring heights to the swaying wet grass we sat amongst. Behind us, a chirping in the trees broke through the intrusive winds, and as if in response a cow stammered her own low tune.

'Such a shame.' Tyler exhaled a long breath.

'What is?'

'Oh, nothin'.'

I didn't push him, but he continued anyway.

'Just thinking of Dad and how much he would've loved that we finally made it here.'

'Was it the country he liked or the snow?'

'Both, I think. He grew up on a farm, not a working farm, but lotsa land. That's where he learned to fly – his dad had a glider.'

'Wow.'

'I know. They had money. I never knew my grandad, though. He died from a stroke when I was a few years old. Gran sold the property, said it was too much for her to maintain, and she gave the glider to my dad, but he had nowhere to keep it, so he had to sell it.'

'What a shame. Was he gonna buy another one when you moved here?'

Pain flashed across his eyes. 'That was the plan. I think he really wanted to give me some of what he had growing up. But he also desperately loved the snow. We came on a family holiday here once, but it wasn't enough. He always dreamed of coming back so we could live the life he wanted every day, not just during the holidays. "Life is about living for today, not tomorrow", he always said.'

'I like that.'

'Speaking of which.' He sat up, leaned toward me, and placing his hands on my cheeks, pressed his lips to mine. They were warm and tasted of sweet chocolate. There'd been no taste or smell to accompany our first kiss in our dream, it was like a 2D drawing come to life. My pulse hadn't slowed since we'd climbed through the fence, and now it grew dangerously close to explosion. He slid his fingers behind my neck, gathering me closer as I lifted my hand to his face, tracing my fingertips over the cool skin on his cheeks.

I dragged my lips away to catch my breath, and it came out in ragged, desperate drags, his scent leaving me wanting more. Tyler trailed his hand from my neck, down my shoulder and the length of my arm, until our fingers connected, sending another shattering jolt through my skin.

'Wow,' he said, and we laughed, our mouths only inches apart. 'That was so much better than the dream.'

I nodded. 'The dream has nothing on that.'

His eyes burnt into mine. 'No. But maybe we should make sure.'

My laugh detonated the air, but before he had a chance to put his test into practice, the sky darkened, and a crack of thunder rumbled around us. The clouds that'd been over the mountains minutes ago were right overhead.

'We don't have long.' Tyler jumped up, hauling me to my feet.

We climbed back through the fence and bolted through the trees, the rain pelting down once we reached the road. We held hands as we raced down the hill, our laughter filling the air as much as the thunder claps. Tyler's hair stuck to his forehead, the rain pouring down his face, into his eyes and the corners of his mouth. By the time we stood across the road from his place we were drenched. My shirt and shorts clung to my skin, Tyler's chest visible under his white top.

'Come for dinner Friday?' he asked with urgency but almost too soft to hear above the wailing wind. He squeezed my hand.

I nodded, and he covered my smile with a kiss before rushing across the road and waving from his doorstep.

Damn it, I forgot to tell him about @Star_Crossed. A bolt of lightning flashed overhead, illuminating the sky. I'd have to tell him another day. Soaked through to my skin, I spun around and started for home.

—18—

M Y SEARCH FOR MORE details on the house fire turned up
nothing. Beverly had two children. A daughter who lived in
Perth and a son in Canberra who visited most days. If I felt the way
I did, I could only imagine his distress and eagerness to find the
cause of the fire that'd killed his mother.

Smoke choked my lungs and burnt my eyes, and all I could do
was squeeze her weak hand when my mind gifted me with another
onslaught of fiery pain that night. Nothing changed; I hadn't come
up with an alternative yet. The weight of her loss, and the magnitude of my failure, seared me along with the fire. But I didn't give
up hope for Beverly; accidents could often be turned around. I just
needed time.

The following day, with Tyler's voice still echoing in my mind
about helping others, I showered and dressed in faded jeans and
a black hoodie, my least 'I have money' clothes, and strode the
soaked footpaths into town. It wouldn't take my mind off Beverly,
but without school to do the job, working at the shelter would do
well to keep me somewhat distracted.

Pleased to have extra hands for the day, Patty got me sorting
through one of the supply cupboards with her, and then after
lunch I played a few games of draughts with Henry.

I enjoyed the interlude. Being productive instead of useless
helped, and when I arrived home, I held my breath and searched

the news again. The air rushed out at once, relief, so much relief. Detectives had traced the source of the fire back to the dishwasher.

I called Tyler and filled him in while I paced my room. Window to door, robe to table.

'So if she just didn't start the dishwasher...'

'Yeah, but most people *do* at the end of the day, don't they?' Tyler said. 'Not sure there would've been a way out of this for her.'

'Maybe, but you know how sometimes they advertise recalls on the news, maybe she saw that, or her son saw it and told her about it.' I paused by my window and ran my hand back and forth on the ledge, bringing to mind all the photo frames in her home, the faces of her children and grandchildren. They had to be an indication she had loved ones who cared.

I stood silently with the warm phone to my ear, contemplating her alternative. Tyler's steady breathing flowed down the line.

I sat on the edge of my bed. 'So how's your day been?'

'Mmm, not the best, not the worst.' He spoke heavily, and my heart cracked a little for the pain behind his words.

'That's sucky, I'm sorry. Do you wanna get out tomorrow, do something together?'

'I'd love to, not sure Mum'd be keen.'

'She doesn't like you seeing me?'

'No, it's not that. I dunno, I feel bad going out and leaving her when she's in a bad way.'

'You sure it's still okay to come round tomorrow night then?'

'Yeah, she's picked a movie for us all to watch. I think she's secretly looking forward to it, doing something normal.' She wasn't the only one, and the longing to see Tyler bubbled within me. But until then I had to erase Beverly's death from my mind, and the only way to do that was to save her. Or at least pretend to.

When I woke the following morning and had my coffee and

pencil in hand, I recalled the strangeness of my dream as the conversation I'd dreamed came to mind.

'Mum, just go and check it for me, will you?' Beverly's son sounded impatient.

'What? Now?'

'Yes, put the phone down, I'll stay on the phone until you come back.'

'All right, dear.' There was a pause and a shuffling. 'Yes, it is a Bosch, John.'

'I know that, Mum, that's why I'm calling. I need you to check the serial number for me,' he huffed.

'Where will I find it, dear?'

'It's usually on the inside of the door, at the top, it's a large number. It'll start with an S.'

'All right, I'll have to get a pen and paper, then.' She set the phone aside, and after a tedious minute of waiting was back on the phone. 'I'm not sure which number it is, there's more than one.'

'Okay, I'll come over tomorrow, see if I can find it. Don't use it tonight, though, all right, just in case.'

'But what about the dirty dishes? I had the girls over for cards today, and we used all the side plates.'

'Don't worry about that, I'll wash them for you by hand if I need to. I've got a meeting first thing, but I'll pop round after that, probably round eleven. You need anything from the shops?'

'No, dear, but thank you. I'll make some lunch for when you get here.'

'Sounds great,' he said quickly, abruptly ending the conversation.

'Oh dear, I'll have to wash before you get here so we have some plates to use.'

*****

I HOPPED ACROSS TYLER'S front yard, the wet grass squelching beneath my Cons, and knocked on the door. I tugged at my denim jacket and held my hands together, sliding the jet bracelet around my wrist with my thumb. I traced the doormat with my foot and brushed my fingers down the hair falling over my shoulders. The door flung open, launching my pulse into top speed. Tyler wrapped his arms around me and squeezed the panic and shyness away.

'Hey,' he said tenderly with a quick press of his lips on mine, giving me all the confidence I needed. I took his hand, and a big breath, and stepped inside.

I followed Tyler into the kitchen, the plain picture-less walls broken only with doorways offering glimpses into stark, sparsely furnished rooms and stacks of unpacked boxes. A couple of lonesome framed photos sat on an otherwise empty sideboard in the dining room.

A woman fussed at the kitchen bench, pouring store-bought popcorn into a white ceramic bowl. A line of orange juice-filled glasses waited beside her. Her dusty brown hair fell in an unkempt, just below the ears bob.

Tyler's warm fingers slid from mine, and he tentatively edged forward placing his hand on her arm to coax her from her trance. 'Mum?'

He was the same height as her, and she eyed him with a slight, somewhat sad rise of the lips before turning to me with a wide, enthusiastic, but quivering smile. Her blue eyes were puffy and blotched pink, evidence of recent tears, or maybe they'd never gone away.

'You must be Lucy.' Her smile settled down a few notches toward normal. 'It's lovely to finally meet you; Tyler's told me so much about you.'

'He has?' Tyler cast his eyes down briefly. I reassured him with a smile to ease his nerves, no doubt on edge like mine.

'Yes, he has, and I've been keen to meet the girl who's been stealing so much of his time.' I shifted uncomfortably on my feet.

'Oh, it's perfectly fine, don't feel bad. You've made him smile again. I should be thanking you, really.' And there was genuine warmth behind the sadness in her eyes.

I had an urge to hug her, to relieve some of the pain that radiated like a tidal wave. Instead I said, 'Ah, well, thanks for letting me come over tonight, Mrs Sims.'

'Just Sally is fine.' She collected the drinks, and we carried the selection of nibbles into the lounge room, placing them on the glass coffee table. Tyler and I settled onto a two seater sofa, while his mum grabbed one of the recliners in the corner and wrapped a pale pink woollen throw over her legs.

'You cold?' Tyler reached over me to a crumpled blanket on the end of the couch.

'I'm sorry it's so cold, Lucy,' Sally said. I eyed the dark and empty freestanding fireplace near the TV 'We haven't organised any wood for the fire yet, and the reverse cycle only blows the already cold air around the room.' With Tyler's presence and the nerves running under my skin I'd been too warm to notice the chill in the air.

'It's fine. I'm used to the cold, love it actually.'

Tyler straightened the blanket over our laps. 'You're weird. Give me the surf any day.'

I huffed out my nose. 'You're only saying that 'cause you don't know any different.'

Jada moped into the room, arms folded across her body, and slumped into the only vacant chair before she spotted me. Lips held tightly together, she reluctantly lifted the edges and offered me an, 'Oh hey.'

Tyler squeezed my knee under the blanket and moved his hand to my fingers.

The pre-movie music started up, and Tyler leaned in to me. 'You have a better dream last night?'

I smiled and nodded. 'Yeah. I came up with something.'

'You feel better?'

'Yes and no. It's bittersweet.' I sighed. 'I won't see it anymore, but she's still dead.'

'Sucks, hey.'

I couldn't agree more and rested my head back on the couch. 'Yeah.'

By the end of the movie I decided there was nothing more awkwardly uncomfortable than being in a room with two weeping women and your boyfriend. I wasn't a movie crier, but was tempted to become one, simply so I wouldn't want to laugh so much. I focused on Tyler's hand in mine, and the tingling sensation it stirred, to distract me from their sobs.

The movie had barely finished before Tyler was leading me from the room. We ran upstairs and closed the bedroom door, moments before erupting in laughter. We collapsed on the bed, heads rammed into the pillows in the hopes it would dispel some of the cackles that might make it under the door and back down to the lounge room.

'I'm so sorry, that was awful,' he said.

'Oh my God, it was, wasn't it? I don't think I've ever found a sad movie funnier than I did tonight. I'm such a bad person.'

We moved to lie more comfortably on our backs. Tyler focused on the ceiling while I gave his room a once over. He'd fitted it out more substantially than the rest of the house, and I imagined this as his refuge from a home still thick with grief. I didn't doubt he held onto his own version of bereavement, but his transpired into something far different to what was on the other side of the door.

His bed was made neatly, well it had been before we crumpled it, and his desk held stacks of school textbooks, language books, and murder mysteries. A skateboard sat propped in the corner, alongside a surfboard, his soccer ball, and boots. Surfing posters adorned the front of his wardrobe.

'Were you that good?' I asked and pointed to one.

'You bet I was.'

A framed photo of him and his dad balanced on top of a pile of books on his bedside table. His dad's arm was draped around Tyler's shoulders, and they both had matching grins. Tyler was a younger version of his dad. It had to be painful for his mum, to look at her son and see the husband she would no longer rest eyes on.

Tyler's eyes flickered to the picture before landing on mine, and we shared a silent acknowledgement of all it meant. He still hurt, and there was nothing I could do to take it away. It just was. The pain wasn't raw anymore, but the wound had only begun to heal, and before that happened it needed to seep and fester some more. I squeezed his hand.

'Have they worked out the cause yet?' He drew in a breath, and I wished I could take back my words. 'Sorry, you don't have to talk about it if you don't want to.'

'No, it's okay. And no, they haven't. The crash investigators are still trying to piece it all together.'

'It's taking a while, hey.'

'Yeah, and I hate it dragging on with no answers. Mum doesn't cope when there's more news or speculation. She's right back there, spiralling down and shutting us out. I want it over. Like maybe then she'll be able to work on moving forward instead of letting it hold her down.'

I asked about his mum when I realised I had no idea what she did, other than cry. Tyler told me she'd been a travel agent in Sydney, but it wasn't long after his dad died that she stopped working. She'd tried to go back too soon, but her sombre expression and mood did nothing to create excitement in her clients, who often left to find business elsewhere, and so she came to a mutual understanding with her boss that it might be for the best if she took more time. She was still taking that time.

'I don't know what she'll do here. She's not looking for work as far as I know. Sometimes I wonder why she even bothered to move us here. I think she had this idea it'd make everything better. Fulfil Dad's dreams and all that. I'm not sure what she expected, but whatever it was, it didn't work, it's only made it all worse.' Tyler's voice trembled as the angry and hurt child who'd lost his dad surfaced. It wasn't something I witnessed often; he kept that part of himself hidden so well.

'I'm sorry, Tyler,' I said, unable to come up with anything else.

'You're the last person who should be apologising. Mum was right, you've made me smile, and if there's one good thing to come out of all this, it's you. I was drowning. Slowly getting pulled under by Mum and Jada. You saved me. I'll be eternally grateful for that.'

Tears formed and I blinked them away. 'You've kept me from drowning too.'

'Looks like we're a good pair then, hey.'

'As long as we don't pull each other under,' I said with a weak one-sided lift of my lips.

'We won't.' Tyler reached out and placed his hand on my cheek. 'Not if we keep kicking.' He stroked his thumb against my skin, and then his mouth pressed against mine. I closed my eyes, weightless with pleasure, and decided this was a feeling I'd be happy to drown in.

'Do you think we'll ever be able to have another dream together?' Tyler asked when our lips parted. 'It's driving me crazy. You're all I think about as I go to sleep, but nothing works. I've even been meditating more.'

'Meditating?' My eyes narrowed, unsure if I'd heard right. 'You meditate?'

'Sometimes. I'm a surfer, remember. At one with the ocean, and all that.' He laughed at my shock. 'Actually, it's got nothing to do with that. We used to do it at school every day, fifteen minutes. Was the quietest part of the day.'

'At school?'

'Yep. We had a very forward-thinking principal. It's actually not as hard as everyone makes it out to be.'

'And you still do it?'

'I sleep better when I do, so yeah. I do it a couple times a week. But don't tell the lads, they'll roast me.' The mattress rocked beneath his laughter. 'It's not working to make me dream though. I thought it'd help, but man, waking up has never been so disappointing.'

I lowered my eyes away from the heat of his confession.

'I'm sorry, I have no clue how we did it in the first place, let alone how to do it again. If I knew meditation would help I might attempt it, but I'd be so bad at that, my mind never shuts up.' I wished I had a better answer. 'Oh crap I nearly forgot again.' I sat up and Tyler joined me, his eyes wide at my sudden energy. 'I checked on a dream forum I'm part of, 'cause the interweb's full of weird people like me.'

He chuckled. 'Any weirdos have any clues?'

'No, but you got your laptop handy?'

Grabbing it from his desk, Tyler flipped it open, and I showed him the question I'd asked when he arrived at school a little over two weeks earlier, and more recently the answer from @ Star_Crossed.

'I know, it's a bit soppy.' I shrugged. 'But I like it.'

Tyler's gaze lingered on me, taking me in. 'Me too. And in case you're wondering, I *am* enjoying every morsel.'

—19—

TYLER AND I STROLLED hand in hand on our way to a planned meet up with the rest of the crew. He had a grey beanie pulled tight over his head, strands of hair curled onto his forehead, and I giggled at his obvious discomfort at the cooling weather.

'I'm not used to it, all right.'

'I know, you just look so cold.'

'That's 'cause I am,' he said, and I rubbed my hand over our entwined fingers to share my warmth.

It was school holidays, and the streets were still fairly quiet for this time of year. No snow on the mountains yet to attract the thousands of punters that swarmed on us during the winter months. They were like a pack of children at a fairy floss stand – queues and high prices couldn't keep them away. I didn't blame them really; the high from the fairy floss was worth it.

It was Friday again, the previous week having passed by in a flurry of activity, none of which included nightmares, or death, or fear. I worked a couple of shifts over the weekend with Laurie, and then spent more time at the shelter. I wanted to spread some of the joy Tyler had given me with those who rarely saw much. It felt good to be happy, and not fleeting, on-the-surface moments, but deep-to-the-bone happy.

Tyler joined me on the afternoons I went for a run, although most of the time we didn't talk. It was too hard if we wanted to maintain an even breath to last the distance, and so we simply ran. I shared my eclectic and vast playlist with him, and Tyler shared with me his love of The Wombats and Arctic Monkeys.

'Okay...ready, set, go.' We'd simultaneously press the play button on our shared playlist and connect on another level, through the music in our ears.

'Good?' Tyler had mouthed to me as the grungy voice of The Wombats lead singer growled. I'd lifted my thumb and nodded with a smile.

When we ran, we ran hard, and then we'd offload our day once we'd caught our breath on our hill. Yes, it had become ours. It ceased being mine the moment new shared memories erased my old lonely ones.

I'd never wanted to get so lost in another person that I forgot to be me. I thought it would be a betrayal to myself, to my identity, but I started to contemplate the possibility of preferring the person I'd become because of Tyler. Like the polished jet on my bracelet – it was what it was because of the saltwater and sediment that smothered it for millions of years. Alone it would've remained a single piece of rotted wood; dull, unchallenged, less loved.

The street hummed with a mosaic of teenagers and tourists, wandering aimlessly in a state of mellow holiday euphoria, but in that moment it was just me and Tyler. We walked in silence, enjoying what still felt like new company but with a comfort you reached from knowing someone a lot longer than three weeks.

We heard the laughter before they came into view; all of our friends around a table, under a bright yellow umbrella outside the local pizza joint, Slice of Heaven.

'They're alive,' Cal called when he spotted us. Amber elbowed him in the side and he laughed hard, and, as if we were a famous celebrity couple strolling Fifth Avenue, she raised her camera and pointed it in our direction.

We ordered our pizzas, the conversation flowing as freely as the soft drinks, but then the inevitable happened – it always did.

'How about that politician's grandkid who drowned on the weekend,' Sean said, and my head jerked toward the source of his disdain. 'He ought to have jail time for that.' I stiffened at the words, stopped chewing my margherita.

'It was an accident,' Amber said. 'You make it sound like he let it happen on purpose.'

'She was a child.' Sean spread his hands on the table, my own clenched into fists in my lap. 'You don't leave a child alone near water, everyone knows that. And this crack is supposed to be helping run the country.' I swallowed the nausea creeping up the back of my throat, but the pizza remained stubbornly in my left cheek.

'You don't know the full story,' Amber said delicately.

'I know what the news said.'

'Precisely.'

'She was three,' Sean said through gritted teeth.

I gulped my food. It may as well have been a golf ball sliding down my dry throat.

'You okay?' Tyler whispered in my ear, placing his hand over mine. I found his eyes, worry and affection painted in their depths.

'Perfectly fine.' I pressed my lips into a smile.

'You don't have to lie to me.'

I shrugged. 'I'm used to it, it's fine.'

He raised his eyebrows all the way to the edge of his beanie. I huffed out a small laugh at his disbelief and snuggled into his shoulder. 'It is,' I said again, because what else could it be if I couldn't change it.

'Call me tomorrow,' he insisted. 'We can talk it over if you want.'

I relaxed a little knowing he'd be on the other side to catch me. 'Thank you. Maybe you could come for dinner tomorrow night? Mum asked me to bring "this boy" over.'

He cracked a smile. 'I'm *this* boy?'

'The one and only.'

I STAYED UP LATE; did the dishes for Mum, watched a movie with Jake and worked on a school assignment until after midnight. My eyes grew weary at my determination to avoid the misleading comfort of my bed. There'd be no comfort under those blankets tonight. At half past twelve, no longer able to fight my exhaustion, I changed into pyjamas with clammy hands.

Perfectly fine, my arse.

THE FAIR-HAIRED CHILD TOTTERED *over to the pool edge, her pink dress flouncing in her eagerness to catch the ball. Oh no. Heart lurching, I spun around. The yard was empty of even a recently vacated chair. No one was watching, not even pretending. Peering through a wide window into the house, I scanned and spotted a figure pacing the length of the room, phone to his ear, an arm slicing through the air. Crap.*

She knelt beside the pool, reached for the ball with her chubby hand, and slipped quietly into the water. I ran to catch her, but she sank like a dead weight, her hair and life flowing up and away from her.

I thoughtlessly jumped in after her, the urge to save her dispersing any pain from the icy water. She stared at me boggle eyed, her mouth sucking in water as her lungs screamed for oxygen. I dove deeper, my feet driving me down, down, until I cradled her in my arms.

I fought to reach the surface, but the water held me under. We were balloons in a pool of lead. Shocked and afraid, I gulped in a mouthful of water, my hair cascading in front of my face. The heaviness of my failure drowning us with the water. The little girl's dimpled hand tangled in the dark strands of my hair, brushing it away, and as if sensing my regret and wanting to absolve me, she smiled. I held tight as her body jerked and grew limp. Her brief and perfect life – over – thrust into a never-ending darkness.

I woke sucking in air. My chest heaved and fell. Wiping at the thin trail of sweat coating my neck, I reinstated myself back into reality. I might've left the chill of the deadly water far behind in my dreams, but I couldn't remove the vision of the dimple-faced little girl; sweet, round...gone.

*****

I READ THROUGH THE news articles to find clues on how to save her. Her grandfather was doing a last-minute favour for his daughter, but still trying to get work done. My guess was he wasn't used to having kids in the house and forgot the outside doors weren't locked. If his daughter made the suggestion to take his grand-daughter for a walk he would've locked the house up and been elsewhere when the call came in. It might be enough to prevent the tragedy.

It did, and she was saved. In my dreams at least...

Seeing the revised outcome brought solace that made me sleep contentedly right through until midday rays broke through my blinds. I woke to familiar, yet unexpected voices at the bottom of the stairs. A smile formed on my lips and I was immediately awake.

I rubbed the sleep from my eyes and bound down the stairs to a barrage of hugs, kisses and teasing about sleeping in so late from Granny Tess and Pop.

'So, what's new?' Pop asked as he released me from his tight hold.

'She's got a boyfriend,' Ollie said, hurtling down the stairs and barrelling into Pop.

'Has she now.' Pop raised an eyebrow. 'And what about you, Ollie boy? Any young ladies I should know about?'

'Nope.'

Pop lowered his voice. 'Any I *shouldn't* know about?' He winked.

'None of them, either, Pop,' Ollie said, ducking into the kitchen to grab a glass of orange juice.

'So, things are going well with...' Granny Tess faltered.

'Tyler is lovely,' Mum piped up. He'd come around the night before, and Mum and Dad both agreed he was lovely – Mum's words – and a great kid – Dad's words.

I turned to Pop, unsure if Granny Tess had filled him in after our phone call. 'He goes to my school, we do Geography together.'

'Is that what you're calling it these days, back in my day we called it–'

'Granny Tess! Don't you dare.' I waggled my finger at her. I didn't want to hear any such words leave her mouth. 'You're worse than Jake.' She stifled a laugh, and warmth tingled my cheeks as I darted out a friendly glare.

'Sorry, I couldn't help myself.'

'I know, you never can. But it's only been two weeks, so yes, it's just Geography.'

'Mmm, if you say so.' Granny Tess lifted her teacup to her lips.

I rolled my eyes and stepped around her to make myself a coffee. 'I didn't know you guys were visiting today.' I shot a questioning look at Mum, she'd normally have told us.

'Don't look at me, I didn't either.'

'It was a last-minute decision,' Pop said, scraping out a chair at the table.

'We came as soon as Edna was able to put some of her cookies in a container for me to go.'

'Mum, that's not why you go to church,' Dad scolded.

'It sure is. I certainly don't go for the God they preach about.'

'That's so bad.' I laughed, and Mum brought her mug to her lips covering her own snicker.

'No, it's not. Church is so much more than that, it's the spiritual connection, the community. And if going for the friends, and the cakes, gets me there, there's nothing bad about that.' She arranged the hijacked biscuits onto a plate and carried them to the table.

She sat beside me and when everyone's chatter grew louder she leaned in and patted my knee. 'You doing all right?' I should be asking her, she'd just lost a friend, but the reassurance she provided by asking felt like sprinkles on top of Tyler's layer of icing.

I offered a genuinely contented smile. 'Yeah, I'm doing all right.' The nightmares left a sour taste in my mouth, but it was bearable when I could swallow it down with a dose of their sweet affection. It would take a true disaster to rob me of this feeling; that I was the luckiest girl alive, finally happy regardless of the desolation my dreams brought me.

—20—

ARLY MORNING SUNLIGHT PEEKED through the trees and
kissed the frosted grass on the soccer pitch as we huddled on
the sidelines, trying to keep warm. I'd travelled into Mayfield earlier with Amber and Max for the boys' fifth soccer match of the new
school term. None of the boy's parents joined us; they'd watched
plenty before, so the cheering responsibilities fell solely on our cold,
stiff shoulders.

May, with its sun-burnt leaves and quiet crisp nights, had
drawn to a satisfying end as it made way for the grey and chilly
winter ahead. It had been a month of some of the happiest days
in my life, but all seasons come to an end, and this one was no
different.

In the five weeks since we'd been back at school, I'd spent each
Thursday night watching the boys at soccer practice. I'd never been
a fan of the game, even though I'd sat through plenty of matches
over the years, but now, well, it'd grown on me.

My life had become akin to the dreams I'd always wished to
trade my nightmarish ones into – pleasant, fun and full of vitality,
the good kind. The nightmares continued, my latest ones being
a gruesome farming accident, a toddler on a bike in a driveway,
and a very public scuba diving accident in far north Queensland,
where a reputable and well-known instructor lost his life. I'd learnt
to live contentedly alongside the grief, and I walked through my

days with an unfamiliar calm. How easy it'd been to fall into this new way of living, this new version of a happier me.

'Hey, Eric, you're out of bed, someone pinch me.' Cal jabbed his teammate as Sean punched Cal in the arm. Eric was the dodgy spare wheel of the team, the one you found flat in the boot of the car when you went to use it.

'Sean bet me I wouldn't make it this early, I needed the money,' he said with a yawn.

Sean slapped a ten in Eric's hand.

'Right, Cal, you're on the bench for the first half. I want to save you for the comeback,' Mr Jeffers said, patting him on the back. 'Alex, you're off too.'

Cal motioned for Amber to meet him at the sideline. He pushed her hair aside and whispered something in her ear. She returned for her backpack and jogged back to him.

The game started, and she popped some tablets from their foil casing into Cal's palm. He downed them with a big chug of water, kissed Amber, and sat on the bench.

'He all right?' I asked as Amber lowered herself beside us.

'Yeah, just a headache. I think that knock yesterday was worse than he's letting on.' Cal had been knocked out during PE the day before, an accident involving a high-jump mat, or lack-there-of, and the gym floor. Tyler had relayed the incident to me after school, but it was more a hilarity than a mishap, like most things with teenage boys.

'Should he be playing today?' I asked, frowning in Cal's direction where he sat jiggling his legs from the cold. He looked like he needed to use the bathroom.

'Like that'd stop him. I'd like to see you suggest he sit this one out.' Amber laughed, fog escaping from her cold lips.

The small crowd erupted with stunted early morning cheers;

Mayfield High had scored. Cal's hands balled at his sides, hating the inadequacy of sitting on the sidelines, but fortunately for the team, his momentum was building – they wouldn't be able to hold him back when he finally got onto the field.

'Yeah, nah, think I'll keep that thought to myself.' I rubbed my gloved hands together and brought them to my lips.

At half time, our hands had warmed up enough to eat some of the apricot and almond muffins Amber had been urged to bring by Laurie. I savoured the taste of the moist cake on my tongue and cursed myself for not thinking to bring a coffee.

It didn't take long into the second half for the excitement and heat of the game to thaw the pitch – and our noses. Cal now joined Sean and Tyler on the field, giving the team a new burst of energy. The intensity of our cheers increased, and within a few minutes Tyler booted a kick-ass goal, evening the score. We jumped up, screamed madly, made a bit of a scene, and gracefully sat down again. I caught a beam from Tyler, apparent delight to be proving his weight with his new team. I whooped again and sent a huge grin dancing his way.

By that point it was game-on – even scores meant even deter-mination to gain the lead. I could smell the testosterone in the air.

Cal raced toward the goal and hit the ball off his forehead, hard. The ball sailed into the goal, while in the same instant his temple collided with the head of a player from the opposing team who'd been running just as fiercely. They both crumpled to the ground, and my hand impulsively reached for Amber's, while the crowd cheered. I held my breath.

The player from the other team eased himself up, but Cal stayed motionless, a huddle of player's bouncing around him, waving their hands above their heads. The piercing shrill of the referee's whistle slashed against my ribcage. Amber's fingers pinched around mine.

The cheers subsided and a quiet murmuring fell over the crowd. Coach Jeffers rushed onto the field. My heart stopped, frozen with fear.

Barely able to see him through the bodies gathering around, Amber and I stood, but he was so far away and unreachable he may as well have been on the moon.

The scene played out, and a dizzying numbness crawled over my skin, distant voices garbled and the world around me fell silent. I wasn't in a dream and yet I felt the same as if I was – useless. So accustomed to my usual position of watch and observe, my feet were fixed firmly to the ground, so when Amber started to move forward, I squeezed her hand tighter and pulled her back. 'Should we stay over here out the way?'

'I can't,' she said, and I followed her lead, her hand still in mine. Max followed close behind and half running, half too damn scared to get any closer, we shoved our way through the thick crowd swallowing Cal. The throng parted and we caught a glimpse of him again.

'Oh my God, he's not moving.' Max sucked in a breath.

Amber clutched my fingers like she held a grenade about to explode, and my heart beat a fast, dull thud behind my tightening chest.

We inched closer to the centre. Cal lay on his back, arms to his side, lifeless on the grass. I caught the looks on the faces around me, but the fear in their eyes only confirmed my own panic.

Tears stung the back of my eyes, and I blinked them away.

Tyler rushed to my side, enclosed me in his strong arms and spoke reassuring words into my hair. Amber's hand no longer sat in mine; she kneeled in the grass beside Cal.

Shivers travelled to my neck at the sound of a siren, far off in the distance. It grew louder as it inched closer and filled the chilly air.

'What should we do?' Max asked, panic overriding her normally calm exterior. 'Should we call Marie or Harry?'

'Marie's working today, she's on with Mum,' I answered. 'Oh God, we need to get there and warn them before she sees him.'

'I've called Jake.' Sean fiddled with his phone. 'He's heading round to find Harry. Amber, if you drive Cal's car to the hospital, we'll wait until he's on his way, then meet you all there.'

'Do you have to finish the game?' Max asked.

'That's a joke, right?' Sean said. 'We'll be right behind you.'

I nuzzled into Tyler's side, and he silently kissed the top of my head. I swallowed the lump in my throat, blinked heavily to clear my eyes, and then let him go as I left with the girls.

The familiarity of the clean, crisp, disinfectant smell wafted toward me as the hospital doors slid open, but I stood dangerously close to the edge of disaster for it to be of any comfort today. Unsure of what lay ahead, a shuddering spread over my body. I stepped onto the thin maroon carpet of the hospital foyer.

I spotted Mum almost immediately, and her sixth sense as a mother knew straight away something was gravely wrong.

She strode across the room, her steps gathering speed, eyes darting from me, to the girls, and back to me, raw, unfamiliar terror in her eyes. She grabbed me by the arms. 'What is it?'

'Cal,' I choked out. 'The ambulance is on its way. He's not moving, Mum, I'm so scared.'

She wrapped her arms around me, and Max blurted out the details.

'Mum, where's Marie? We need to tell her before they arrive.'

'I'll go find her. It might be best if you girls stay here until she knows.' She squeezed my arm and hurried down the wide corridor. We collapsed into chairs lining the white walls at the entrance, momentarily able to catch our breath but still unable to breathe easily. I clutched my head in my hands and closed my eyes, willing myself not to cry, not yet, not here. This couldn't be happening. *Please, someone, wake me up from this god-awful nightmare.*

I shifted my head toward the spine-tingling blare of sirens at the other end of the hospital. Cal had arrived. I caught sight of Marie, the mum, not the nurse, as she ran full pelt back along the corridor. She sprinted toward us, anguish and panic all over her face, and turned sharply to head down an identical corridor.

We waited in those seats for what felt like hours, and once Sean and Tyler joined us we migrated to the chairs in the wide corridor outside the emergency department. I jumped out of my seat when Jake and Harry burst through the doors. Harry's wide eyes barely rested on us before marching around the half wall and into the ER.

I paced the small area, unable to sit still and wait for the news that never arrived. I twisted my fingers and tightened my jaw, anything to contain the urge to run through the hospital and demand to know what was going on.

A few minutes later Harry stepped into the tight space. He took three determined strides to reach us. With strained blood-shot eyes he said, 'He's not responding. Doctor wants to do a scan. He asked if he's consumed any alcohol recently, had any medications, Aspirin, Ibuprofen, that kind of thing, or illicit drugs? Kids, you have to tell me anything you know.'

'I gave him some Aspirin this morning, before the game,' Amber said quickly, her voice wavering.

'What for?'

'He had a headache. From the knock yesterday, I think.'

Harry's eyes widened. 'What knock?'

Sean spoke up. 'He hit his head in PE. Blacked out for a second, then he was fine.'

Harry closed his eyes. 'Anything else?'

A few head shakes and then he spun away.

I dropped back into the chair, my head growing fuzzy.

'Was the Aspirin a bad idea? Should I have given him something else? It's what Dad takes. It's all I had in my bag.' Tears fell freely down Amber's cheeks.

I placed my hand over the fidgeting fingers in her lap. 'It's all right. You did the right thing.' Did she? I knew some people weren't supposed to take Aspirin, but I couldn't think why. My throat grew dry and I tightened my grip on her hand.

Silence descended, too shocked to speak, the distant clangs and shuffles from the ER the only sounds filling the rapidly stifling air.

A stretcher bed rolled around the corner, the rattle of metal and wheels on linoleum bursting through our quiet dread. I wavered in my seat, my hand flying to cover my lips. Cal. So still and lifeless. Not our Cal. Marie and Harry trailed behind and stopped while he disappeared from sight.

Clutching onto Harry, Marie's hollow eyes reached out to each of us. They shuffled to a seat, supporting each other so they didn't fall. Sitting hunched, Marie's head rested on Harry's chest, his arm around her shoulders, his hand running tenderly over the golden strands of her hair; it mirrored the way they'd held each other in comfort over their other son not so long ago.

I focused, unblinking on the plastic white clock on the wall. Each jerking movement of the hands offering the only evidence that time had, in fact, not ceased since Cal's collision.

Mum stopped by with some sandwiches. They remained unopened on the peach table beside the *National Geographic* and *Time* magazines.

Thirty minutes later, the doctor returned.

'Mr and Mrs Brooks, would you like to come with me so we can speak in private,' he said calmly but with concern.

'Oh God.' Marie let out a sob.

The doctor reached out a reassuring arm. 'Nothing's changed, he still hasn't regained consciousness, but I'd like to talk about our next steps. Unless you don't mind doing it out here.' He scanned the room.

Marie blinked and shook her head, then nodded. 'Yes yes, that's fine.'

'Your son is in a critical condition. It's rare and extremely unusual for someone his age, but he's suffered an intracranial haemorrhage. Our best guess is that the previous concussion and Aspirin have contributed to the severity in this case. He's going to need immediate surgery to stop the bleeding on his brain and repair the damage.'

His words fly-kicked me in the stomach, and I swayed in my seat. Tyler reached out to secure me. I sought his other hand, winding my fingers around his. My mind whirled, only registering some of the doctor's next words; helicopter, Canberra, consent, risk.

I realised all the waiting so far would be nothing compared to what lay ahead. I clenched my jaw, angry at the doctor for not giving us more, even an ounce of hope to cling to in the hours ahead. But he gave us nothing.

My chest heaved, emotions swirling into an uncontrollable tornado. Not wanting everyone to see me break apart, I ran from the room. Automatic doors slid open at the end of the corridor, and frigid air slammed into me, adding to the pain of this agonising day. Tears fell. I couldn't hold back my sobs, all my fear and tension escaping, pent up since Cal's body struck the cold damp earth that morning.

Had it really only been that morning? It felt like a lifetime ago. Would today be the end of his life?

Tyler's arms wrapped around me and he pulled me to him. My legs buckled. He held me, and we knelt on the concrete together, a big crumpled mess.

'He can't die, Tyler. He can't die.' My body shook. 'They've already lost Richie, and Cal's the only thing that's kept 'em going. If he dies, it'll kill 'em. He can't die.'

Tyler whispered in my ear. 'I know. Just breathe.' His words and the strength of his hands layered me in more warmth and comfort than any blanket could provide. He guided me to the cafeteria, where I stood for about five minutes in front of the vending machine, struggling to choose between a plain Twirl or a Picnic bar. I felt guilty to be making such a simple decision as if it were any ordinary day, as if Cal wasn't hanging on for his life. Cal might never wake up, but hey, let's carry on as normal.

I chose the Twirl; it'd take less to get down.

We headed back into the cold, away from the sombre faces filling half the room. We sat on a garden bench beside a row of pink rose bushes.

'It's not fair. Richie's already been taken from them, why can't God find a different family to pick on. I feel sick.' I dropped the half-eaten chocolate bar next to me on the bench.

'I don't think it works like that,' Tyler said with a sympathetic frown.

'Well, it should.' I scoured, projecting some of my anger onto him, immediately regretful. 'Sorry.'

'No, it's okay. You're allowed to be angry. I get it. I tried it for a while, still do every now and then. I've come up with every possible reason why life could be so cruel. I blamed God too, even though I don't believe in him, but sometimes you gotta blame something. You're allowed to feel this way, but the truth is, nothing can change what's been done, life's as random as a frickin' lottery ticket. It's completely and utterly messed up.'

'You got that right. I've seen it too many times. It doesn't stop me from wishing it could be different, wishing I could change it, wishing to make it better. Half my life is daydreaming about the what-ifs, but they're as useless as these damn tears.'

'Those tears show the world you care. And you do make it better. Just not in the way you want to. It's not all your responsibility, as much as you feel like it is. There's nothing you could've done today to change any of this.'

'I know, but the wanting hurts so much.'

'Well, as my mum always says, "I want never gets".' He raised his eyebrows, and his attempt to lighten the mood worked; I managed a small grin.

'She can't be all right,' I teased back with a sniff. 'You wanted me and you got me.'

'Nope, wrong again.' He shook his head. 'I didn't want you. I needed you.'

By the time we made it back inside, Cal was in the chopper, and Marie and Harry were speeding behind in their car.

Still in shock, and exhausted from the strain of the unknown, the rest of us staggered back to my place. We crammed into the lounge room and fell onto the couches. I flicked on the TV, so there'd be something to distract us from the nasty place our minds wanted to take us.

I lay awkwardly along the length of the long couch. My head rested in Tyler's lap, and he stroked my hair. Amber lay on my legs, her head rested on my thighs, and her hand reached above her head to hold onto mine. Lulled by the warmth and comfort of their closeness, I closed my eyes and slept.

I WOKE AND LAUNCHED myself upright, letting out a loud gasp before I realised where I was. I hid my head in my hands so I wouldn't have to see the embarrassed looks on the faces around me. Tyler's head lowered to rest beside mine.

'Are you all right? Did you have a dream? Of Cal?' he whispered.

'Yeah, the accident.' I tried to shake away the images of seeing the collision again, these ones with far more zoom than the originals. I could still hear the crack of Cal's skull against the other player and the thwack as his body hit the wet ground. I trembled, and Tyler placed his arm around my shoulders. 'How long was I asleep?'

'Maybe half an hour?'

'Have you heard anything yet?' My heart accelerated, sudden panic forging itself on me. What had I missed?

'No news yet, no.'

I found the clock, both hands were on the two – he'd left over three hours ago.

'Is that normal? Should it take this long?' I asked anxiously.

'I don't know, but I think brain surgery can take a while.' I drew strength from the smooth confidence in his voice and the calm in his eyes.

Still, a shiver ran down my spine, and a ruthless ache stabbed at my heart. I scanned the faces of my friends. Everything had been so empty when Richie had passed, and I couldn't imagine life without Cal to brighten our days. He was the effervescent bubbles in our soft drink, and without him everything would turn flat and dull.

No, he had to be fine. I couldn't think like that.

Tyler held my hand, and we continued to wait. I startled and caught my breath each time the phone rang. By three pm I was a trembling mess, at four I'd almost worn a patch in the carpet, and at four-twenty-seven when Mum stepped from the kitchen with the phone to her ear, I squeezed Tyler's hand so tight I may have left bruises.

My heart slammed as I tried to decipher the conversation.

Mum's eyes fixed on the floor, one hand on her cheek.

'Okay, I'll let them know.' She stumbled and grabbed onto the back of the office chair, the phone fell from her fingers, and her glistening eyes met mine. Her head barely moved when she shook it. 'He didn't make it.'

My cry tore itself from my lungs, my body hurling forward as I clutched onto my knees shaking my head, the sobs tumbling out.

Amber fell onto her knees and crawled to the phone as if she could somehow retract the message. 'No, no, no.' Each word came out like jagged, pain-filled barbs, tears streaming down her face. She curled onto the floor, tapping at the phone, blonde hair tangling over wet cheeks. Mum shuffled over and pulled her into her arms where they wept together.

Max huddled into Sean, her shoulders shaking violently, clutching his hand. Sean stared straight ahead, trails of tears sliding from his chin.

A deathly pulse resonated in my ears, and my vision blurred, the tears coming in uncontrollable torrents. I found Tyler's gaze, locked onto him. He tugged me into his arms, but I pushed him away. 'I can't...breathe.' I tried to suck in a breath. Panic engulfed me.

Tyler pressed his hands to my face, forcing my eyes back to his, grounding me. He didn't say anything, just inhaled deeply and then exhaled, imploring me to do the same.

My breaths returned, the tears continued to flow, all the while my heart wailed. *Why Cal, why? You can't leave us. We need you.*

Sometime later in the blur of the night, Tyler helped me climb the stairs to my room. With swollen eyes, and a chest that felt like it'd been stabbed, kicked and hollowed out, I climbed under the covers.

Warm lips pressed onto my forehead and my heavy eyelids drifted over.

—21—

I DRAGGED THE BLANKETS up around my neck and sank further into their warmth. Was it morning yet? I cracked open an eyelid. Soft orange light filtered through the unopened blind of my bedroom. I scrunched my eyes from the early morning glare, making way for the memory of the previous day.

A whimper escaped with the deepening sorrow of our loss, and I folded myself into a ball and let the tears fall.

The agony of my dream surfaced. I'd dreamed that Eric slept in like everyone expected him to and Mr Jeffers put Cal on for the first half where a different accident played out. Cal lunged for the ball in his usual enthusiastic manner, which normally put him at an advantage, but on this particular day, would always be to his detriment, and he landed on his ankle, fracturing the bone. The ambulance took him to the hospital and far away from the pitch before he had a chance to collide with the other player.

The what-ifs had never hurt so much.

With a painful heart I dragged myself out of bed and plodded downstairs in my pyjamas. My night was such a daze I couldn't even remember changing into them. Mum stood at the kitchen bench spooning yoghurt over her muesli. She glanced up, concern and shock etched in her brow. 'Honey, are you okay?'

My eyes welled up before I had a chance to shake my head. Mum hurried to wrap her arms around me.

'What is it?'

I frowned through my tears and sniffed. 'What do you mean, what is it? Cal. He's gone.'

She held me away from her, a strange look in her eyes. 'Gone? Where? He was at home just yesterday.'

My heart stopped, panic gripped at my sides. 'Home? No, you're lying.' I pushed her away.

'Lucy. You're freaking me out.' She reached for me and dropped her arms, but I stepped further away.

'I'm freaking *you* out?' I wiped at the hair stuck to the side of my face. 'If he's at home I want to go around there right now,' I challenged. What the hell was going on? Why was she toying with me like this?

She slanted her eyes. 'Okay? Just let me get changed.' She was still in her pyjamas, I hadn't even noticed, no way would she be ready fast enough.

Waving my hand to stop her, I backed out of the room. 'Never mind, forget it. I'll just run over there.' I bolted upstairs, changing into my jeans and blue hoodie, and ran from the house.

Confusion barrelled into me with every pounding thump on the bitumen. Cal was dead, wasn't he? How could he be at home? He died yesterday.

Marie opened the door shortly after I rang the bell, and with her usual large smile brightening her face, stepped aside to welcome me through the door. 'Lucy, how are you?' A turbulent breeze blew in from behind me, and she patted her hair down.

How was I?

Ignoring the question, I glanced over her shoulder, scrutinising the scent of frying bacon and the appearance of a regular Sunday morning.

'Are you all right dear?' She had similar worry lines Mum had worn ten minutes before.

'Cal?' My lungs surged in agony. They needed more air.

'He's here, love.' She spoke like she was talking to an injured animal.

'He's here? He's okay?' I choked out, a big lump wedged in my throat.

'He's fine, would you like to see him? Oh, Lucy.' She wrapped her arms around me and I silently wept on her shoulder. But he was dead. If he was here, what happened yesterday? Was I dreaming? If I was I never wanted to wake, not to a world without Cal.

Marie pulled away and wiped at a stray tear on my cheek, squeezing my shoulder. 'Come on. Let me take you to him, he'll be able to cheer you up.'

We walked down the familiar corridor toward Cal's room at the back of the house and through his open door. I resisted the urge to run across the room and lunge myself at him. He was sitting up, pillows propped behind him, eyes locked intently on the television screen perched on the tallboy against the wall opposite his bed.

'Lucy's here to see you, love.'

His eyes darted quickly to me with a faraway smile and a 'hang on', his full attention held by the pretend world in his video game.

Marie rolled her eyes. 'I'll get you some water, dear.'

'Oh...thanks.' I turned to the form on the bed, still in shock at what sat in front of my eyes. I wiped at the tears trailing silently down my cheeks – joy, relief, fear.

Cal lost the game, plopped the handset beside him, and shuffled on the bed, poking at the pillows behind his back.

'Luce. Whatcha doing up at this hour on a Sunday?'

Swallowing back the uncomfortable lump of denial and confusion, I searched for the time. The clock beside his bed said 09:33. I shook my head, frantic to understand what was going on and ignored his question with one of my own. 'You're okay.' Actually, it was a statement, shrouded with query.

'Of course I'm okay.'

Well, yeah, you're not dead.

'So how you feeling? How's your head?' Which was a stupid question because he looked nothing like someone who'd had brain surgery the day before, like someone who'd died.

'My head? It's fine. My ankle's another story. Speakin' of which.' He plucked a box of pills from beside his bed and popped a couple into his hand, throwing them back with a glass of water.

My vision grew blurry, my head spun, and my legs almost buckled beneath me. I swayed and reached out aimlessly to grab something to hold me up.

'Hey, you right? Here sit down.' He winced as he shuffled his foot aside to make room on the edge of the bed. I ignored his obvious pain and sat on the side, afraid I'd end up on the floor if I didn't. My pulse thundered in my ears, so loud Cal could probably hear it, but he spoke like everything was perfectly normal.

'I have to stay home for a few days, wait for the swelling to go down. Then they'll put the cast on. I'm thinking fluorescent pink, whadya think?'

Painful as it was, I found a smile. 'Pink's good,' I said with barely an ounce of Cal's enthusiasm.

His forehead scrunched with concern. 'What're you doing here, Luce? Has something happened, you don't seem normal.'

'Since when am I ever normal?' I joked as I attempted to plaster a big fake 'everything's fine' look on my face. 'I just wanted to make sure you were okay, you had us all worried. But now I'm here, I'm not feeling that great.' I wrapped an arm around my stomach. 'I think I'll go before I pass anything on. You right if I leave?'

'Um, sure. I think Sean's comin' round later for a video game sesh.'

I stood. 'Great. Well have fun.' I placed my hand on the doorframe, ready to bail, and almost bumped into Marie with my glass of water. 'Oh, sorry, Marie, I'm not feeling well all of a sudden, I have to go.'

I didn't stay to hear the worry in her voice. I didn't want to listen while another person asked if I was all right.

I dashed through the house and out the front door. I ran hard and ran fast, afraid that once I stopped I'd have to confront myself with the reality that I was most definitely not all right.

But I did stop, a few times to vomit. I staggered home to bed and the spinning began to slow, the reality catching up to me. It hit me with the force of a high-speed collision – one I should've seen coming.

My life buckled and crumpled around me in the most gut-wrenching sensation, the blow sending pain shattering right to the outer inches of my body. I'd known since that morning – when I woke wearing pyjamas, and saw the confusion etched on Mum's face – that something was wrong, out of this world, *X-Files* wrong, but nothing could truly prepare me for the all-consuming realisation of what I'd done until the fullness of it hit me.

I was a ticking time bomb, about to implode. I cocooned myself in my bed and hoped the blankets would shield the people around me if I did shatter to pieces.

I slept, and when I woke, panic forced itself over me with the strength of a pro-wrestler, and I cried until I fell asleep again. I only ventured out to use the bathroom.

Did I do what I thought I'd done, or was I going crazy and only imagined the collision, the head injury, the painful agony at hearing Cal had died? No, they were real. As real as the crinkled covers on my bed, as real as the rustling wind outside, and damn it, as real as my beating heart. I squinted at the sliver of light peeking through the blinds, reminding me that the world continued to rotate, even if mine stood still. My body grew numb and weightless as I drifted into a state of insanity. I had no more tears left, they'd all dried up. Was this how people found themselves in mental asylums? Did they even exist anymore? Maybe I'd soon find out.

Darkness fell and Mum checked on me before she left for work. I apologised for my earlier outburst and blamed it on something I'd caught. I'd become limp and bleary eyed, and the bucket on the floor meant she didn't even question the lie. I hadn't eaten, and I'd barely had a drink all day, my head throbbed like someone had been at it with a jackhammer. I tried some Panadol, but it may as well have been a tic-tac. My eyes were puffy, the standard symptom of a day spent crying.

I couldn't feign a stomach bug for too long though. Besides, this was a much bigger, much more dangerous and formidable bug that needed serious quarantine. Yes, that was it, my best idea in a long time – if I quarantined myself, if I stayed locked up somewhere, way away from anyone and anything, no more harm could be done.

But there'd been no harm done. I'd saved Cal's life, and in doing so, Marie and Harry's. But that in itself was dangerous, wasn't it? What other damage had I caused?

My stomach churned again. I thought of all the people I'd dreamed of in the last weeks, months and years, at all the lives I hadn't been able to save, perhaps this really was my imagination playing the dirtiest trick of all, giving me hope that I had the power to change the ending.

But what if it wasn't? The urge to know poked at me, prodded, and pushed me to reach for my laptop and search up the last death I'd dreamed. The farming accident. I hit the enter button. Scrolled. Tried a different search…scrolled some more – nothing.

My pulse thundered in my temple, and I reached into my bedside draw for my book, flicking frantically for the most recent pictures I'd sketched. The child on her bike. My search brought up a lot of driveway accidents, but I couldn't find the one from last week. It wasn't there.

I flicked back a page, scanning the scrawled image of the scuba diving instructor who'd lost his life two weeks ago. I searched the web, but all I found was his business page. I inhaled, sharp and deep. I blinked and clicked on the link to his Facebook page. A page not full of the expected commiserations at his passing, but one he'd been active on yesterday.

Holy cow. No friggin' way!

I ran my hands over my head. This wasn't real, it couldn't be. My book slid off the bed and landed with a thud on the floor. I caught a glimpse of the sketched faces on the opened page. Dreadlock Lady and her son. Why hadn't I been able to save them?

Placing the book beside me, I looked up their story, just in case – nothing had changed. What was different about these deaths? What had changed?

I bit my thumbnail and trailed my eyes over the postcards on the wardrobe door, a kaleidoscope of colours from around the world; The Rhine in Germany, a print of a Monet painting, the surf at Bondi. I sucked in a breath.

Tyler.

He's what had changed. Had my feelings for him blossomed and grown into something more powerful than I ever imagined? We'd known each other for two months, but in many ways, not only for the dream at the airport, it felt like I'd known him forever. He knew me, the authentic, crazy me. And his trust opened in me something that had lain dormant for so many years. Maybe it had been waiting for him.

What would he think of all this? He saw and understood more about the part of me I'd always downplayed with everyone else. He'd never seemed remotely put off by my weird ability, and maybe it was why I trusted him, because he simply believed me. But now? He might have an equally strange knack for shared dreaming, but surely this would test the limits of his acceptance.

But of all the people in my life, the only person I wanted to talk to – to tell – was Tyler.

Picking up my phone, I pulled up my contacts. My thumb hovered over his name, uncertainty paving the way to my hesitation. I couldn't do it. Not yet anyway. I needed to test my ability again.

If I'd been able to do it already, what was my limit? I stared at their faces, willed myself to redream the alternate ending to that horrific train crash again and bring them back to life. But first I'd need to fall asleep. Being high on adrenaline made that about as easy as putting a frog to sleep.

I tossed and turned, threw my blankets off in a huff, and circled my table in a sleepy, yet aggressive shuffle. I yanked a pencil off the table and crawled back into bed, letting the stroke of the pencil shading their faces lull me, so that by two in the morning I eventually left the day behind.

I couldn't move when I woke, crippled with fear at my lack of success. I did nothing but stare at my white ceiling for what felt like a thousand years. I wanted so badly to have saved their lives, as ludicrous as the concept sounded, so as long as I didn't search it up and have my hopes crushed, I could stay in my little bubble of optimism.

Once I heard the house stirring I dragged myself out of bed with the idea that if I kept myself busy I wouldn't have to think about the potential what ifs. Mum stood with her hands in a sink full of soapy water. She wore her usual pale-blue uniform, no doubt counting down the minutes until we were out the door so she could take a shower and crawl into bed for the day.

'Morning, honey.' She picked up a tea towel and dried her hands, while I spooned coffee and sugar into a mug. 'Feel better this morning? Sleep all right?' she asked tentatively. Mum worried far too much when we were sick, always did.

I kept my eyes on my mug. 'A little,' I mumbled, stirring the coffee. She passed the milk, and I hitched onto the kitchen stool, inhaling the sweet and bitter aroma of my coffee before taking my first glorious mouthful. It was exactly what I needed, a stimulant to help my body forget it had barely had five hours sleep. 'Think I'll stay home today, though.'

Mum took a sip of tea from her favourite gold-rimmed tea cup. 'That's a good idea. Don't want to pass anything on.' Not a chance. I covered my huff with a cough.

I needed to keep busy. After watching a movie, I went for a short run, and then had a shower. I'd ignored my phone all day, afraid of the avalanche of questions, and when I returned to my room I picked it up with shaky fingers to see the damage.

Cal: *Dude u really weren't good hey, rest up*
Max: *Hey hon, Cal said you were acting weird, I told him it was normal, but are you ok??*

Amber told me to get better soon.

Nothing from Sean. And then four messages from Tyler and two missed calls.

You're not here, feeling sorry for myself :/
Sorry, I should be feeling sorry for you, Cal said you were sick x

Missing you, tried to call, I'll try again at lunch xx
No answer again...you ok?

Ignoring everyone else I responded to Tyler's last message.

No yes no...don't know...can you come over after school?

He replied immediately.

Of course x

LATER IN THE AFTERNOON Mum opened my door, and the smell of baked pie wafted in as uninvited as her.

'Feel like a visitor?' she asked quietly, and I tried to peer around her, hoping it was the one I wanted. My breath hitched, Tyler stood directly behind her. She opened the door, letting him into my room, her weak smile reaching out to me before she backed away, leaving the door half open.

Tyler stood at the foot of the bed. His eyes scanned the room and came to rest tenderly on me as he held out my favourite cupcake. I couldn't help the slightest hint of a smile that crept onto my lips. I really should've been concerned about my appearance – damp, clumpy hair that desperately needed a brush put through it, and I wore my daggy trackies and t-shirt that'd seen better days – but I didn't. I sat up straighter on the bed and crossed my legs.

'Thanks for coming.'

'Cal said you were sick, said you acted strange when he saw you yesterday. You okay?' He took a step closer. 'Or should I stay back here?' He laughed, eyeing the clean but still present bucket on the floor.

'It's not contagious.'

'What's going on, you seemed fine on Saturday.'

'I was,' I said, uncertainty cracking my voice.

Tyler lowered himself onto the edge of the bed, eyes full of questions and concern. His obvious care giving me determination to continue. 'This is gonna sound really weird, but do you think you could remind me what actually happened on Saturday?' My voice wobbled, and new tears gathered heavily behind my eyelids.

'Okay, now I really am worried.' He lifted one of my trembling hands and placed it in both of his. 'We played a game of soccer. You came along and watched. Cal broke his ankle, and we spent the afternoon at Max and Sean's. Then you came back to my place for burritos.'

I rubbed my forehead, the pain behind my temple intensifying to a whole new level.

His fingers brushed my cheek as he pushed a thick strand of hair from my face. He looked me squarely in the eyes and frowned. 'You don't remember any of this?'

I shook my head. 'My memory of Saturday is slightly different.' I scrunched the sheets in my hands.

'Different?' He waited, and I fixed my eyes on my lap, terrified to speak. Afraid if I said it out loud, I might actually have to believe it, and afraid that he wouldn't. 'It's all right, Lucy, you can tell me.' He spoke with a gentle confidence, no idea what I was about to hit him with, just pure belief that telling him wasn't a choice, that I had to do it.

'Can you shut the door?' I asked. 'Mum cannot hear what I'm about to say, I'll be put in a strait jacket and dragged out of here before you can say fruit loop.'

Tyler closed the door quietly. 'She wouldn't do that.'

'You might not think so after you hear what I'm about to say.'

'Does this have anything to do with your dreams?'

'I think they're changing...um...things,' I stuttered.

'What does that mean?'

'It means that two days ago, for me, started out much the same as it did for you. Except in my memory, Cal slammed his head on another player's, and was knocked out. He had bleeding on the brain, and they flew him to Canberra for surgery. He died, Tyler. Cal died.' The tears fell; big, fat drops slid over my nose and landed in my lap. The tears were good, I couldn't see Tyler's face through them, couldn't see his disbelief. I used the back of my arm to wipe them away and continued, 'I fell asleep on Saturday night and dreamed of how different things could've been. I was desperate for him to be okay, and dreamed of an alternate ending.' My eyes found his, and I drew in a deep breath. 'I think I changed the ending.'

—22—

TYLER'S EYEBROWS WERE EXACTLY where I thought they'd be, raised in disbelief, but instead of calling my bluff he said, 'Wow. I knew you were awesome, but this is way beyond that.'

'You believe me?' I asked shakily.

'Yes.' He shook his head with a grin and nodded. 'Yes, I believe you.' He held my hands and squeezed gently.

'But why?'

'Why not? Trust until proven otherwise, remember? I can't think of a single reason not to trust what you say, I mean why'd you make something like this up? So it's as simple as that. I trust you. I believe you.'

I let out a long slow breath, and my whole body, so tense since his arrival, finally relaxed – he'd done it again, given me air to breathe.

He shuffled closer and tugged me near, his arms full of acceptance.

'My one in seven billion,' I said.

'Huh?' He pulled away and looked down at me.

'You're my one in seven billion. No one else in the whole world, except Granny Tess, would ever believe what I just said, but you did. You're my one in seven billion.'

'And you're mine, *ma petite rêveuse*.' He kissed the side of my forehead and gathered me back to him.

He'd come unwanted into my life, but I now needed him as much as the oxygen running through my blood. Sometimes I felt so weak for needing him, and other times I was so happy he was there, it didn't matter if it made me weaker or stronger, or anything in between.

A half hour later we sat widthways on the bed, backs against the wall, our feet dangled off the edge. We'd finished the pie Mum had brought up for us and shared the cupcake, because it was hardly fair to eat it on my own, not when it had become Tyler's favourite too. I had my appetite back, much to Mum's delight, and I caught the look of appreciation she sent Tyler as she left the room with our empty plates.

We sat silently, enjoying the quiet for a few brief moments, before Tyler spoke. 'Do you think any of your other dreams have come true?' My heart skipped a few beats as he spoke the thought that mirrored my own.

I nodded. 'Some have.'

'Shit, really. Only some?'

'Yeah, all the ones since the little girl who drowned. I didn't save her.'

'From a few weeks ago?' His brows furrowed, head tilting as if he were trying to recollect a lost memory. 'There haven't been any since then.'

'What're you talking–' I clapped a hand over my mouth, the sting on my lips shocking my skin as much as the realisation. 'You don't remember our conversations...they never happened if the events changed.'

'You've kinda lost me.'

I pulled my book onto my lap and flipped to the back. 'See these,' I said, pointing. 'And the dates. We talked about them. It's all changed.'

Tyler hooked a leg under himself and grabbed the book, taking a closer look at the words and pictures. 'Shit.' He muttered. 'But not this one?' He held out the page of the little girl.

'No. Not yet. But I might be able to. See I couldn't help myself yesterday, I tried to go back and save someone from weeks ago.'

'Who?'

This was it, the moment of truth. I hesitated.

'What is it?'

'I'm too scared to say it, to find out if you remember them or not.'

'But you're the girl who has to know all the answers.'

'I know, but I want this so much, or at least I think I do. It also scares the crap out of me. All the lives I could change without knowing the repercussions.' I slid off the bed, taking my sketch-books off the bookcase, and dumped them on the table, along with the current one. My hand sat protectively on the top of the four books. Nearly a year in each one. 'This is what's made me sick. I mean, look at them, what a responsibility.' I thought of all the dreams I'd had over the years, but instead of feeling lighter, happier, that I might be able to save some of these people, I felt as if a huge burden had been given to me. A burden I wasn't sure I could carry.

'Okay, so we could sit here all day coming up with reasons why it's a good thing or a curse, but shouldn't we start by finding out what we're dealing with?'

He said *we*, as if it was his problem to deal with as well. As if it wasn't even an option. My shoulders relaxed; every step ahead would be with him by my side. It gave me the little bit of strength I needed to move forward and figure this out.

He squeezed my hand and grabbed the stool below my window and we sat at the table. 'Let's see if you did it.' He opened my laptop, and clicked on the browser, his hands waiting on the keys. He laughed. 'You're going to have to tell me who they are, you know.'

I swallowed, took a breath. 'It was a train accident. At a level crossing, a mother and her son were killed.' His face remained blank. 'You don't remember it, do you?'

'No.'

'Ugh, it's so weird. Those conversations are just gone.'

'You're tellin' me. You talk like I'm supposed to know what's going on and I've got no memory.' Tyler's eyes wandered to the right-hand page, at the face peering up at me. The faces that haunted me in detailed perfection, until, with my pencil acting as my crossing over, I sketched the memorised lines. He pointed to the page. 'So this was her? Where was it?'

I peered at my almost illegible, early morning scribbles depicting the dream on the bottom corner. Only three letters: NSW.

'New South Wales, at a level crossing. Wollongong from memory. But it was still an accident, so there should be a story online somewhere.'

'Here it is. Victoria Street in Wollongong. One person killed after a train collided with an SUV that ran through the boom gates.' Tyler brought up the news article from the accident, and my heart hammered at the images from my dream, the second one.

An orange SUV Ute smashed to pieces by the force of the train. Images of the carriages that had derailed on impact, of the crew as it worked to clean up the mess, and there in the second picture, sat a car. I couldn't see if anyone was in it, the picture wasn't clear enough, but I knew it was *the* car. The little white Nissan Pulsar.

My eyes glazed over. *It really worked.* 'It was originally two people, the lady and her son. I killed the man.' I squeezed my eyes tight, held them closed.

'No you didn't. He was way over the limit.' Tyler shifted on his seat and wrapped an arm around my shoulders, his mouth resting on my hair. As right as he was, the enormity and fault still hit me hard.

'That's them,' I said.

'Who?'

'The lady and the boy.' I pointed.

'What, Dreadlock Lady from your book? I can't see her.' He leaned into the laptop with a squint.

'No, but that's the car they were in when they were killed in my dream. The one she was in with her son when they were killed.' And the one they were in when they weren't.

'This is kinda cool, but should I be freaked out?'

'Probably. You're not though, are you?'

'Not really. Just a bit awestruck.'

'Lucky you,' I said, envious I couldn't feel some of the same easiness with the situation.

'You saved someone's life, Lucy. Aside from the strangeness of it all, you have to agree that's pretty awesome.'

'I do agree,' I said. 'It's a lot to take in. I've spent years wanting this. Two days to get used to playing God isn't much time.' I gave a half-hearted smiled. 'You know, seeing what I've only seen in my dreams is really freaky. A bit like how I felt when I saw you. But at least with you I couldn't deny it, not with you standing right in front of me. And what if I didn't make things better? Only worse? You know, like some kinda damaging butterfly effect.' I screwed up my face, the dilemma crawling under my skin. 'I'm not touching that book again until I'm sure I've done the right thing.'

He scribbled down the number plate. 'What if we could find her? To ask what happened. She might be able to tell you what you're needing to hear. That she's happy to be alive, to really see that the details you dreamed actually came true.'

'Well, it did. Look.' I nodded at the screen. 'It's the other car that's smashed.'

'I know, but in the flesh, like with me. You could go see her and be sure.'

'And how do we find her? Head to Wollongong and walk around until we bump into a chick with blond dreadlocks?'

'Well, that's one way. Or I could pull in a favour from my aunty who works at Service NSW.' He held up a scrap of paper with a grin on his face. 'Fancy a road trip?'

'To Wollongong?'

'Mm, hm.' His smile reached the outer edges of his face, deepening the dimple on his chin. 'And of course we'll have to go to Sydney so you can cross that city off your list.'

I sank in my chair. I'd love it to be that simple, to jump in a car and take off as easily as everyone else. 'I dunno. I don't really do travel, remember.' I interlocked my fingers, tightened them, relaxed them.

Tyler swivelled on his chair and faced me, dropping his shoulders so his eyes could meet mine. 'But it's just Sydney.' There was doubt in his eyes, because for someone who'd never experienced even a taste of what I choked on every day, it couldn't be easy to comprehend.

My eyes pleaded with his. 'It's not the distance.'

'What is it then? Explain it to me. I want to understand.' His hand rested over mine.

I gripped his fingers, knowing it would be like trying to explain colour to the blind, but I had to try. 'It's the unknown, not being able to control what happens around me. What I see or hear.' I brushed off a shudder. 'See, when I'm here, even when I see something horrific, at least everything else is normal. But out there' – I flicked my head toward the window – 'nothing around me is familiar. And that terrifies me. Like I'll fall into some deep black hole, like really deep, and not be able to climb out.'

Tyler was silent, digesting my words. He rubbed a hand on the side of his face. 'What if we made sure we knew exactly what'd happen? We could have everything booked, stick to a tight schedule, have it all worked out.' His enthusiasm crept across his face, lifting his cheeks. 'Wouldn't it be worth it? You know, like seeing her, seeing the reality, and even better, seeing the world?'

'Maybe, but I don't know if I'm brave enough to find out.'

'What if I was with you?' He swivelled his shoulders like a peacock showing off his feathers.

I giggled. 'That is tempting. *You* are tempting, but even you can't make me forget everything–'

His mouth covered mine, my lips curving upward beneath their warmth. He cupped a hand around my neck, his fingers tangling in my hair, and fireworks exploded behind my eyelids, sending electrifying jolts all the way to my toes, and I did forget.

With his face inches from mine, he whispered, 'You sure?'

—23—

I SAT IN THE back of Cal's car, my body pressed into Tyler's side. His arm draped around me as he stared out the window. Almost a week had passed since Cal's accident.

With an empty long weekend to fill, and my parent's permission, I agreed to go to Sydney to see Dreadlock Lady, knowing how important the trip could be to help rid my doubt and maybe answer some of those nagging questions. Although with Cal sitting in the front seat of the car, I found it hard not to truly appreciate all that'd happened in the six days gone. Despite my continued dreams, and the grief I still carried with me each day, I felt the small quiver of happiness. I was snuggled against Tyler, but not only that – for the first time in my life, I was headed to Sydney.

True to his word, Tyler talked his Aunt into looking up the records for the number plate he'd scribbled down. We contacted the owner and teed up a time for an interview – under the guise of doing a research paper for level crossing incidents across New South Wales. Blond Dreadlock Lady's name was Cara.

To ease my anxiety and fear, Tyler had an hour-by-hour schedule prepared for the trip. 'And where our plans stuff up, I'll be right there,' he said.

We'd left school early, planning to drive straight through to Sydney. Counting lunch, toilet breaks, and Friday afternoon traffic, we probably had five or six hours ahead of us.

The boot was full of camping gear for our two nights in Sydney. Somehow, with the long weekend, we managed to score ourselves a campsite, which, even though unpowered, we considered a small miracle.

We'd be staying with Granny Tess and Pop in Canberra on our way home. I'd called her a few days after Cal's accident and told her my news. I had to hold the phone from my ear as her screams flew down the line. If ever she'd been my cheerleader, now was it. When I decided to go to Sydney I called again, knowing she wouldn't let us drive by without a visit.

Amber was driving us in Cal's car. He couldn't drive yet with his foot, so he sat beside her as navigator-cum-driving instructor-cum-annoying front seat passenger.

'I know how to drive a car, Cal,' she said. 'That's why they gave me a license.'

'Yeah, but you don't normally drive a manual.'

'I learnt to drive in one. I'll be just dandy, thank you very much.'

'Yeah, but will we?' He craned his neck and stuck his tongue out with a chuckle.

'Hey. Why don't you focus less on what gear I'm in and find us a decent radio station?'

We'd asked the others if they wanted to join us, but Max had a comp on, and Sean said he wasn't interested in another trip to Sydney. He already had to go enough to visit his dad, but more importantly, didn't want to miss the predicted early snowfall over the weekend. I didn't blame him, I almost used it as an excuse to back out myself. But Tyler was so excited for the trip, and I'd geared myself up so much already I chose to push forward.

'Hey, I got you something.' Tyler reached into his backpack and retrieved a small white jewellery pouch, his eyes wandering across my worried face. He smiled reassuringly. 'Don't panic, it's nothing exciting, I just thought of you when I saw it and had to buy it.'

'Now I'm curious,' I said with a tentative smile. I wasn't a jewellery person, Tyler must've noticed, so I was genuinely intrigued by what could be in the bag. He placed it into my hand.

'Open it and I'll explain.'

'Okay?' I slid my finger in the top of the bag and loosened the drawstring.

'You know how you're always wearing the black one.' He looked down at my wrist, and I followed his eyes. 'And you're remembering the bad dreams, well, the people in them.'

I tipped the contents into my hand. An almost identical bracelet to the one on my wrist but with white gemstone beads fell out. I lifted my gaze back to Tyler and he continued, 'For the days after your good dreams.'

Tears sprang to my eyes – happy tears. I quickly wiped them away and placed the bracelet on my wrist.

'Tyler, it's perfect. Thank you. Where did you get it?'

'It was in the second-hand joint near the servo. I figured a bit of balance is always nice. Bit of happiness alongside the Queen Vic melancholy, 'cause our dreams are ones you don't want to be forgetting, right?' He smirked.

'Right.' And he was – so very right.

Traffic delays on the outskirts of Canberra, and a lunch break involving a pleasant, but unnecessary, wander through a local car museum, had us way behind schedule. Add to that a driver who was especially keen for every photo opportunity along the way. I swear we stopped at all the scenic lookouts, and she didn't just want photos of the view.

'Come on, lovelies, just one more,' Amber said, her voice pleading for us to hop in the shot.

'That's what you said last time.' Cal hobbled from the car on his cast.

'I know, but I didn't know this was coming up.'

Six and a half hours later, we reached the outskirts of Sydney for a fun game of 'can we get out of this alive'. One GPS wasn't enough for us to safely navigate the inner maze of the Sydney roads: Amber had a GPS on the dash, and Tyler had his open on his phone to help from the backseat. I don't know how Amber kept her cool so well. She stayed calm, even when every piece of directing, technical and otherwise, sent her up a one-way street with nowhere to turn around.

'See, I told you I knew how to drive,' she said, and we all laughed.

A short while later she pulled Cal's car up to our campsite.

Miraculously, it only took an hour, and a few curse words, to get the tent up and beds ready, and then, all completely knackered from the long drive, we climbed straight under the covers.

'Meet me at the tree, *ma petite rêveuse?*' Tyler whispered from his bed beside mine. My heart fluttered and my eyelids closed.

'I'M SCARED,' I SAID. *We sat with our backs to the tree, exactly like our first dream. Tyler held my hand, the stroke of his thumb on my fingers easing me into the dream.*

'What of?' he asked.

'Everything. Seeing them for real.'

'Yeah, but it'll feel normal soon, once you get used to the idea.'

'That doesn't seem possible. I don't feel like I'll ever feel normal again.'

'No, but then you're not very normal, are you.' His mouth curved in a lopsided grin.

'Thanks,' I said, my voice oozing sarcasm.

'Normal's boring and bland. You're unique and interesting. Who wants a plain canvas when they can have Picasso?' Tyler said.

'I wouldn't mind plain and boring sometime. I love that I'm saving people's lives, but the dreams are horrible.'

'Not this one,' Tyler said.

I couldn't help my smile as I admired the peaceful school grounds and the unclouded brightness of the sky, so perfect it must've been airbrushed. These dreams weren't anything close to horrible. Not even a semblance. Most of my mind was filled with pain, death, horror. Tyler had taken me by the hand and led me down the dark passage in my mind, through the doorway to a secret room I'd never known was there. It's hard to see the light when you're so focused on the darkness.

It was like walking into the sun after being holed up in a pitch-black room. All my senses intensified. I felt awake, even though I was asleep, but most of all, there was no sadness.

'Thanks, Tyler.'

'What for?'

'For giving me these dreams. They make it all so much better. I wish we could do it every night and not only when we're near each other.'

'Yeah, I know what you mean. God, I hope we figure it out.'

Tyler leaned into me and pressed his warm lips onto mine, and every fear, every worrying thought floated away.

I nestled into his side, and he kissed the top of my head and stroked my hair. We spent the rest of our dream like that. No soap skating or swimming. A close togetherness, unblemished by the parts of our usual life that required our attention; those things that shifted our focus away from what truly mattered – connection.

*****

'THAT'S IT.' WE STOOD under the thin canopy of a wisteria tree, three houses away from the home in my dream. My left hand pressed around the small toy dinosaur in my pocket, the other gripped Tyler's hand, pulling him to a stop. We'd come here for this, but the muscles in my legs chose that moment to bail on me. Their heaviness rooted me to the cement footpath. 'Number fifteen. And that's her car.'

Crippling fear converged around my lungs, pushing in at the walls.

'Breathe, Lucy.' Tyler gave my hand a squeeze.

The vibrations in my temple were heavy, the blood pulsated and screamed 'don't panic, don't panic', reminding me I was already panicking.

'I can't.' The words surfaced in a strangle, jagged and sharp.

'Lucy, look at me. You can. There's nothing to be afraid of. You already know what you're going to see. This is confirming what you already know. It won't change anything. It already is.'

His voice and gaze were hypnotic, and I drew from his strength, willing my heart to slow the flow from gushing river to gentle spring. His calm tone washed over me, and I managed to take in a big breath and move my feet forward.

Tyler knocked on the door. We stood on the porch of the exact same house I'd only ever seen in my dreams. Until now.

It was real.

And as Cara opened the door and welcomed us into her home, and every detail I'd dreamed, from her small frame to the frizzy dreadlocks and painted nails, surged to life around me, I stood face to face with the realisation that she was equally as real.

Cara led us through her sparsely furnished house. It was a 'just enough' home. Just enough chairs, just enough cupboards, just enough plates. Any more would create the usual unnecessary clutter most homes had. We walked into the kitchen and sat at a round pine table.

'Can I get you a drink?' she asked.

'Water would be great, thanks.' I clasped my shaking hands

together in my lap. Tyler nodded agreement, and placed his hand over my trembling ones. She extended a small but genuine smile, her dreadlocks flicking outward as she spun to reach into the cupboard.

I blinked hard. I'd never met someone from my dreams before, other than Tyler. It was like standing in front of a television celebrity when I'd only ever seen them on the screen; raise my arm and I'd be able to touch them.

Cara placed two glasses on the table and took a seat.

'Thanks,' I said, my throat clogging the way for more words to escape. Not that I'd know what to say, all rational thought had vanished.

Tyler gave me a reassuring nod and eased his fingers from mine, lifting his glass, his elbows resting confidently on the table. 'Can you tell us what you saw that morning?' He didn't need to act, all our questions could be applied to both dream investigation and fake research paper.

Cara told us what she'd witnessed the morning of the accident. Being first on the scene, she'd called for help, and left her son, Benji, in the car so she could assist. The driver of the vehicle was still alive.

Her shoulders sagged and she shook her head. 'He wasn't conscious for long and died later in hospital. He'd been drinking. It was a forty zone, but they've said he was going over eighty K. I don't even know how it's possible to go that fast 'round here. Such a shame, but it's lucky he didn't kill someone else.'

'Makes you wonder what might've been if you were at the crossing before him.' I stumbled over the words, speaking before I realised what I was doing.

'I know, I'm the same, nearly every day.' She heaved in a breath and then her strained face lifted in a smile. 'Hey, Benji, come and meet our visitors.' A little boy bounded into the room, and Cara hoisted him onto her lap. The curls I remembered so well bounced around his ears and brushed against his shoulders.

'Hello,' he said, and my heart sang with joy at the sight of him – so cute, so bubbly, and so alive.

'Hello, Benji.' My smile grew with his. 'I wonder if you could tell me...' I paused and his eyes grew wide in anticipation. 'Do you happen to like dinosaurs?'

'Yes.' He nodded enthusiastically. 'My favourite is the diplodocus.'

'Is it? What about this one?' I tugged at the toy in my pocket. 'Do you like this one?'

His smile wrapped around my heart. 'You can have that,' I said and sipped my water.

'You know,' Cara said, jostling Benji on her knee, 'I think it was this little fella who saved our lives.'

I didn't dare move. I couldn't miss a single detail that might shed light on the specifics of her morning, the bits that weren't in any online articles.

'I was in a massive rush that morning. I'd started a new job the week before and couldn't be late. I mean, who can? But I had to get Benji to pre-school before I started my shift and seriously, if I ever get a stomach ulcer it'll be from that freight train. It goes over the crossing at around ten to seven, if I don't get out the door by six-forty I'm screwed.

'Benji asked me to do his laces up and I fobbed him off, said we'd do it when we got to pre-school. We were rushing out the door, and he tugged at my arm. I was seriously annoyed, we didn't have time for muckin' about, but he spoke three words that I'm pretty sure saved our life. "I love you".' She pressed a firm kiss onto his chubby cheek. 'Sometimes the universe gives us a sign to slow down. I think this was one of those moments. Benji's such a sensitive soul, he hates the rushing, and he had tears in his eyes. Kids cry over the silliest things sometimes, for him it was undone shoelaces that morning. But instead of screaming or arguing with me, he did the one thing that weakens me more than anything in the world, he spoke those words.'

'I learned how to tie my laces now, Mummy.'

'Yes you did, clever boy.' She ruffled his mop of curls. 'At that point, I no longer cared about getting to work on time. I gave Benji a big hug, wiped away his tears, and of course while I'd bent down I did up his shoelaces.' She laughed softly at the absurdity of it.

After thanking Cara and Benji for their time, and invaluable assistance with our 'research paper', we headed for the train. I left the toy dinosaur for Benji, but he'd given me something far greater to line my pockets with – clarity and belief.

—24—

THERE WERE ONLY A few other passengers in the carriage with us, and I shifted away from everyone and looked out the window. I couldn't decide if I should be elated or afraid. Should I laugh, cry, scream, or curl up in a ball and rock back and forth? It seemed fitting with the current insanity status strung around my neck.

Tyler asked if I was okay. I nodded, and with the squeeze of my hand he allowed me the time I needed to absorb what I'd witnessed.

Somewhere between Wollongong and Sydney, I finally broke the silence. I had no idea where, because the buildings outside my window were as blurry as my thoughts. I couldn't focus any more on those than I could on the racket inside my head.

'Do you think you could bring me some of Laurie's peanut butter, chocolate cupcakes to the asylum, I don't think they serve very nice food in those places.'

Tyler took one look at my serious face and burst into laughter. Big convulsive chuckles.

'That's what you're worried about? That you won't get good food if you're locked up?'

'Well yes, but specifically good cupcakes, they probably don't serve them at all.' I kept my mouth straight. This was a serious concern.

Tyler laughed again, placed his hands on either side of my face, and pressed his lips on mine. I startled from the sudden shift in emotion, but I liked this feeling so much more than the last and went with it. I ignored the fact we were on a train surrounded by strangers and kissed him back.

'Okay, now first of all,' he said as he pulled away, 'you're not going to end up in some asylum, I won't allow it. And second, if you do, you can count on me being your personal peanut butter, chocolate cupcake courier.'

'Thank you,' I said, content that at least I wouldn't be lacking in the 'fine food' department, even if I had to be locked up forever.

'So, other than being worried about your supply of cupcakes, tell me how you're really feeling?' he asked, intensity in his eyes.

I caught sight of his seriousness and huffed out a small laugh. 'Freaked out. Seriously freaked out. But I'm also thrilled she's alive. I watched her die and I don't think she deserved that. She seemed really nice, didn't she. And Benji, so cute.'

'*Oui.*'

'And they look exactly like I dreamed. Everything did. It was exactly how I imagined, how I dreamed it.' I shook my head. 'It's absurd. Will I ever get used to it?'

'I dunno. Would you want to? As soon as it becomes normal, you stop seeing the wonder in it. Don't you think?' Tyler's lips pursed as if he was questioning his own wisdom.

'Yeah, but I think you're starting to sound as nuts as me. You'll have to join me at the asylum.'

'That wouldn't be a bad thing, but then who'd bring us cupcakes?'

'Ooh, that's a problem.' I tilted my head to the side.

'All right.' Tyler sat up straight, and slid his phone from his pocket. 'We're right on schedule. Opera House, lunch at Circular Quay, bridge, then Bondi. Sound good?'

Despite the tornado we'd survived, a sudden eagerness to enjoy all of Tyler's plans swirled. 'You sure we'll fit it all in.'

He held up his phone. He'd listed each location with the time we'd spend there and how long the walk or bus to the next stop would take. 'I've been planning this for days.'

I snuggled into his side, wrapping my arm around his. 'You're amazing.'

He didn't disappoint. The sites might've been obvious choices but he showed them to me better than any tour guide – they generally didn't steal kisses from their patrons.

He shared stories of his time in Sydney while we climbed the steps of the Opera House. Then we walked, hand in hand, across the Harbour Bridge and peered over the side into the water far below, where white wakes trailed behind the tiny boats.

We wasted away the last of the afternoon at Bondi beach. I settled in the sand between Tyler's legs, the rise and fall of his chest against my back. The temperature dropped as dark clouds loomed out at sea, and because of the undesirable beach weather, we nearly had the place to ourselves. Tyler's arms enfolded me as we watched the surfers ride the waves.

Not far from us, a surfer, clad in a black and red wetsuit, plucked up his surfboard and ran into the water. 'Wish I had my gear so I could join him.' Tyler's chin rested on my shoulder.

'We should've thought about that, hey? Could've thrown your board on Cal's roof.'

'Mmm, not sure he would've liked that.'

'No, you're right, he would've hated it.' I laughed at the thought. 'Hey, you should be catching up with your mates while we're here. I've been so selfish, I didn't even think about what it might mean for you to be back here.'

'No, it's all right. To be honest, I wouldn't know who to catch up with anyway. My best mate moved to Brissy two years ago, and after Dad died, I kind of lost a lot of my friends.'

'Really?'

'Yeah. I used to go surfing with my mates at least twice a week, more if the weather was good. But then we lost Dad and I couldn't do it. Couldn't bring myself to enjoy anything, and couldn't leave Mum at home crying on her own. More than that, my mates distanced themselves as much as I did. I mean, what do you say to the kid whose dad killed a plane full of people, and what do I say to them? It got awkward, and by the time I was ready to surf again I made sure I came out here on my own. It was easier that way.'

'That must've been hard.'

'Mmm. You know, at first I was annoyed with Mum for wanting to leave, I mean where's the surf in the mountains, but then I realised it could be an opportunity to become Tyler again, not the pilot's kid. I think that's what Mum wanted too, for her, and for us. Not sure it's working out for her, though.' His half chuckle vibrated onto my back.

What would it mean for Tyler and his family to have his dad back? They'd be whole again, not floundering in the raging sea of grief currently trying to drown them. My chest tightened and a lump formed in my throat. *Nope, not going there.* And no point worrying about it when I couldn't help anyway. But even if I could do it, would I?

I coughed, clearing the way for air to fill my lungs again, and shifted my thoughts to those I could help.

'You know, seeing them like that today has really helped, thank you.' I brushed my fingers over Tyler's clasped hands on my stomach. 'Now I know I didn't do the wrong thing.' I paused, drew in a big breath. 'I think I'm ready to go back and save more lives.'

Tyler's hair skimmed my cheek with his gentle nod of solidarity, and his warm lips pressed against my neck at the same moment the clouds chose to follow through with their threat of rain.

* * * * *

I PEERED UP AT the Bondi sky, a perfect luminous blue. The sun reflected off the water like diamonds floating on the ripples. If this were a normal day, a real day, the sand wouldn't be visible beneath the beach towels spread along its length, but it wasn't a normal day. It was a dream, and I stood completely alone, my only company the gulls cawing overhead. We'd agreed to meet here, but I couldn't see Tyler anywhere. I turned around to the vacant car park, restaurants and parks, the end-of-the-world empty roads. The waves crashed rhythmically on the shore behind me.

'Hey, gorgeous.' I spun. Tyler stood in his wetsuit, feet in the water and surfboard under his arm. He gaped at me, appreciation in his eyes – I wore a navy blue two-piece. My cheeks warmed at the attention, but I smiled and approached. Tyler placed his free arm around my waist and pulled me in for a kiss. Our lips moulded together. I could've stayed like that for hours, but I reminded myself we were here to surf, or at least Tyler was.

'Okay, mister, time to show off your skills.' I shoved him away, and he grinned while wading deeper into the water.

I eased myself onto the sand and admired the view as moist grains oozed between my toes.

Tyler glided through the water. He was good, seriously good. He twisted the board almost effortlessly and propelled himself through the waves. With those skills, he'd pick up snowboarding in no time.

'Want a turn?' he yelled from the water.

'Nah, you keep going,' I yelled back, flicking my hand in the air.

My toes cooled as a wave rolled in, and I recalled childhood days at the beach, running away from the waves with squeals of delight when they caught me. I pressed my hands into the sand and rubbed the exfoliating grains through my fingers. I looked up right when Tyler waved to me. With sandy hands, I waved back.

My body detached from the dream, a buzzing started in my ears, and I felt myself floating away. The walls of the dream closed around me, shifting, narrowing, converging, until the only thing left was the sight of Tyler on the waves. I wanted to stay there with him, but I had no control of the rippling out-of-body sensation that surged through me from the evolving dream.

I no longer had sand on my fingers, but the arms of a chair, an aeroplane chair. I closed my eyes and swallowed back the lump of a scream lodged in my throat. I ached for my earphones, for my music, to help drown out the sickening wails surrounding me and penetrating every morsel of my being.

I knew what came next, but that knowledge did little to comfort me. Take me back to the beach. I didn't want to be here with all these human carcasses. That's what they'd be soon enough. They were about to perish, to disintegrate with the remains of the plane. For once I couldn't bear to look around me. I didn't want to see their faces.

My heart pounded beneath my ribs, and my breathing grew rapid as I struggled to get the air in. I closed my eyes and pictured Tyler's face – the face I'd soon wake up and see.

I fixed my eyes on that man again, the one I often remembered when I thought of this dream. I wished I'd had a different seat. One where I didn't have to see into his hauntingly dark eyes. He freaked me out and I had no idea why. Something about him disturbed me, unnerved me. He delivered that crooked smile again, but this time, I noticed the harsh scrutiny in his eyes that accompanied the rise of one side of his face. A small shiver ran down my spine.

I closed my eyes and twisted to face the old lady, and a sense of overwhelming sadness crept over me again as she repeated her chilling words. 'She needs me, she needs me.'

The captain's voice, Tyler's dad's voice, crackled to life, and I braced myself for the excruciating and instant pain that signalled the end of the dream for me, but death for everyone else on board. It came and sent me spiralling to the other side.

I bolted upright with a scream so loud it would likely wake a few neighbouring tents. Rain poured down outside and it took Tyler's arms for me to realise I wasn't about to die. I choked on the erupting sobs and clutched his top in my fists.

'It's okay,' Tyler said into my hair. 'You're okay. You were having a dream. I'm here.'

Tears fell down my cheeks and my breathing slowed. Tyler laid me gently back down.

'The waves were good,' he whispered.

'I'm sorry I left. I didn't mean to. I wanted to stay with you.' My voice trembled.

'I know. It's okay. You're here now.' He kissed the tears on my cheek, stroked my hair, and held me close. And as I held on to him I drifted back into a dark and empty sleep.

—25—

A
MBER PULLED THE CAR up to the front of the small sand-coloured home at the end of the cul-de-sac and tooted the horn. I jumped out, ran to the side gate, and called out to Granny Tess and Pop. Pop warned us they'd likely be in the back yard for the afternoon. Moments later they strolled through the gate, waving their soil-covered hands and grinning from ear to ear.

'You made it,' Granny Tess said.

'Miracle of miracles.' Cal climbed out the car as Amber shot him a friendly glare.

'He still giving you a hard time?' Granny Tess asked.

Amber gave Granny Tess a quick hug. 'I'd be worried if he didn't.'

'I can't believe he let you drive his baby,' Pop said, patting Cal on the back with his clean hand.

'I didn't have much of a choice.' Cal stuck his leg out.

Granny Tess had her red hair up in a bun, messy tendrils dancing around her face as she twisted toward Tyler and me with her arms wide. 'And you must be Tyler, I've heard about you.' She hugged him, bending her wrists to keep her hands away from his clothes. He gasped and stiffened, but quickly moulded into her welcome embrace. 'How's Geography going?' She winked over his shoulder, and I choked back a laugh, my cheeks flaming.

'Shit yeah.' Cal shoved his phone into my face. 'Check it out.'

The snow report from home filled the screen. 'It's snowing.'

Excitement swelled within me and an uncontrollable grin spread across my face.

'I can't believe I'm gonna miss half the season because of this thing.' Cal lifted his hindrance of a leg off the ground.

'Sucks hey.' My eyes softened, displaying the sympathy he craved, while inside a flood of gratitude surged for his broken leg.

We stumbled into the thick heat of their cosy home, and the unease of the previous two days settled amongst the familiar sights and smells. A bunch of freshly picked roses sat inside a green glass vase on the sideboard of the entry way, their aroma blending with Granny Tess' beloved essential oils.

Many a school holiday had been spent here, alone without my brothers, doing nothing but idling the days away building puzzles, going for walks, and eating ice-cream with Granny Tess and Pop. They preferred to have us one at a time, they said; not because they couldn't handle three at once, but so they could spoil and get to know each of us as people in our own right. Once a year each, for five days. We'd always go home gloating about all the wonderful things the others had missed, unaware we all had it as good.

An hour after we'd arrived, Cal, Amber, and Tyler left with Pop to pick up dinner, Thai take-away, and I was alone with Granny Tess in her art-slash-sun room. Despite the rapidly disappearing sun, the room radiated warmth. Paint fumes fought with the three vases of roses around the small room, coming out a clean winner from sheer volume. Canvases coated with seasoned brush strokes in every imaginable colour leaned against any and all supporting structures in the room; the doorframe, table, window sills, and propped against the stool I hitched myself onto.

'Tyler's a good-looking boy,' she said.

'Ah yeah...he is.'

'Kind of reminds me of a young James Dean.'

'Thought you might say that.' I couldn't help but smile. 'I thought the same thing.'

'What, you don't anymore?'

'Well yeah, but now he's Tyler to me.'

'Right, yes of course.' She lowered herself onto the window bench seat, resting her hands one on top of the other. 'So tell me, how are you...really? I've been dying to hear everything. Are you coping? What you're doing is huge, Lucy.'

I agreed with a small smile. 'It's bigger than Russia, but yes, I'm okay.' I hesitated, tapping my fingers on my legs. 'I'm going to save Beverly.'

Granny Tess inhaled and placed her hand to her mouth. Tears sprang to her eyes and she muddled her words when she spoke. 'How...do you...you can do that?'

I nodded. 'Yes, I think so. I'm sorry I haven't done it yet, but I was waiting to be sure.'

'You don't have anything to be sorry about. You have a good heart, Lucy, I knew you'd use your gift for good.'

I pressed my lips together, fiddled with my fingernails. 'Did you ever ask yourself, why me?'

'Oh, all the time. Then I decided, what did it matter? That made no difference whatsoever in my ability to do what I could do. You could spend your entire life trying to figure it out or you can take it for what it is; a chance to play God and do something good in the world.'

'So I'm God?' I laughed.

Granny Tess gripped the bench on either side of her legs, her eyes narrowing as if trying to come up with an explanation. 'No, just the essence of what God is – goodness, love.'

'But you don't believe in God.' It was a statement but also a question.

'Yes, I do. Maybe not the version of God they preach about in church, but that's not why I go. I go to church for the spirituality and the friendships...oh, and the free food.'

I rolled my eyes and laughed as I imagined Granny Tess sitting in the pews ignoring the minister and then smiling only thirty minutes later with a plate of food in her hand.

'I believe God is within us. You've heard me say that before, haven't you?' I screwed up my lips, before agreeing with a nod. 'It's the part of us that's innately good, the purest part of our very being. You don't have to call it God, but it's the part of us that shows up in every good thing we do and in every kind word we say. We all have that goodness – that love – deep within us. For most people it's a whisper. But not you, yours is roaring.'

TYLER AND I NESTLED on the couch, fingers entwined, my legs tucked up and resting on his knees. The movie credits scrolled up the screen.

Granny Tess collected the empty mugs from around the room and carted them to the kitchen.

'We're off to bed,' Amber said with a yawn and tugged Cal from his spot on the couch.

'Night all.' Cal slid his hand through hers and hobbled behind Amber from the room.

Pop slapped his hands on his knees and groaned, easing out of his seat. 'That's my cue. Think I'll leave you lot to it.' He kissed Granny Tess goodnight, planted one on my head, and lifted a hand to Tyler.

Granny Tess lowered herself back into her recliner. 'So, it appears you two are a couple of clever clogs. Tell me about this dream where you saw each other.'

Tyler's fingers tightened around mine, and I flicked my eyes toward him, reassuring him. 'That dream wasn't much. But the ones we've had since have been pretty incredible.'

She sat up straight, eyes wide. 'You've had more?'

I smiled and looked to Tyler. 'Three?'

He nodded.

'Well, that gives meeting the man of your dreams a whole new meaning, doesn't it?' she said with a wide grin.

'We haven't figured out how we can do it though. So far it's only when we're near each other.' My stomach fluttered, it wouldn't be long until our minds carried us to our imagined world again later that night. 'Were you ever able to do it, when you used to dream?'

'No.' She paused, eyes assessing, taking us in, our bodies and hands weaving comfortably together on the couch. 'I'd say it's something to do with the connection you two have with each other. It's strong, isn't it?'

We looked at each other, our eyes lingering, searching, communicating without words. Our lips rose in unison and we spoke at the same time. '*Oui.*' – 'Yes.'

'Thought so.' She sighed, content with our answer. 'Do you have other dreams too, Tyler?'

'No, only ones with Lucy.'

I reached for the last square of chocolate in the bowl in front of us, and plopped it in my mouth. 'Do you know if there's any way to control the dreams more? At the moment, even though I'm consciously thinking it, I don't feel like I've got any control.'

'You and your control.' Tyler nudged me with his elbow.

'What? It's not a bad thing.'

'I didn't say it was.' He laughed and twisted away from my retaliating elbow.

'What exactly are you wanting to control?' Granny Tess asked, narrowing her eyes.

KRISTY FAIRLAMB

'I dunno, nothing really. I just want to know everything.'

'You can. Well I could. But be careful. It's usually a selfish desire that drives that motivation, and that's dangerous.' Her mouth quivered, and she folded her hands into her lap. What had she done that was so dangerous? 'Keep your thoughts unselfish and everything will fall into place, like you're already doing.'

'Lucy, selfish? Not possible.' Tyler stroked the back of my hand with his thumb.

'You didn't see me steal that last bit of chocolate before?' I turned serious again, my lips pinching as I absorbed all the wisdom Granny Tess had gathered through the years of doing what I could, except for saving lives of course. 'Okay, so as long as we're not controlling the dreams to do something selfish, it's all right?' I'd never even thought to do something that only I gained from.

'Yes,' Granny Tess said quickly.

'So, you gonna fill us in on the secret?'

'What secret?' she asked, uneasiness settling over her.

'How I can actually control the dreams? Not that I want to, I just want to know how.'

'Oh. It's not a secret. People have been doing it for centuries.'

'Meditation,' Tyler added.

'Well I'm screwed.' I threw my hands up.

'I can teach you.'

Granny Tess' brows shot up and I laughed. 'He meditates. Would you believe?'

'That's perfect,' Granny Tess said. 'If you can learn the art of meditation, you'll perfect the art of controlling your dreams. And maybe even share more dreams.' *Now that I like the sound of.* 'When you get good control over your thoughts while in a meditative state, the same principle can be applied in your dream. But don't expect to learn it quickly or easily, it took me many years of frustration to learn how to meditate properly. I've no doubt you will master it well though, my dear.'

'So why am I able to already turn my thoughts into dreams, I've never meditated in my life. I've never even tried to do what I do, it just happens.'

'That's your subconscious working. Clever, isn't it?'

That was one word for it.

'I'll bet it's the running...or the drawing.' Tyler broke into my thoughts, and I recalled the night I wanted to return to save Cara and Benji, and the rhythm of the pencil on the paper as I sketched their faces before sleeping. Was that part of how I could do what I did? And all those days of running; where my mind drifted away, making me more dazed than awake.

'You could be closer than you think, Lucy,' Granny Tess said.

Tyler and I eventually made it to our room in the early hours of the morning. I changed quickly and shivered as I climbed under the covers. I welcomed the furnace radiating off Tyler when he returned from the bathroom and joined me.

'You cold? Come here.' He opened his arms, and I shifted my body as he wrapped me in a blanket of his warmth. I inhaled his familiar scent, his breath warm on my forehead.

'Your Granny Tess is so cool.' Tyler trailed his fingertips down my arm and found my hand under the blankets. Our fingers meandered together before closing around each other's.

'I know, right. She knows so much about dreaming and how it all works.'

'I wasn't talking about the dreams.'

'Oh?'

'Do your parents know she lets her teen guests have their own room?'

'I don't think they've ever thought to ask.'

'Good. We'll have to visit her more often.' I laughed and shoved him in the side. 'Warm now?'

'Very.' He had no idea.

'Mind if I steal a kiss?'

'You don't have to steal one.' Heat warmed my cheeks and I moved my hand to find the sharp lines of his jaw under my fingers and his soft lips under my thumb. We shared the same breath. His was mine and mine was his. Tyler stroked my hair from my face, closed the gap, and eased his lips onto mine.

'OKAY, TELL ME SOMETHING,' I said. 'If we can control our dreams, why are we just sitting here?' We repeated the dream of two nights ago – school, tree, blue skies.

'What's wrong with sitting here? I love sitting here with you.'

'Yeah, me too.' I relaxed into him in a position I'd grown used to. I fit into his side as if I was designed to be there.

'I still can't figure out why we can only have shared dreaming when we're near each other physically,' Tyler said. 'It doesn't make sense. We didn't meditate before falling asleep tonight. Why does it matter if we're near each other if we're connecting on a spiritual level, in a different paradigm or whatever?'

'Now who's the one who needs all the answers?'

'Don't you wanna figure it out so we can do it all the time? No need to sneak around in the night, we simply meet at an agreed rendezvous in our dreams.'

'Or at Granny Tess's.'

He smiled. 'Or at Granny Tess's.'

I loved the idea of spending each night with him uninhibited.

'More meditation, maybe?' I suggested with a shrug.

'More? Gee, the things we do.'

'Yeah, well, it's not a bad price to pay for this, is it?' I stretched my arm *out at the view.*

'Or this,' he said and placed his fingers on my lower cheek to turn my chin. His eyes met mine as he leaned in to kiss me softly, dreamily, and the sensation awakened all my friendly butterfly friends. 'Bargain really,' Tyler teased, his breath warm on my lips. 'It's virtually a steal.'

'For me it is, I literally, pay nothing, do nothing…it happens easily.'

'You're just a freak of nature,' he said. I nudged his arm with my shoulder, and he laughed. 'Whereas I'm normal.'

'Normal, ha.'

He pulled a face, looking anything but normal, but then grew serious again.

'You actually pay quite a high price, Lucy. You've lived nightmare after nightmare.'

'True. And then you came along,' I said.

'Was it worth it?'

I let out a deep sigh. 'Yes.'

'But you'd still rather not have those dreams.'

I inhaled, long and deep. 'I'd give anything for them to go away. Anything but you. You make all my days…and nights worthwhile.'

*****

'WHAT ARE YOU THINKING about?' I asked Tyler as we took in the passing hills from the backseat of Cal's car. He twisted the white beaded bracelet around my wrist, a pleasant reminder of the night gone. Music poured from the speakers, and Amber sang along to her own version of the lyrics, providing enough background noise for us to have a private hushed conversation.

We were on our way home.

'Tomorrow.' He paused. 'Tomorrow it'll be one year.'

I wrapped my hand around his in as much understanding as possible from someone who'd never lost a parent.

'You gonna be all right?'

'I have to be, don't I?'

'No, you don't. You have every right to be anything but. Should I come over after school?'

'Not sure that'll be wise. Our house'll be more depressing than anything you've ever seen.' I turned toward him and raised my eyebrows. 'Okay, maybe not, but still, probably best you keep your distance. Besides, the mountains are calling, you can't miss that.'

'I can if you need me.'

'No way, I'm not going to make you suffer with us, but I might call you after dinner though. You can tell me all about it.'

'Sounds good,' I said.

'Ugh, I hate this song, it's so irritating,' Amber said, jabbing at the radio to change station.

'Hey, I'll do that, you'll get us all killed.' Cal shoved her hand away and attempted to find a station with the right tune to take us home.

'Grab my phone, we'll connect to my playlist.' She pointed to Cal's feet. 'It's in my bag.'

Cal leaned forward to rummage at his feet, leaving the radio on a random station that, even without hearing perfectly, I knew was the news. The sound pulled with the relentless strength of a magnet, and my heart raced in anticipation of what was coming, but with the recent insight of what I could do, my ears pricked up with an interest I'd never had before.

'The body of missing six-year-old Toby McPherson has been found this morning after a three-day search. An extensive search has been underway since Saturday afternoon, when Toby disappeared from his family's campsite. Authorities feared for the child's safety as temperatures dropped and heavy rain fell overnight. A coroner's examination is underway to determine the actual cause of death.'

I sagged into the seat, squeezing my eyes closed out of pain and frustration for what'd happened and what I would soon see.

Tyler squeezed my knee and leaned in close. 'You okay?' His stormy eyes were as tender as his voice.

I drew in a deep breath and shifted in my seat with a tight smile. 'Perfectly fine.' And although the words were normally a lie, this time I meant them. I might not be looking forward to the dream, or the draining thoughts that came afterward, but if that's what I needed to endure in order to save little Toby, then I was perfectly fine with that.

—26—

I HELD MY BARE hands up to the campfire flames, rubbing them together in an attempt to distribute the warmth up my arms.

'Hey, Dave, can you take the boys to get more firewood for later?'

I turned and saw a woman on the other side of the flames near the tent. Toby's mum? Without seeing me, she returned to chopping vegetables.

Two little boys ran in circles in the dirt, kicking a soccer ball with a man twice their height – Dave, their dad I guessed. The oldest, who I assumed was Toby, dashed for the ball. Soft wisps of blond hair escaped from under his green baseball cap. His turquoise blue eyes glistened with excitement.

He belted the ball, and it rolled between a plastic bucket and a tree stump. 'Score!' He ran in a wide circle, his arms raised in the air.

'Come on, boys, let's see how much we can find tonight. First one back with arms full wins. Let's go!' Dave headed off for the edge of the tree line, and Toby and his brother scuttled behind him.

'What does the winner get, Dad?' Toby asked.

'Two extra marshmallows to toast on the fire.'

'Only two?'

'All right, make it three.' The smile in Dave's voice was evident even though all I saw were the backs of their heads.

They worked together to pick up the sticks scattered across the ground. Their handfuls grew as they chatted away, and then their search had them going in separate directions. Toby walked deeper into the woody trees, and it wasn't long before the others were out of view. Twigs cracked under his feet, and a stillness surrounded us, but he was so determined to get those marshmallows, he'd drifted even further away before he realised how completely quiet and alone he'd become.

'Dad?' he called and stepped slowly around in a full circle, then with a worried look on his face, eyes darting all over, repeated frantically in the opposite direction and called louder. 'Dad! Mike!'

I twisted on the spot – left, then right – everything in front identical to all that lay behind. We were in the middle of the bush, with nothing to distinguish one way from the other. I was as lost as Toby.

Still holding onto his little bundle of sticks, he trudged away from me, his trembling calls echoing quietly through the trees.

Stacks of walking later and we neared the edge of a creek. Toby made a right and followed it upstream. Maybe he knew it'd lead him back to the campsite; maybe he'd seen it before. A twinge of hope prickled at my skin, and then my stomach dropped as I remembered the news headline. 'The body of missing six-year-old Toby McPherson has been found...' I shuddered as a cold shiver ran down my spine. It didn't help that the temperature had dropped. The sun now barely showed through the trees, and a grey haze settled around us. I wanted desperately to wrap my arms around Toby, to offer some kind of assurance. I had nothing. He'd long since discarded his pile of firewood, and his pace slowed considerably, no longer darting hurriedly to find his way out of the maze.

He rubbed at his arms and hunched his shoulders. The wind grew fierce, whistling through the trees, whipping up my hair and stinging my cheeks. Toby held his hat down, and I pulled my jumper sleeves over my hands, lifting them to my face.

Brush crunched under our feet, the crack of wood the only sound accompanying the cawing echoes of the crows. My dreaming body grew sleepy; we'd been trudging through the thick dense bushland, ducking under branches and endless trees for an eternity. Were we walking uphill? I couldn't tell.

The sun dipped below the horizon, and I couldn't see between the trees to the sky – to the scarcely lit moon we so badly needed to guide us. My body grew numb from the chill seeping into my bones. It became too hard to see far in front of our feet, and little Toby kept tripping on the branches as he shuffled along.

I stayed with him until he found somewhere to rest; in a little hole, dug out into the side of the hill, protected from the cool winds by a covering of bush outside the entrance.

'This is why they couldn't find you, this is where you died,' I said, but knowing he couldn't hear me.

He lowered himself into the hole and curled into a tight ball. I lay beside him, wrapped my arms around his tiny frame, and ached for him to feel my warmth. Tears rolled down his dirt-stained cheeks, and I wiped them away with my thumbs.

Time shifted to a new day, but we hadn't moved. He was like a baby possum, cocooned in his pouch. Except this one wouldn't give him life; it would bring him death. Was he breathing? I couldn't hear him anymore. My own breaths, thick with anxiety, came heavily; I didn't want to watch him die. He was so tiny.

The grip of reality pulled at me, and my body roused.

'I have to go now, little man, I'm so sorry,' I whispered into the air. 'But I'm coming back. I'll make it all okay, you'll see.'

My eyes fluttered open. They were wet, and I lifted my fingers to smear away the tears. Little Toby's death had been and gone, but it didn't stop the incredible rush of guilt from surrounding me – I'd left a child to die.

I hoped to see daylight easing in at the edges of my blind, but the cloak of night still hung on the other side. I stretched blindly past my lamp on the table to find my jet bracelet. I slid it onto my wrist, rolled over, and contemplated how I'd be able to save his life.

First thing in the morning during Geography, I opened my laptop and found the story of Toby. I hadn't stopped thinking of him: while I showered, dressed, drank my coffee, and drove to school, my mind was on him, in that little hole, unseen, afraid.

I clicked on the story, and his face covered a corner of my screen. Laughter creased around the edges of his eyes as they peered back at me. It was a picture from his birthday. Six candles poked out the top of a cake. I clenched the mouse. I wouldn't let that be the last birthday he had.

Tyler's hand landed on my shoulder, and I jumped in my seat.

'Shit, Tyler, don't do that.'

'Sorry.' He pressed his mouth into an apologetic smile and kissed me on the cheek before plonking himself at the table beside mine with a soft groan.

'How are you today?' I asked, biting my cheek. Was that the right thing to ask?

Tyler shrugged. 'I'm all right, I guess. Mum's a mess. Jada stayed home. I can't believe it's been a whole year. It feels like yesterday. But hey, let's talk about something else.'

My mouth scrunched up, eyes full of sympathy when no words would do, especially when what he needed was a distraction. 'Yeah, sure.'

Tyler nodded at my laptop screen. 'What did you find out? Anything not in the news?'

I tapped my feet against the table leg. 'Yeah, the reason they couldn't find him was 'cause he hid himself so well.'

'In what?'

'In like a little dugout hole under a tree in a hill. I think it might've been some kind of burrow. And then when it rained so hard he wouldn't have wanted to come out, and he didn't hear the calls.'

'Have you worked out how to save him?'

'Not really.' I shook my head. 'More instructions from the parents? Brighter clothes? Leave something outside as a sign?'

'Like what? If it was that cold he wouldn't wanna take off any clothes.'

I lifted a finger, beaming at Tyler. 'You're not bad, Robin.'

'Why thank you, Batman. I'm your very own superhero sidekick. Maybe I'm not so dispensable after all.'

'I never said you were. But that's it. He had a hat. He could've left that out for them to see. If he put it out before he hid away they'd have found him in time.'

'Then do that,' Tyler said. 'You can, can't you?'

Anticipation trembled with my excitement for what lay ahead, and I beamed one of my rare full smiles. 'I can do anything – apparently.'

Tyler grinned. 'You're finally enjoying your superpower, aren't you?'

I tilted my head, darting my eyes away. 'Maybe.'

'Admit it, you love it.'

'Only this part.' My shoulders dropped. 'I wasn't smiling last night.' My eyes fluttered closed, and the cold, harsh emptiness of the dense bushland returned to me.

'Sorry.' He grasped my shoulder, and with the tight pressure of his fingers, his understanding stilled my racing heart.

*****

WE REACHED THE TOP of the first slope where we stood without the need for introductions; we knew the snow and the snow knew us. It flurried around us, dumping fresh, white goodness all over the peaks. We lined up and clipped our boots into place on our boards. Only a small scattering of other skiers and boarders dotted the mountain side. Their yells and the mechanical whirl and clang of the ski lift were the only sounds louder than the blasting wind.

First snow was my favourite time of the year, I waited months for this feeling, and I welcomed it like a flickering fire in the cool of the night; but with the death of Toby resting on my shoulders I struggled to enjoy it as much as usual. How do you have fun when that meant ignoring someone else's pain? We flew down the mountain, the snow thick and soft under our boards, but all I could think about was the shadowed pain in Tyler's eyes when he insisted I go out without him, and little Toby in his burrow waiting for me to bring him back to life.

—27—

I RETURNED AGAIN TO *the campfire with the small, young family, and for the first time I stood at the beginning of my dream consciously aware of what I was doing. I had a plan. I guess I always had, but this time, I grasped onto the bigger picture and the power of my plan with both hands.*

I followed little Toby again, watched him stumble and fall, and saw his bottom lip tremble when he realised he was lost. And as he reached his final resting place, I watched him think, take off his green hat, and lay it on the ground before he stepped inside, away from sight.

I almost curled up beside him again, but before I could get comfortable I stood by the now barely smouldering fire. Why did they let it go out? The darkness enclosed around me, and I rubbed my hands vigorously to get the blood rushing.

Crowds of people darted around, shouting words I couldn't hear clearly through the commotion. The sounds of crying nearby squeezed my heart, their desperation evident. Was it still the same night? It had to be. This much panic could only mean one thing. Fear for the little lost boy, and a hope he'd be found quickly, but in that moment I realised, along with everyone else who had no clue where to find little Toby, I also had no idea where he'd ended up. The only advantage over anyone else was the knowledge that he'd left his hat out to be found, but that was it; I still didn't know how to get to him.

My heart raced with dread. The thought of time ticking away bringing us closer to his eventual death made my stomach roll. I didn't want this responsibility. What if this didn't work? What if I couldn't save him after all? Panic set in, my eyes shot around, frantic.

'Do something!' Come on, people. I darted from person to person, in the hope I'd find some sign of progress being made. Police officers and volunteers, some in uniform, some not, stood around, but no one was doing a damn thing.

'Okay, everyone, if you can all gather round for a moment.' Finally. 'We've ascertained that Toby is somewhere in this vicinity.' The police officer pointed to a large map spread over a makeshift table.

I tried to peer over a shoulder to get a closer look. 'It's been three hours since he wandered off, so we need to act quickly. The parents have already searched nearby, so we need to go further afield. We'll split into three groups. Harrison, you take your team down toward the creek over here. Berson, you search here.' He circled the map with a pen. 'And I'll take my men down into the gulley over here. This isn't going to be easy. It's dark out tonight and the rain is only gonna get heavier. Stay safe everyone.'

In my frenzy I hadn't noticed; water rushed down my forehead onto my nose and into the corners of my mouth, I wished for the full weatherproof coveralls those around me wore.

People started to move away. I stepped toward the table to get a glimpse of the map, but it was useless. I had no idea where he'd gone, how far we'd walked, but then I remembered the creek. With no clue how far from there he'd travelled before he eventually stopped I likely had no more chance at sniffing him out than anyone else, but I still decided to follow Harrison and his team as they headed out.

The glow from the torches crisscrossed, and people called out desperately for Toby, myself included, even though I couldn't be heard.

Rain fell all night; big, fat drops in an endless stream that soaked right through my thin layer of clothing within minutes. My hair hung wet in my eyes, and I struggled to keep my footing in the mud.

The temperature dropped further and brought with it a cold wind that *pierced my sodden skin. My teeth chattered and my body shook hard. The wind grew fierce and whistled in my ears. I couldn't hear anything other than the shrieking gusts around me. The trees bent and crackled. Branches and leaves whipped me in the face, stinging my eyes.*

I groaned. I'd made a mistake. I should've stopped him from going out with his dad to begin with, not just put a hat out. This wasn't Hansel and Gretel, it was real life. I cursed my stupidity. Tears mixed with the rain and mud on my face, and I fell once more.

Daylight arrived, and new people joined the search. I ached for some dry clothes and followed one of the new groups as they headed out. I counted ten people, each with fresh motivation. They moved fast, and my drenched self struggled to keep up with them. Although the thick mud slowed us down, we still covered more ground than we had during the night.

I climbed upon a huge, dead tree lying on the ground. The rain continued to fall, and my feet slipped on the log, but I managed to stand and take in a wider view. That's when I saw it. The little green hat, drenched and almost entirely covered in mud, right beside the hole where Toby hid. They needed to look here, but the men were walking further away. I spun around. Maybe more volunteers would be coming from the other direction.

My feet slid and sent me sideways, and I plunged toward the ground. My shoulder hit the log with a jarring force, but I reached my arms out in front of me in time to stop my head from smashing into the ground. The side of my face squelched into the soft mud, followed by my body and legs, and I lay in a crumpled heap covered completely in the thick, brown sludge.

I craned my neck, lifted my heavy body out of the mud, and yelled with everything left in me.

'Aaahhh!' I screamed until my head hurt. 'He's over there!' I pointed. Spinning round, I called in every direction, but it was useless, no one could hear me. I wasn't really here. 'Don't go. He's right here. Come back,' I whimpered. I was Rose, they were the lifeboats. I wished I had a whistle.

My throat stung, my tears falling in an unrelenting stream.

It didn't work. I'd failed him.

The rain drowned out the sound of a man, but as he walked past me, almost through me, and headed in the right direction, I collapsed again. Relief washed over me with the rain.

I lifted myself up and followed him, my eyes blurry. He stopped, picked up the hat, shot his eyes around, and began yanking at one of the branches.

He spotted Toby. 'He's here! I've found him.' Then realising his useless attempt to be heard over the weather, snatched out his radio.

He returned to the boy, and in his desperation to reach him, became a madman as he pulled and pushed at the branches.

'Toby. You're safe, Toby.'

I stayed while Toby's limp body was carried onto the stretcher and up into the sky away from harm. I watched from a distance, comforted by his safety even as my body shuddered and the lingering tears made tracks down my mud-stained face.

I shivered beneath my heavy blankets, no warmer than if I'd stayed rain-drenched in my dream, sniffing as the tears continued to roll down my cheeks onto my pillow. I whimpered into the air and carried with me the chills of the cold night as I tossed back the covers and stumbled to the bathroom. I turned on the hot tap in the shower, and contentment spilled over me as warm water ran over my body. I scrubbed at my muddy face, but the water ran clear.

It was almost six when I returned to my room. I flipped open my laptop and typed two words into the browser – 'Toby McPherson'.

It had happened recent enough to be the top story. I clicked on the article from two days ago.

'Missing six-year-old Toby McPherson has been found this afternoon after an almost twenty-four hour search. The boy had been missing in the Blue Mountains since late Saturday afternoon. Search and rescue teams have

kept up a constant search since Saturday evening, fearing for his safety as temperatures dropped severely overnight and heavy rain fell. The boy has been airlifted to safety and remains in a stable condition at the Prince of Wales hospital in Sydney.'

I shuddered as I recalled the mud and bitter cold and my heightened doubt at my ability. The knowledge that I could change it had given me an intense pressure to truly make it happen. I visualised Toby's sweet, round face, and smiled widely and triumphantly to myself – he was alive.

I'd saved him.

I punched the air. 'I did it.'

* * * * *

I RUSHED TO CATCH up to Tyler. I wanted to talk to him before we had the others around. 'I did it.' I jumped in front of him and skipped backwards along the path. My smile from earlier still stretched across my face, the elation of saving Toby giving me a bigger high than a bag full of jelly beans.

Tyler laughed. 'Did what?' He crooked a hand under his bag strap, and I fell into place beside him.

'Saved him, the hat worked. They found him.' I hopped a little in my step.

Tyler scrunched his brows, the lines around his eyes deepening. 'What are you talking about?'

My stomach lurched. I sucked in a breath and stopped walking.

'Woah.' Tyler grabbed hold of my arms. 'Are you all right? And don't say perfectly fine.'

I pressed a hand to my forehead. 'You don't remember any of it, do you?' Of course he didn't. Why did I think he would?

'If I knew what you were talking about, I might be able to answer that better.'

'Toby,' I said slowly, peering directly into his eyes, imploring him to remember. 'The little boy lost in the wood. I'm Batman, you're Robin. You helped me figure it out. He left his hat out?'

The confusion on Tyler's face told me everything. 'I have no idea why you're Batman and not me, but sure.' He let out a laugh, cutting it off abruptly, probably from my glare. 'Are you talking about the kid from last weekend? The one who got lost?'

'Yes!' Finally. But he wasn't remembering anything we'd discussed about it. He was only remembering the updated news headlines. 'Aargh.' I slapped my forehead. Where had all our conversations gone? And why couldn't I remember the new pieces that filled these blanks?

I tugged on Tyler's hand and dragged him around the corner to a bench attached to the orange brick building. I told him all the parts of the story I'd erased because of my dream, and watched his face go from concern and confusion to understanding and pride.

'Incredible.'

'It is. But damn frustrating too. How am I supposed to act in a conversation when I can't remember half of what people are talking about? If this keeps happening I'm gonna have to seriously work on my poker face.' I slid my hands through my hair and groaned.

He laughed. 'You've mastered "perfectly fine", I'm sure you'll manage the "in the know" look just as well.'

'I haven't mastered "perfectly fine".' I nudged him in the side. 'You had me figured out straight away.'

'I'm just special.'

'True.' I shook my head, trying to figure it all out, straighten out the bumps and gain control of this new way forward. 'Actually, you're the only one who I talk to about this stuff, so you'll be the only one who can't remember the conversations.'

'So in a lot of ways it'll be just as hard for me.'

'Um, yeah.'

'All good. I am your sidekick after all.' He wrapped his arm around me, and I leaned into him. 'So who's next? Who will you save now?'

'I have to go back and save Granny Tess's friend.'

'The lady in the fire?'

'Yeah. I know how to do it. I just have to do it again now that it'll definitely come true.'

The bell sounded.

'And I won't have any memory of this tomorrow, will I?'

'I don't think so, no.'

'And what about this?' He pressed his lips to mine. 'Will I remember this?

I laughed against his mouth. 'I hope so.'

*****

'These are for you.' I held out a small bunch of white daisies for Sally. They weren't much, nothing extravagant, a simple gesture. She lifted a hand to her mouth and the other clasped hold of the flowers.

Tears sprang to her eyes and she pressed them to her chest. 'When we talked about moving here, we wanted to get a place with a little bit of land, pretend we were farming people.' She let out a little laugh and sniffed. 'I wanted a cottage garden. With paths and flowers, and Charles said he'd plant me a whole heap of white daisies, because that's what you have in cottage gardens, right.' Her lips lifted with a quiver, but no happiness flashed behind her smile. She wasn't remembering a fond memory; she was grieving a lost one. One that would never be.

My heart tightened. I blinked back my own tears. 'I'm sorry.'

'No, please don't be.' She placed her hand on my arm. 'These are perfect, truly perfect. Thank you.'

'I'll plant you some daisies,' Tyler said.

'You wouldn't know how to garden to save your life.' She swatted him on the arm and reached into a cupboard for a vase. 'But thank you.'

Later that night, after we'd eaten dinner – burritos again – because I enjoyed them so much the other time apparently, we helped clean up and retreated to Tyler's room.

I slumped into his desk chair. 'She didn't seem too bad today.'

'There's only so many bad days a person can put out. I think the flowers made her happy.' Tyler propped himself against his headboard.

'Really? I thought they upset her more.'

'Nah, I reckon they gave her something nice to think about.' His gaze drifted away and the room fell silent.

I lifted and wedged my foot under my knee, toying with the hem on my pants. 'Why didn't you get the house with the land? If that's what they'd wanted, this is far from that.'

He rubbed his fists along his thighs. 'Dunno. Maybe it was too hard, I'm not sure. I'm gonna plant those flowers though. Gotta be a video on *Youtube*. Shouldn't be too hard. I can't bring him back, but I can give her that at least.' He looked away to the blackened window and the few bright stars visible through the glass.

My throat constricted. Did he think *I* could bring him back? I knew I couldn't, not without knowing how the plane went down. And even then, could I – would I? I slid out of my seat and hopped onto the bed, the mattress sinking when I lowered myself beside him.

I opened one of his fisted hands and twined my fingers with

his. 'I wish I could bring him back for you.'

He sighed heavily. 'I'm sorry, I didn't mean it like that.' His thumb grazed the back of my fingers, and with tenderness in his eyes, he brushed the hair behind my ear. 'I know you can't.'

I rested my head on the soft spot under his shoulder, my ear pressing above the steady beat of his heart.

'You know, I always thought I'd give anything to have my dad back, to see his face again, hear his laugh, see Mum laugh again. But I don't think I could anymore. Not if having him back means I never met you.' Tyler twisted to face me, his eyes glistening with tears. 'I'm terrible for thinking it, and it makes me feel sick to say it, but I don't think I could give you up.'

'You don't have to. You're not going anywhere.' I couldn't bear to think of the alternative. I swallowed back the ball of unease in my throat and patted his leg. 'Especially before we've got you on the slopes.'

*****

'You're gonna love it.' I squeezed Tyler's hand. We sat in the back of Jake's van as we wound up the road toward heaven.

'I know. Although I'm slightly worried you guys've given me a false sense of confidence by telling me I'll be a natural.'

'Nah, you'll be fine. Besides, your teacher's one of the best around.' I grinned sideways at him, my legs jiggling from the cold and excitement at finally being able to share the mountain with him.

'Really? You don't think her good looks might be a bit of a distraction?'

'It's possible. But if you're that easily distracted we might have to find you someone else.'

Sean leaned forward and talked across me. 'Happy to be of assistance.'

'Thanks, mate, but I'll pass,' Tyler said, and turned his attention back to me. 'He doesn't look half as good as you in ski pants.' I couldn't hold back my smile that escalated into laughter.

Tyler *was* a natural. His surfing skills translated almost perfectly onto the snowboard. The afternoon passed with the expected falls and frustrated curse words, and by the time Saturday rolled around and we returned for his second lesson, he managed to glide down the slopes with an ease most would take a lot longer to master.

Colourful tourists and locals dotted the side of the mountain, much more than earlier in the week. I preferred the less obstacle-laden courses a little further afield, but this period would be temporary. I could tell from Tyler's determination we wouldn't be stuck on the packed learners slope for long.

We sat in the snow at the top of the slope, almost ready for another run.

'Oh, hey, since you didn't ask, because you don't remember it, I cracked another one the other night,' I said, tightening the clip on my boot. I'd called Granny Tess the moment I woke. I could hear the agitation in her voice as she tried to recall a fire at Beverly's place, and then her ecstasy when the realisation hit her. And even though Tyler was clueless, I still wanted to tell him. 'An old lady who died in a fire. Granny Tess's friend actually. You helped me with that one.'

We were a seriously cool superhero team.

'You're welcome?' He turned to me with a vacant look in his eyes before lighting up. 'And since you didn't ask...hang on. When did she die, I mean, not die?'

'Oh God, I don't know, maybe two months ago?'

'Right, so you've missed out on a bit then, it's a shame you missed it really.' He had a straight face, serious eyes, and I gave him my rapt attention even though I hadn't missed a thing. Nothing except the conversations involving the accidents or dreams ever changed. It didn't stop Tyler's charade though. 'Everything was pretty ordinary until yesterday when I had a chopper come pick us up from school, take us to the top of that mountain over there and drop us off.' He pointed into the distance, an adorable smirk on his face.

I tried to keep a straight face.

'It was incredible,' he said.

'Of course it was.'

'I beat you down the mountain...in case you'd forgotten.'

'Okay, now I know you're lying. Helicopters I'd believe, you beating me – never.'

'Never say never.'

We hauled ourselves off the ground and carved our way down the small incline of the beginners run.

'Speed up, Pops,' I yelled as I curved my board around Tyler and stopped in front of him. He wobbled, arms flailing at his sides, before he grabbed hold of me and yanked us both to the ground. We threw our heads back, our cackles mingling with the chorus of yells and laughter on the mountain.

Tyler's arms wrapped around me, and we snuggled in the comfy blanket of snow surrounding us. He drew me in for a quick kiss, before he jumped up and pulled me to stand beside him.

'I can't wait to do this in Canada with you,' he said, as if it was already decided, and kissed me again. He launched himself away and left me standing there. I started to speak, started to call out and remind him I didn't do travel, but visions of the Canadian slopes interrupted, and my whole body tingled with excitement. How amazing that would be, to board the longer, unknown runs – and with Tyler. I gasped. Was I really considering it? Tyler's encouragement already got me to Sydney, could I go further? Maybe I could step out from behind my hodophobia label. If all it did was tell me I couldn't do something, maybe I should listen to Tyler instead.

A smile rose to my lips, so content in that moment I thought I might burst with the fullness of it. Embers of hope grew within me, that maybe, after all the turbulence, things were truly headed in the right direction.

—28—

TYLER STARED ME DOWN, concern etched into his face. 'You need a break,' he said. We sat on the library sofa, pretending to be busy working, but my eyes were heavy and I didn't have the energy to read the words in front of me.

It had been two weeks since I'd saved Beverly and life had shifted into a new norm. Each night I sat with my book and flipped back through the pages to another old face I could work on. Drawing helped bring their stories and deaths back into mind-shattering focus, so when I closed my eyes I was there again. Sometimes I even repeated the pattern in the middle of the night, frantic to make the most of my night time hours, because I had a whole book I needed to bring back to life.

I'd saved the little girl who drowned in the backyard pool, the man who died of the heart attack, and the woman hit by the rock. I'd gone all the way back before Tyler had shown up at school, twelve weeks of dreams in two.

'Are you sleeping?' he asked, the worry evident in his eyes.

'Is that your way of saying I look like crap?'

'No.' He brushed his thumb under an eye, peering into them mischievously. 'Besides, these dark circles suit you. What do you call 'em?'

I swatted his hand away. 'Bags.'

'How many times did you wake up last night?' His deep voice

turned serious again, tender.

'Only two. At one in the morning and then again at four thirty.'

'You need to give it a rest. For one night at least.' He was right. The relentless visions and constant yearning to help tightened around my chest. The increasing pressure made it hard to catch my breath. 'No buts. Tonight I'm coming over and I'm gonna teach you how to meditate. If I can keep you away from your dreams by having my own with you, then that's a sacrifice I'm willing to make.'

I laughed. 'So thoughtful.'

He came around after dinner and I tried, I really did. But having Tyler beside me while I attempted to shut off my mind from the dreams and his close proximity was like sitting on a hill in a thunderstorm and expecting me to ignore the blizzard and bolts of lightning striking around me.

The following day he gave me a pep talk before we went our separate ways. 'Remember, don't rush, give yourself time.' He rested his hands on my shoulders and rubbed in circles. 'Let it go.'

'Thanks. Now I've got the *Frozen* song in my head.'

I tried again that night, but it was hopeless. One minute in and my mind ran off like a dog chasing a stick, and I was left behind to watch, hoping it'd eventually come back. I struggled competing with my overactive thoughts, and chose to instead consume myself with the one thing that always stilled my mind.

'Ready?' Cal shouted above the wild breeze, his cast pressing into the compacted snow where he'd remain before returning inside. We all nodded, poised for flight at the top of the slope. 'Set.' His voice rang across the terrain. 'Fly!'

I lifted my board, pulling my body with it, and started down the slope. Heels, tilt, toes, I weaved my way down, gathering momentum, my heart pulsing rhythmically with the movement of my board.

We yelled ecstatically to the wind, and it whistled a chorus of elation into our ears. I sensed the other guys around me, but I was all on my own – me and my board and the mountain. The wind whipped the falling snow past my face, blowing my loose hair behind me and piercing the exposed skin. But I felt nothing but exhilaration. I was alive and in control and my rampant thoughts slunk into the shadows.

After a morning of pure exhilaration, I waved to Sean and Max on the ski lift above and tapped on my wrist. Lunch time.

'So which run next?' I said, reaching for a fry, my hands warming around a mug of coffee. The scenery outside the floor-to-ceiling glass stole my breath, but with Tyler across the table from me, I barely noticed. 'You guys reckon Tyler's ready for "The Intrepid Shelf"?'

'*I'm* not ready for The Intrepid,' Max said. 'You're nuts if you take him up there'.

'If he's ready for that slope, he's ready for Whistler. May as well pack his bags now, 'cause he'll be bored here in no time,' Cal said, reaching for a corn chip.

'I'm not ready. This is just Lucy's way of saying how incredibly slow I am.'

'No, it's not. If I was going to say that, I'd just say it.' I cupped my hand to the side of my mouth and whispered to the others, 'He's really slow.' Chuckles erupted around the table.

'I heard that.' But he joined in the laughter. 'You might be faster than me, but you watch me master and hone my skills. I'll be ready for Canada in no time.'

Cal tapped a hand on the tabletop. 'And with school holidays around the corner, you got heaps of time to practice. And I'll finally be back on the slopes.' He grinned around a mouthful of cheesy nachos.

'Who's going to Canada?' Amber peered at Tyler.

Tyler's dark eyes glinted, the sides of his mouth lifting. 'Lucy.'

Hang on, what? I never actually *agreed* to it.

'Seriously? Luce's gettin' on a plane? Since when?' Sean asked.

Tyler's eyes reassured me with their inviting depth. 'No details yet, but I know she really wants to go. Sometimes that's the only detail you need.'

'Yeah, but about the plane.' Max widened her eyes as if to say, 'Wake up, tell him how much you don't want to do this'. 'That's a pretty big detail.'

Tyler shook his head. 'Minor.' I stared in wonder and suddenly saw my desire to travel through a different lens. I'd been so focused on the details that scared me – the plane, the faces, the new dreams – when the only detail that mattered was being in Canada.

I turned and smiled at Max, and with eyebrows raised and a shrug, it told her everything she wanted to know.

'MEDITATION SUCKS.' I SLID my goggles onto the top of my head, unclipped a boot, and skated up to the back of the ski-lift queue. Tyler was ready to try a new blue slope.

'You just have to keep practising, you'll get it eventually.' He reassured me.

'Easy for you to say, Zen master.'

'You're used to being good at everything. Gotta be something I can beat you at, even if it is having a quiet mind.'

'I'm sick of trying, I wanna give up.' I leaned my backside against the metal railing.

'But you're not a quitter.'

'Unfortunately.'

'And surely the payoff will be worth it, getting to see me day *and* night?'

'The payoff will be worth it if the payment doesn't drive me to madness first.'

'Can we give it a try anyway? To dream. If we believe we can do it instead of thinking it's not possible...I mean it has to be, doesn't it? Why should our subconscious need our physical bodies to be close, it's only our logical brain that's thinking that. If we can shut that part of our mind up.'

'Easier said than done.' I shoved off the railing and we scooted into position for the chair-lift.

'I know, but I like a challenge, don't you? I mean, look where I am.' The chair hooked under our backsides and we landed into position, the bar falling into place over our laps.

'I'm looking.' The ground disappeared beneath our snowboards.

'So let's do it then.'

'Do I have a choice?'

'None.' His face brimmed with that all-consuming smug-filled smile I loved. 'Meet me here tonight?'

'I'll try.'

Satisfied, Tyler put an arm around me, and I rested my head on his shoulder. A stupid grin spread over my face at being able to share this magnificent mountain with him.

I didn't have a stupid grin on my face later that night in bed as I tried to visualise being on the snow-covered slopes with Tyler. It seemed impossible, yet Tyler had to be right. Surely the possibility was similar to being in the woods with Toby, or watching a train wreck when over four-hundred kilometres away I lay sound asleep.

My struggle once again to calm my racing thoughts led to me pulling my book onto my lap and flicking back another page. How could I leave these people in here? Their families needed them, just like Tyler needed his dad. My fingers trailed the edges of the paper, fanning the pages like a flip book, and stopped right above the picture of the old lady on the plane. Her words still haunted me. 'She needs me, she needs me.' I stopped myself. Slammed the book shut. I needed Tyler.

I need Tyler.

My heart rammed into my lungs. Oh God, I couldn't, could I? It wasn't possible. Surely that was too long ago. Fear lodged behind my eyes and tears welled. I would learn how to meditate if it was the last thing I did. *I need Tyler.*

I pulled out a clean, crisp sheet of paper, sharpened my pencil, and drew the face of the person who'd given me so much more than he'd ever know. Half an hour later, when I set the picture aside, I was able to relax my muscles, slow my breathing, and close my eyes. Nothing interrupted my thoughts, nothing but Tyler, and for the first time since I began my painful attempts at meditation, I actually believed I could do it. My head sank heavily into the pillow. I inhaled and exhaled, finding comfort in the rhythm of my breathing, and after my best attempt so far at meditating, and with Tyler's face in the forefront of my mind, I drifted off to sleep.

'Woohoo,' Tyler called across *the snow, arms raised in triumph as he carved his board in swift bends down the mountain.*

I couldn't help but yell right along with him as I kept up to his escalating speed. My hair flew in a dark tangle behind me as the wind blew across my face and whipped at my cheeks. The snow, with its dream-like perfection, shimmered beneath our boards, as if we soared down a mountain of diamond-coated powder. I bent and plied at the snow, grabbed a thick handful, and threw it in Tyler's direction. It landed squarely on his back.

'Hey!' he yelled over his shoulder.

He slowed, formed his own ball of snow, and propelled it straight at my head. I ducked and missed the snowball, but not the trap of his arms as I glided past. We erupted in laughter and he tugged me in close.

*****

I CLOSED THE BOOK and shut my laptop. Relieved I'd completed the two large assignments set for the school holidays, I reached for my sneakers. I shot off a quick text to Tyler and let him know I was heading out for a run. His reply appeared almost instantly.

Sorry, Mum needs me x

He didn't give a reason – that was reason alone.

I headed up the hill, past the newly inhabited homes that now overflowed with constant noise and beat-up hatchbacks. The sun edged toward the horizon, and the street lights flickered on. I'd need to make it a quick run if I didn't want to be stuck out in the dark. I tucked the earphones in my ears and slowly, methodically, and meditatively formed a rhythm between my heart and my feet, my feet and the earth.

Tyler was right. Running was a form of meditation. Now that I'd managed to snatch actual glimpses of it I could see that. Since our first shared dream from a distance three weeks ago, we'd done it again three times. Still catching up on my book full of dreams, we made an agreement; one week of saving lives earned us a night of shared dreaming.

The music flowed through me, and I immersed myself in the thud of my feet on the damp track. It helped to dispel some of the unease that occasionally crept through me, that the seemingly perfect life I'd been living was all an illusion. What was the saying? *If it's too good to be true then it probably is.*

Where was Tyler when I needed him? He had a knack for saying the right thing to make my insecurities go away. I couldn't be irritated at his mum though; she really did need him more than I did.

It had been barely over a year since he'd lost his dad, he hid his grief from everyone so well, but it reared its nasty head every time he spoke of his mum. Her grief was his to carry. Hidden beneath the layers of smiles, banter, and caresses, his scars were red raw. It was like his mum kept picking at the healing scab, encouraging it to bleed, reminding him of the pain. I wanted to take it away like I could for so many others, but it was to me as insurmountable a challenge as Everest would be to climb. I questioned, not for the first time, how he managed to care for everyone so well, when he hurt so much himself. I knew the answer too well, it mirrored my own. It was simply who we were. To help someone in need came as naturally as breathing, but we shared a mutual relief to give to each other what we couldn't receive from anyone else – fresh air to breathe.

I reached the crest of the hill and the fence became visible not far ahead. My phone vibrated on my arm. I stopped running and instinctively smiled when Tyler's name appeared on the screen.

Tyler: *Come over on your way home?*

I'd already turned around.

Me: *Sure, what's up?*

Tyler: *Have you heard the news?*

Crap. It had to be bad if he felt the need to tell me.

Me: *No, should I have?*

I waited nervously for the phone to beep back at me. I ran on the spot, not overly keen to find out what my nightmares would be made of. Even now with all the new possibilities, I dreaded the impending calamity.

Tyler: *They've found the cause of the crash.*

My heart stopped. I swear it actually stopped beating for a few seconds. It waited until I'd reread the message to start again, and a lump wedged in my throat. For a moment, I thought I might be sick. I stepped off the path and braced myself against a tree. I wanted to smash my phone into pieces, but instead stared at the seven words I'd been dreading for the last two months. I couldn't go over there. I couldn't find out the truth. Finding out would send my mind down a path I didn't want it heading.

My thumb trembled as it hovered over the screen.

Me: *I'm coming over, but you can't tell me any details xx*

I turned and ran in the direction of Tyler's house. He opened the door, his eyes sunken and downcast. The reminder of what their dad had been through, of the nightmare they continued to live, couldn't be easy to deal with.

He stepped onto the porch, and under the flickering moth-riddled light he held me tight. His arms crushed me with the weight of his burden, and I took what I could, but as he pulled away and spoke, I lifted my hand and placed my fingers over his mouth.

'Don't say it,' I said quickly. 'I can't know what happened. You know what it'll mean.' The urgency of my voice caught him off guard, and the question in his eyes, the pain on his face, tore through me. He tugged on my hand and led me across the lawn.

'Here,' he said gruffly, and we sat at the edge of the grass on the cement curb. 'Away from the noise in there.'

I crossed my feet on the bitumen roadside and wrapped my arms tightly around myself. I felt weak, pathetic, useless. Tears fell, unwanted, down my cheeks and I brushed them away. 'I'm sorry. I should be comforting you, not crying on your doorstep. Oh, God, Tyler, this is a disaster.'

He lowered his eyes. 'We had to find out eventually.'

I hooked my arms around Tyler's legs, resting my head on his lap, and he folded himself over me. We stared up the hill, at the sun falling steadily below the tree line.

'I know this is hard for you. But you have to promise you won't tell me.'

Tyler's chest rose and fell on my back. 'I promise.'

I dreamed of the plane crash that night. It was all the same, except for one thing. The man across from me opened his mouth to tell me something, but I interrupted him and repeated what I'd said to Tyler earlier. 'I can't know what happened, I can't.' I lowered my body over my knees and placed my fingers in my ears to block him out. 'Please don't tell me. Promise you won't tell me. Promise me.'

—29—

I woke full of dread the next day. The thought crossed my mind to stay in bed, but what was I going to do: stay in my room until the story died down? Climbing into the shower, I reminded myself of Tyler's promise.

I arrived at school on edge, my shoulders already aching from the tension. Fearing the worst, I stuck my earphones in and locked myself safely away in my own little world. I couldn't learn the cause. I couldn't risk it – I couldn't lose him.

Tyler broke through the barrier five minutes into our lunch break. I sat against the tree, book in lap, pencil in hand, listening to Jack River's 'Limo Song'. He sat beside me and removed an earphone. 'Hello in there,' he whispered, sending tingles through me, and I slanted my face up to him before I switched my music off.

'Hi.'

'You all right?'

'Perfectly fine.' *Liar.*

'And that's why you're here, while we're all over there?' He pointed to our friends only a few metres away at the table, but could've been on another continent for the space I'd made between us.

'I'm trying to get this finished off before class, that's all.' Another lie.

'You've been hiding all day. You really don't want to risk hearing anything, do you?' He saw straight through me and my lies.

'No. I don't. Sorry, I can't. You understand, don't you?'

'As crappy as it is, yeah I do. I'm not sure they do, though.' He nodded toward the table. 'They're all wondering why you're sitting over here on your own in what, they've said, is a typical Lucy tactic of avoidance, getting a wet bum from the soggy grass too.'

'Crap. I am too.' We'd come to that time of year where no matter the hour or how much the sun shone, everything remained wet. Tyler helped me up and I tried in vain to wipe the moisture off my pants.

I placed my hand on Tyler's arm. 'How you doing? You okay?'

'Not really.' He shifted his feet, casting his eyes down.

'Oh.' I didn't know what to say; I couldn't ask for details – I didn't want them. I cared, but I simply couldn't do anything for him – as useless as a band-aid on a bullet wound. 'Sorry, Tyler.' I dropped my hand from his arm and, like a traitor, wished to be anywhere else but beside him.

'Yeah. Me too.'

I grew increasingly scared. The what-ifs haunted me from a different angle this time. What if I lost Tyler?

I spent Monday and Tuesday afternoon at the shelter, helping Patty so I wouldn't have time to think of the crash. It didn't work, and on Tuesday night I dreamed of the plane crash again.

MY HEART SLAMMED INTO *my chest. A flurry of activity surrounded me as flight attendants rushed to lock trays into place and return potential missiles safely behind locked doors. Only one door stood between me and Tyler's dad.*

I wanted to hurl, but instead I swallowed back my unease for what lay ahead.

The plane pitched downward; it had already begun.

I unnecessarily ducked out of the way as a flight attendant reached above me – I was invisible. I fell forward and hit my head on the metal cupboards overhead. Then, with unsteady feet, I stumbled with the slope of the plane to the door leading to the cockpit. My hand trembled as my fingers clutched the doorknob, and as it turned, the door flew forward and I tumbled into the cockpit with a scream. I landed heavily into an ungraceful pile on the floor.

'Oh God, my leg! Friggin' hell. That hurts.'

No one noticed my sudden arrival or my obvious agony, my leg sat twisted at an odd angle. I didn't move from where I'd landed, but I managed to brace my arms behind me and pushed myself into a half-sitting position. I looked straight across at Tyler's dad and recognised him immediately. It could've been Tyler twenty years from now. Beside him, directly in front of me, another pilot with Ken-doll hair, far too clean and shiny, worked in a state of panic. He had a young voice, full of inexperience and maybe a touch of fear. They threw words around, words that made little sense to me.

'Altitude data isn't working.'

'Disable the autopilot.'

They were controlled, swivelling in their seats to administer some sort of operation.

The plane pitched up, and my body slammed into the back of the cockpit door.

I WOKE WITH AN overwhelming sense of failure. All those people died, their lives over, and I'd woken in my bed ready to start a new day, all the while avoiding the truth that might save them. It felt wrong, and the desire to do something about it surged. I slammed my fist against the wall. No. I wouldn't. I couldn't. I'd rather watch them die ten thousand times than lose Tyler.

I was being more selfish than I'd ever been in my life, because this plan, to keep him here, prevented him from truly being happy. He'd have his dad back, and his mum would be whole again. Regardless of what he said to me, they were his family, I wasn't.

He could live without little ol' me, but would he ever be fine again without his dad?

It went against every instinct to make others happy. I heard Granny Tess's voice in my head, her warning not to use the dreams for selfish acts. But this was different. I was being selfish by preventing a dream. Surely nothing was wrong with keeping things how they were?

Tyler meant everything to me. I had Granny Tess, and she understood what I lived with, but without Tyler, who would I be? I didn't want to return to the person I'd been before he made me a better version.

He'd shown me how to dream good dreams, not only at night, but in reality too. I dreamed of a future where I didn't have to hide from the world, and I dreamed of a future with him. This selfishness would only be temporary but felt like a necessary stance to take, because there was no way in hell I'd be giving him up without a fight. *En garde.*

* * * * *

WE WALKED SILENTLY BESIDE each other, heading inside to find a table, the others not far behind. It had been a fun morning of gliding down the mountain together, but boarding was a silent sport, and most chatter went on inside your own head – easy to pretend everything was normal when we didn't have to speak.

The week had left my body aching from a strain so taut, not even a run could ease it. I'd become jumpy and paranoid whenever anyone spoke to me. I worked on Thursday and Friday night, again hoping the busyness would distract me from my thoughts. But all it did was give me a different place to think, and on Friday night I was there again, in the cockpit, and then in seat 41H as the plane went down.

I missed Tyler. Missed seeing him, missed being with him, so when Max asked if I'd be joining them on Saturday on the mountain, I remembered his promise that he wouldn't say anything, and said yes.

But now we were alone, and without the shield of goggles, gloves, and beanies, we were exposed.

'Are you going to talk to me at all today?' he asked.

'What do you mean? I've talked to you.'

'You know what I mean. You're running away, and I haven't even given you any reason to.'

'Yes, you have. You know and I don't.' I stopped and turned to him.

'So you *are* not talking to me on purpose. If you don't talk, I won't talk, is that it? Lucy, I haven't given you any reason not to trust that I'll keep my promise. What happened to our agreed trust until proven otherwise?'

'That's not safe in this situation and you know it. It's probably not safe in any situation, actually. Ever see *Silence of the Lambs*?'

'I am not Hannibal Lecter.' He started to laugh, and the fight in me wavered. I walked through the doors into the crowded cafeteria and spotted a table.

I had to raise my voice to be heard over the din. 'I'm talking Buffalo Bill. The guy who lures women into his truck because they have no reason not to trust him.'

'I'm not luring you into a trap, Lucy, even though every part of me wants to talk to you about this, I wouldn't do it, not when I know how important it is not to. And if you think I would, then we're in big trouble.'

'I don't think that, Tyler. I do trust you, I'm just afraid,' I said, slumping at the table. 'There's something I haven't told you.'

Tyler dropped into a seat opposite me, waiting for me to continue.

'You remember the dream in Sydney, when you were surfing and I left?'

'Yeah?' He watched me intently.

'I didn't just go. I ended up back on the plane again. And then Sunday night when we...you, heard the news I dreamed of it again. Then again on Tuesday and again last night. That's six times.' My eyes pricked with the fear and sadness of what that meant, and my voice caught. 'I'm afraid I'll keep dreaming it until I change it. Like that's what's meant to be.'

His eyes moistened, and he blinked back his own heartache. 'You really think you'll change it if you know?'

'I don't know. But just in case, I need to lay low while the world is frantic over the story. Will you let me do that?'

'Of course I will,' he said. 'But what do I do in the meantime? Pretend you're not here? Pretend there isn't someone who will make me feel better just by being there? Act like everything's normal?'

I couldn't help but notice the sadness and maybe a touch of bitterness in his words. I wished I could take away his pain. I wanted to be the person he needed and deserved – I couldn't. I was afraid my voice would tremble when I spoke, but I had to answer him.

'Yes.' The word came out soft, painful.

I jumped when Sean dumped his gloves on the table. 'What got into you two?'

'Shut up, Sean.' I couldn't help it. I didn't want to hear or see his gratification that things in paradise had gone to ruin.

Across the table, the unmistakable hurt in Tyler's eyes sliced through me like a barb. I wanted to rip it out, to take it back, but it was stuck. Like the fish hook I caught in my leg as a child: it would be equally as painful to remove it, but eventually it had to come out – it couldn't stay there forever.

—30—

'I S EVERYTHING OKAY WITH you and Tyler?' Max cornered me as I arrived at school the following Tuesday.

'Yeah,' I said, slowly turning toward her in time to catch the disbelief in her eyes. 'No, it is,' I found a fake smile to go with my fake words. 'I'm going through a little something right now; it'll be all right soon. Nothing to worry about.' My smile turned into a half-genuine one. I truly believed everything would be okay with a bit more time.

'Why do you insist on pushing everyone away right when it seems you need them the most?' she asked.

'I don't push you all away.'

'You sure about that? You're not the one left wondering when your friend'll be back,' Max said with more than a hint of hurt in her voice at my inconsistent, but persistent disappearing acts.

Where'd this come from? She knew me well enough to know my coping mechanism – I removed myself, always had. She'd seen it before, but I'd never noticed the effect it had on her.

'I'm sorry,' I said as we dodged the school crowd. 'I don't mean to hurt you. I need some time to work something out. You know me.'

'I do know you.' She frowned. 'But does Tyler?'

'What does that mean?'

'You distance yourself like this, and he might not be waiting around for you when you've made your way back to him. He's been very quiet this last week, you both have. We know you like to go into hibernation occasionally, and *you* know, as much as we miss you and don't understand it, we'll still be there when you come back. We've known you a long time, we know what to expect, but you can't assume everyone will accept it.'

'Will accept *me*, you mean?' I snapped.

'That one aspect, yeah.'

'Why not? I'd accept every part of him. Why is it too much to expect the same of him?'

Was it too much to assume he'd wait around, or had I been too blinded by the walls I'd placed around me to see clearly anymore? Regardless of what Max said, I was sure he'd wait for me, give me the space I needed.

I kept my music in my ears during my runs, at home, and out of class – and even in class if I could get away with it. My world had shrunk to the size of the space between my ears. It was the best form of protection I could come up with, and I didn't care what anyone thought. It was a temporary fix to what could be a permanent problem. A problem I wouldn't let happen.

I needed Tyler more than I'd needed anything in my life. I missed him, but I wished he could be more understanding about why I needed to keep to myself, why I had to avoid the knowing. He knew of my ability; I thought he'd want to protect us as much as I did. I couldn't understand why he wasn't on my side, and the lack of understanding began to form a big wedge of distrust between us.

Our world had never been filled with so much awkward, silent avoiding, both with him and everyone else. They all sensed something was up; you'd have to be deaf and blind not to feel the tension. Still, they pretended nothing had changed, because no one had said otherwise, but each day Tyler would be up one end of the table, me up the other. He, with a fake 'all's-cool' smile on his face, me with earphones in as I pretended to keep busy – no one was fooled. I wished I could say it didn't ache as much as it did. Every now and then we'd share a smile – the sad kind, where your mouth said smile and your eyes said cry. Every time I looked into his eyes I'd remember how much I missed him, how much we'd shared. We didn't talk, we barely spoke at all anymore, we'd become a semblance of what we'd once been. Each time I saw the pain in his eyes I had to remind myself of what could be lost so I wasn't seized by the enormously confronting fear that I'd made a huge mistake.

I'd been so confident in my decision that this was the only way through the shifting sand, but as Tyler distanced himself, my certainty wavered.

It had been two weeks since the news broke. Alone in my room at the end of another lonely day of avoidance, I wished I could be at work, so I wouldn't have to think about how much I missed Tyler, and how much I'd messed things up. I'd begged Laurie for an extra shift, but she had enough staff on, and I'd already had heaps of extra hours recently. I considered sending Tyler a text, to tell him I missed him, but I wasn't sure I had the right to. I didn't know what to do. I lay on my bed, absently examining the paint on the wall. Maybe I could just lay here and infinitely feel sorry for myself.

Or maybe not.

A soft, unfamiliar tap on the door alerted me to the fact that someone other than Mum stood on the other side of it. I drew in a breath as I swung the door open to find Tyler there, and had to hold myself back so I didn't leap into his arms.

'Can I come in?' he said, shifting nervously on his feet.

'Um, yeah, of course.' I held the door open and he stepped into the room, stunned. My heart beat a nervous, unsettling beat. 'Is everything okay?'

'Yeah, I just needed to see you.'

'I haven't gone anywhere,' I said softly.

'Are you sure?' His eyes glazed with tears.

The accusation that I hadn't been there for him winded me like a kick in the guts. Except it wasn't an accusation – I hadn't.

'I'm sorry, Tyler.' We sat on the edge of the bed, leaving enough room for a third person between us. He didn't say anything.

I broke the silence. 'How are you? How's your mum?'

'Are you sure you wanna know?' he asked with more of a questioning tone than an accusatory one. He was genuinely unsure if he was allowed to speak. I cringed inside. What a heartless bitch I must've seemed. Had I ruined something amazing by shutting him out? Had I ruined us in an attempt to save us?

'Yes. I'd like to know how you are. I want to know you're okay.'

'But you don't wanna talk about it, about *that*?'

'No.' My eyes flickered to the bedspread between us.

'Do you realise that by you not knowing, I can't be okay. I can't share with you how I'm feeling because I can't say what I need to. You'll stop me before I start, and it's like I'm keeping something huge from you. Like there's a big secret between us, but I never put it there, and I really don't want it there.'

'If that secret doesn't stay where it is, then you won't stay here.' My eyes filled with tears, begging him to understand.

'What's the point of being here if you keep pushing me away?'

'It's only for a little while; it won't be like this forever. Eventually, people won't want to talk about it anymore.'

'You think it's only some news story for me? This is my life. It's my dad we're talking about. It won't ever be something I don't want to talk about. You can't have me when you want me, then push me away when you don't. I've always been there for you, but now that I need someone, you shut the door in my face.' He spat the words out, like a dragon breathing fire, and the heat burned. Suffocating shame engulfed me.

'What do you want me to do?' I asked, afraid of the answer.

'I want you to know.'

'Do you know what you're asking? If I know, I might change it, and then you'll be gone.'

'You said might. With the might, comes a might not, and I'm betting on the might not. It was a year ago. Maybe that's too long. I can't live like this. I lost my dad, I can't lose you too.'

'You haven't lost me, I'm still here.'

'But you're not. You're hiding away behind your earphones, and I'm afraid you'll never come out. I may as well not even be here.' I could hear the pain on his quivering voice.

'Don't say that. You being here is the best thing that ever happened to me. Even if it's not quite the same at the moment, it's still better than the alternative.'

'Really? You're not the one being pushed away.' His words impaled me like a knife, and I grabbed hold of my stomach.

'You'd rather not be here?' I choked the words out, my voice cracking.

'It hurts every time I see you and you walk away. Tell me you wouldn't prefer to escape that pain.'

'Of course I would. But I don't get a choice. I'm the one who'll be left behind. If you're not here, you'll get to go on and live your life, you won't even remember me. But I'll still be here, alone. You'll be gone, ripped away in a single moment, but every wonderful, painful memory will stay right beside me. How am I supposed to live like that?' Tears dropped onto my cheeks, and I blinked to see Tyler's own moist eyes. 'I would rather have you here and never speak to you again than lose you so completely without a trace.'

Tyler pulled me into his arms, right where I needed to be, and I sobbed. How could I lose this? This warmth, this love – him. Was it possible I'd already lost him, though? If we never spoke, what chance did we have of maintaining this closeness?

And just like that, I understood it perfectly.

I'd retreated, and without the sharing of every aspect of our lives, he'd pulled away too, and the intimacy had gone. We'd never get it back as long as I kept him at arm's length. As always he made perfect sense. We couldn't live like this, and I had to do something about it.

'I don't want to lose you, Tyler.'

'I don't wanna lose you either.'

'I don't want to know, but if that's what I need to do to keep you for now then I'll do it, I'm listening.'

'It's not only for now. I mean, I know you're amazing and all, but don't you think you're being a little bit cocky to think you're this powerful?'

'Thanks a lot.' I shoved him, and we laughed.

'You're beautiful when you laugh,' he said and warmth rose beneath my cheeks. 'You're always beautiful, but I like these creases.' He placed his thumbs on the edges of my eyes, adding pressure as he drew me in until our mouths met. I entwined my fingers in his hair and pulled him closer. He kissed me urgently, tenderly, and I melted into him. His lips were ecstasy, and I imagined a world without this, without him, as new tears formed.

We broke apart, but Tyler's forehead rested on mine, and he brushed away the tears with a single stroke of his thumb.

'What if you stayed here each night,' I said, my face still inches from his, fingers still in his hair. 'We'd dream together and I'd be kept too busy to dream of the plane.'

'I think I could live with that.' He gave me one of his wicked smirks. I'd missed that look. We laughed and I felt more at peace than I had since the news broke.

I folded my hands in my lap. 'So what now?'

'You find out, I guess.'

'Do you want to tell me?' I asked nervously.

'I don't think I can.'

We fired up the laptop, and I went online for the first time in two weeks. I sat on Tyler's lap; one chair wasn't so bad when you had the right person to share it with. His arm rested around my waist like a seatbelt. He said he didn't think I had the power to do it, but the pressure of his arm around me indicated he had some reservations; he'd buckled the seatbelt in tight, ready to hold firm for the oncoming collision. My heart thundered wildly, and as if he felt it through my back onto his own heaving chest, he whispered in my ear.

'It's going to be all right. Whatever happens...it'll be all right.'

I squeezed my eyes closed, sucked in a breath, and as I opened them, clicked on the third news story down the page.

My job is one of the easiest in the world. Balance a tray of perfectly prepared-earlier canapés around a room full of strangers, and smile. My only threat to society, if I trip up, is a shirt full of blue cheese and tomato tart.

The repercussions when other professions stuffed up had the potential to leave a stain too permanent to be scrubbed away. Paramedics, surgeons...pilots. I'd seen the dangerous wake left in the operating room of a not-so-skilled surgeon. It didn't take much for a surgeon's role to deviate into that of the grim reaper. One slip of the scalpel, one misguided move, and their hands were potentially the touch of death.

For a pilot, the wake if they tripped up had fatal consequences for countless others.

Tyler's dad had tripped up; he'd made a misguided move.

No wonder Tyler wasn't okay.

The words in the article were like another language. Even Tyler, with his linguistic skills, struggled to fathom the complexities of it all. From what I could decipher and get my head around, a lot of things went wrong that day.

Apparently it all came down to a cup of coffee and a spill they determined had occurred on the pilot's side of the centre console. Spilling his drink had toppled the first domino.

'Coffee? Shouldn't the equipment be strong enough to withstand a coffee spill?'

'Obviously not. That's why they make the rules, I guess.'

'What rules?'

'The pilot's supposed to receive his drinks from his left side, from the outside of the plane.'

'Maybe it was the steward's fault.'

'Recordings say otherwise,' Tyler said. 'I don't understand it. He was so good at what he did, why did he do something so reckless?'

'It was coffee, sounds more like a lapse of concentration. Or maybe he was in desperate need of a caffeine fix.' I huffed out a half-laugh, instantly letting it fall away. 'Sorry.'

I continued to read the article.

The liquid in the console eventually played havoc with the navigation equipment, giving the plane, and the pilots, incorrect data on the altitude. The plane, automatically correcting the position, had sent the nose pitching up. I remembered being thrust back in my seat in my dream.

The biggest problem, in the end, all came down to a misunderstanding, both technical and human. And when the pilots failed to correct the plane, they contacted the one place that could have helped them confirm their correct altitude – air traffic control.

Such was their luck, and that of the other three-hundred and twenty-five souls on board, their tactical contact at ATC was busy, and fumbled her reply. With her co-worker distracted with an email instead of double checking her numbers like he was supposed to, the error hadn't been picked up. They could've saved them, but instead they knocked over the last domino that sent them straight into the sea.

'So it wasn't only your dad's fault, not completely. The air traffic controllers were supposed to help; I'm putting blame on them. If they'd actually been doing their job properly, your dad would've been able to bring the plane down safely. It's so many things. You can't blame him.'

'I know. But they do, and that's almost worse.' He sounded broken-hearted, like a child told he wasn't good enough for the team.

'Oh, Tyler, I wish I'd known. I'm so sorry.' I turned around on his lap so I could see him. How could I have been so selfish?

'It's okay. I know it's been hard for you too.' The sadness in his eyes remained but his mouth turned up. 'You know what I keep thinking?'

I shook my head slowly.

'How pissed he'd be. Seriously pissed off. He'd be so annoyed at himself for this. And the other guys. Dad had such a high work ethic, he'd be fuming.'

Tyler's gaze grew distant. I'd made the right decision to learn the cause. He couldn't talk openly with his mum or sister without upsetting them. I was the only person who understood him. The realisation only made me feel worse for not letting him talk to me.

Not anymore. Tonight it'd be all about him. How he felt; how angry he was at his dad, how upset that his dad had to leave like this, with it hanging over his name, and how it wasn't fair what the reports were saying.

'He was a good man, accidents happen every day. His just had bigger consequences than most. He wouldn't have wanted this. I feel like I need to talk to the family members of the victims, to tell them how sorry I am. Then I'm angry at Dad that I feel like I have to, but I need to tell them how wonderful he was too, so they don't continue to see him as a monster.' I gripped Tyler's fingers and pressed my lips into his shoulder – the only support I could offer, because nothing I said would help.

I listened all night. We lay in each other's arms until we were almost asleep. Until Mum tapped on my door and told us the time, suggesting Tyler needed to head home.

I didn't want him to leave, if I let him go, it might be the last time I saw him. Fear tightened its hold on me, constricting my lungs.

He walked out of my room with a promise that he wasn't going anywhere, and I believed him. I believed him enough to fall asleep, even though it was the last place I should be heading with the knowledge I now possessed.

—31—

I DIDN'T HAVE A second to panic. I landed in the cockpit as the plane dived and pitched, throwing me around the floor of the cabin. I screamed as my body slammed into the door and straight into another part of my dream.

My breath caught, struggling to keep up with the sudden shift. I stood in a room, surrounded by the flickering glow of rows of computer monitors in the crammed rooms of air traffic control. My head spun as voices crackled to life around me, familiar voices – Tyler's dad's.

'We have a tech problem. Can I get an altimeter check?'

A lady with a thick bun on the back of her head received the call. She flicked her eyes toward a man at a nearby computer and groaned. Adjusting the headset in front of her bun, she said, 'Standby,' before swivelling on her chair to tend to another issue, even though nothing could be more important than this one.

I scanned the room. The man sat to her right with the back of his buzz-cut head to her. He glanced up before returning to his email. Across the room a suited gentleman stood with a foot propped into a set of glass doors, finishing off a conversation with another man walking backwards away from him. Buzz-cut shot another peek over his computer screen, and I wanted to smack him over the back of the head and shout, 'Do your job'.

After what felt like a hundred years the lady shifted her attention back to Tyler's dad and, as fate would have it, distractedly gave him the wrong information.

I groaned and waved my hands. 'No, look properly, concentrate!' I yelled at her, my hands on my head. She didn't hear me – no one could.

I whirled in disgust, back to the plane cockpit. My heart rate accelerated; anxiety clutched at my chest. I knew what happened next, and yet, I still held onto a hope – I was on the Titanic and we were going down, but maybe, just maybe...

I shifted my weight in a futile attempt to get a better grip of the handrail at my side. My clammy fingers slipped, and I jammed my foot into the back of Ken-doll's chair. It held for a second, until the plane veered into a steep dive, and I was flung, like a ragdoll, back toward the door.

They flicked switches and tried to get the aeroplane to co-operate. Their voices strained, and although I'd never say as much to Tyler, his dad sounded panicked. It ricocheted around the walls of the cockpit and filled the small space with air too thick to breathe until the indecipherable words around me became ones that needed no explanation.

'Mayday, mayday, mayday, flight S108 is going down.'

The speakers crackled. The captain's last words – Tyler's dad's last words – pierced my soul as deeply as the first time I heard them. 'Brace for impact!'

But I couldn't brace myself any more than Ken-doll could. And as the plane dove toward the sea, I flailed about like a tattered rag doll.

*****

FIRST THING IN THE morning, Tyler met me in the library for our free. My heart somersaulted at the sight of him, gorgeous and carefree and here. I stared as he crossed the carpeted floor, determined to commit every detail to mind: his long stride, the way he hooked a hand under his bag strap so it didn't slip off his shoulder, and as he drew closer, the tender smile and softening of his eyes, as if I were the most beautiful sight he'd ever laid eyes on. I didn't want to forget a single thing.

'Hey you,' he said, dropping his bag and rounding the table to wrap his arms around my shoulders. He pressed his mouth firmly to mine. 'It's so good to see you.'

I mumbled an agreement, too transfixed in the sight, scent, and feel of him.

He dragged a chair right up to mine and sat. 'Anything?' Anticipation and worry lined his forehead.

I stared, unsure if I should tell him about the dream. It seemed like a clear indication that things had progressed, and my mind was steadily moving forward, toward a destination he still denied existed. I told myself the dream proved nothing, and that I was overreacting. Though a remorseless murderer trying for a 'not guilty' charge would've been more believable in front of a jury.

Just the thought of telling him terrified me. Saying it made it true.

'What is it?' Tyler asked.

My throat dried up, I couldn't speak. I ran my hand along my neck. Tried to swallow, nothing.

'Really? You're gonna play that card? How old are you again?'

I grabbed my water from my bag and chugged a big mouthful. I held the bottle in the air and coughed. 'Same as always. Sixteen years, four months,' I croaked, my eyes growing wide as a thought occurred to me. 'You won't be here for my seventeenth birthday.'

'Of course I will. When is it?' he asked.

'March twenty-fifth, you'll be long gone by then.'

'Hey, what's gotten into you? Where's this come from?' He placed his hand on mine. 'You *did* have a dream.'

My shoulders sagged. I had to tell him. 'Yes.'

'The plane? Was it different?'

I squeezed my eyes shut. 'Yes.'

'But I'm still here,' he said, like it was a triumph, something we'd overcome and won.

We hadn't.

'It was just a new dream, different view, same story. You're still here because I haven't altered anything yet. I needed to see the whole story first. Now I have. Now it's only a matter of time.'

'Stop talking yourself into it. I'm gonna pinch you every time I see you daydreaming today, how's that sound?'

'Painful. You do know how much I daydream, right?'

He screwed up his face. 'Please tell me you haven't already come up with a solution?'

'Nothing concrete yet.'

'What do you mean...yet?' He pressed his fingertips to my cheeks. 'How do we stop you from thinking? There must be a way to ward off your train of thought.'

I wished there was.

Tyler's hands fell away when my face remained straight – if I knew a way I'd have already used it. 'I'm sorry.'

He balled his hands and dropped his eyes. 'No. You knew this would happen. I should've listened to you. I didn't...I'm sorry.'

'No more sorrys. It is what it is.'

*****

'WHAT WILL IT BE like if you go back to your old life? What was it like?' I stood, and looked out my bedroom window at the neighbouring houses and mountain peaks in the distance.

'Why would I wanna go back to my old life?' he said. 'I like it here.'

'Yeah, but if something happened you would.'

'If you brought my dad back from the dead, you mean?' He shook his head and stepped over to stand beside me.

I scowled. 'Don't shake your head, I'm serious.'

'I know you are. I can't imagine it, that's all.'

'You don't have to, I do.' The weight of the responsibility was heavier than all my dreams stacked together.

'I know. I'm not being fair, I'm sorry.'

'So, tell me about your life. I want to know, so I can imagine all the things you'll be doing when you're gone.' It was only a matter of when for me. There was no if.

'You really believe it's gonna happen, don't you?'

'Yeah...I do.' I swept my fingers through my hair. 'And I know it's hard for you to understand why I'm so paranoid, but you haven't felt what I've felt. When I saved Cal, when I woke up and everything had changed, it was horrible.' Tears stung the back of my throat. Afraid they'd erupt if I continued to speak, I swallowed. 'I can't explain it, Tyler. I was the only one who'd lived something different the day before. It was scary...seriously scary. I was terrified, thought I'd lost my mind. I'm scared to do it again. And I'm scared to lose you. You won't have existed to anyone but me, and I'll have to act like I'm normal, but I won't be, because you'll be gone.' The tears fell fiercely, and I wiped at my sodden cheeks. 'But if I know you're okay and happy in Sydney, I'll be okay. I can live with that.'

Tyler pulled me to him, and I cried into his shoulder. I held onto him tightly, as if the harder I gripped, the better chance I had to make him stay.

He held me and told me everything I needed to hear about his old life in Sydney. About the almost daily afternoon surfs during the summer and his mates, who would be his mates again. Then he reassured me that even though he missed the surf, he really didn't want to go back.

'Who wants that when you can have ice-cold snow and frost-bite.' My shoulders shook with laughter.

He shared stories about his dad. All the things he'd do if he got the chance to see him again.

'Except, I wouldn't be seeing him *again*, I'd just be seeing him, same as I always had. I wouldn't be seeing him in any new special, "Oh my God I almost lost you" kind of way. He wouldn't have gone anywhere in my mind, would he?' he asked, frowning.

'No, he wouldn't. It'd be as if nothing'd changed.'

'Then nothing will've changed. I'd still barely see him. I'd still choose surfing over tinkering in the shed with him. Don't get me wrong, I loved him, but back then I hadn't realised how much. Why don't we realise it before it's too late?'

'I don't know.'

He kissed me then, gently and earnestly all at once, then slowly pulled away. *'Je t'aime*, Lucy, I love you.'

I'd known it long before he said it. I felt it in his words, the way he held me, kissed me, and more importantly the way he looked at me, his eyes peering into my soul and sharing a piece of his with mine.

I'd known, and yet my breath still hitched when he said the words out loud.

So many people struggled to say those few words, refused to succumb to the power they held. A certain vulnerability existed with the proclamation of love. It said, 'I need you, don't ever leave me, you are my world'. It shouted desire and devotion far greater than anything physical. It shocked the fundamental core of your being, and if removed would take your breath away – as if it were the air in your lungs. And the biggest problem of all, if you admitted you loved deeply, you opened yourself to an equally deep pain. But the admission didn't alter how you felt. If you loved, you loved, regardless of whether you said it out loud or not, the pain would still be the same on the other side. I'd once thought love weakened a person, but it didn't, it was the loss of love that brought people to their knees.

I was afraid of so much more than that, but I absolutely, without a doubt, loved Tyler – I needed him, I never wanted him to leave. He was my world.

'I love you too, Tyler.'

We fell asleep that way, me in Tyler's arms, resolved to memorise every part of him as I held onto him tightly. As I held on for dear life.

—32—

I WAS BACK AT *the lake. We loved the stunning maple, but it was a perfect night for something different.*

Tyler stood before me at the bottom of the grass, beside the jetty that led to the lake, hands in his pockets and adoration in his eyes. He was so beautiful, I could look at him all night – or day; depending on which reality we were talking about.

Dusk hovered over us, the sky overflowing with purples, blues, and oranges, showing off like a flirting peacock. Pink clouds floated on the horizon and reflected off the crystal, still waters of the lake. I sighed at its beauty, and Tyler strolled up the grass and placed his hand in mine.

'I'm gonna miss the pink clouds,' he said.

'No, you won't. You'll never have seen them before.'

'Ah, yeah.' He sounded pained at the realisation.

'Oh my God.' I spun and faced him. 'You won't have had the cupcakes. You'll go back to not knowing the joy of peanut butter, chocolate cupcakes.'

He laughed, and I joined in, happy for a second of bliss in an otherwise sombre moment.

'No, this is serious, Tyler, your life is going to be so much worse for the lack of those little pieces of heaven.'

'It's true. Life as I know it will be one big, fat lie.' He had a mischievous glimmer in his eyes. 'But there'll be something much more heavenly I'll miss.'

He tugged on my hand, and I stepped into him as he lowered his lips to mine. I agreed completely and wholeheartedly – this was heavenly.

When we surfaced for air, we decided a swim was in order. We immersed ourselves in the cool, calm water and floated like two starfish, arms and legs outstretched, under our real-life Monet painting.

'So I've been thinking. I know I've been acting like this was never gonna happen, as if it wouldn't if I just believed it wouldn't, but there's a part of me afraid of it too. I think of what it might be like for you, but I can't even imagine it. I know I'll be clueless on the other side of what's to come, but I wanted to do something for you. I dunno; give you something to hold onto. I can't give you a letter, or a gift. Anything from me, that's a part of me, will be gone. But I've found something. Something that was here before I arrived and will stay after I've gone. Something you have to promise you'll only go to find if this really does happen – I'm still hoping it won't, you know.'

'Me too,' I said. 'With every ounce of willpower, I'm hoping.'

'So there's a book in the school library. Right next to our back corner table, in the European history section.'

'Okay?' Where was he going with this?

'It jumped out at me one day; it's called Queen Victoria.'

'As in this Queen Victoria?' I held my arm up, and my bracelet slid down my wrist.

'Is there more than one?'

'Probably, don't they rotate names over there?'

'Ha, yeah, but yes, that's the one. If one day, you find you've done the unthinkable and dreamed me out of your existence–'

'Hey, don't say it like I'm some heartless ogre.'

'Sorry, just saying it like it is.'

'You're mean.' I shoved a handful of water into his face.

Tyler splashed me back. 'I know, but you love me,' he said with a grin, and my smile faded with realisation again.

With a solemn face, I said, 'Yes, I do love you.'

Tyler pulled me into his arms as we kicked our legs to stay afloat, even *though every part of me wanted to hold tight, still my feet, and sink to the bottom of the lake with him. Buried in the murky brown water we'd still be together, I wouldn't have to worry that he'd leave me.* Romeo and Juliet had some truth to it after all, as he'd once said. Their story played out every day by lovers desperate to do anything to keep from being torn apart. My shoulders heaved as I held my tears at bay, I refused to let them out, I didn't want to ruin this moment.

'Oh, Lucy, it's going to be all right. I promise. Somehow, I'll make my way back to you. We're meant to be, Batman and Robin belong together.' He smiled against me, and I laughed. 'We'll find a way of getting back here. You just have to wait for me.'

I didn't know how he thought it possible. If he had no recollection of me, no idea I even existed, what chance was there he'd make his way back to me? I wanted to say so, but I pressed my lips together, determined to keep the words from escaping, because I too needed to believe in that tiny, fragile chance.

I'd been ripped from dreams before, woken suddenly in the middle of a nightmare, with only half the story played out. There were times I had the strength to keep from leaving a dream, but sometimes the traction was too strong to fight.

I wasn't being woken, but the pull trying to wrench me out of Tyler's arms had an energy I'd not come up against before. Tyler held onto me, he kissed my lips fiercely, and gave me the fight I needed to stay a little longer. I closed my eyes as I breathed him in for the last time.

'I don't want to go. I can't do this without you,' I cried. 'I won't do it, I won't change the crash.'

'You're too selfless not to, Lucy. And you're going to be great, I know it.' His hand slipped from mine. Tears poured from my eyes. His face filled with fear, and he cried too. 'It's on page fifty-five.'

The force yanked me entirely from his hold, but our eyes stayed locked together, and when I could no longer clearly see his face, he called one last *time to me. 'Thank you for bringing my dad back.'*

Then I left.

I returned to the artificially bright rooms of air traffic control. My legs shook, trembling from the aftermath of where I'd been, of what lay ahead. I'd arrived before the call for help, but before that happened I needed to make sure Bun Lady wasn't left alone this time. She'd need to use the annoyance I sensed in her last time, to speak up and deter her colleague from leaving her side.

Buzz-cut slid out his chair and stood, and she pushed her headpiece back and cranked her neck. 'Don't you dare, Dave. Get your ass back in that chair, I'm getting swamped.'

Alerted by her voice, the suited man in the doorway, who I suspected was some kind of superior, entered the room. It was the last thing this Dave guy needed to prevent him leaving his desk. Job done.

The call came in from Tyler's dad, and together, as a fully alert team, air traffic control was able to authenticate the correct altitude. But with failing equipment the pilots still needed to bring the plane down for an emergency landing.

My head swirled, and moments later my hands held onto armrests I'd grown well acquainted with, surrounded by familiar faces, in a seat I'd frequented more than I'd have liked.

The panicking hadn't yet ceased, a few oxygen masks dangling from the ceiling only increasing the fear. Heads were still bowed in prayer. Little did they know, the God they prayed to had handballed their request, and the girl in seat 41H had already answered their prayers – maybe, we were yet to see. My heart pounded with belief that I may have done it. I still held onto the possibility and hope that I hadn't and I'd wake up in Tyler's arms. But as I considered my surroundings, the mother and child in the seat diagonally across from me, the two ladies next to me, even the creepy-looking dude across the aisle, I knew, just as Tyler did, I couldn't be selfish, not when all these lives were at stake. I wanted to save them all, but why did I have to choose them over him? I shut my eyes from the unfairness of it, clenching my teeth together, holding back the trembling.

I gripped the armrests as the plane began to dive, and then righted itself, before Tyler's dad's voice boomed through the plane, alerting the passengers that the plane was heading down for an emergency landing at Kona International Airport in Hawaii.

My heart pounded heavily with the rocky decent, the cries around me like a drill to my head. The plane jolted sideways, jarring an overhead compartment loose, sending an overly stuffed backpack onto a man's head, followed by a small suitcase thumping into the aisle. More cries.

Lights flickered in the cabin, the wailing coming and going with the intermittent darkness. I glanced out the window and caught the lights from the buildings below, a whir of orange and yellow. Shit, we were coming in fast. Terror coursed through me. I swallowed the bile in my throat.

My head slammed into the back of my seat as the plane lurched up, loosening more oxygen masks from their panels. The elderly lady continued to mutter to herself, words I could no longer hear above the roar of the engine. Releasing my hold on the arm rest, I gripped her hand. Her wrinkled fingers squeezed tightly, and she lifted her tear-filled gaze to mine.

The lights flew past the window, larger, brighter, and I held my breath. The nose pitched up again, slamming me back in the seat, before the deafening crunch of the tail smacking the tarmac. We lifted off the runway and smashed down again, tail, then wheels, then nose. My head whacked the seat in front of me as I was thrown forward, a sharp pain stabbing into my stomach from the seatbelt. Grinding metal thundered as we careened for an eternity, eventually coming to a stop.

My head slumped back, and I started to breathe again.

Huge cheers erupted, and the cabin filled with joy. I glanced around the plane, at the ecstatic faces surrounding me. I tried to scrounge up some happiness for these people, but it was an elusive ask. I wiped my moist hands on my legs and caught the eye of the man opposite me. He smiled, a disturb-

ingly crooked arch that I wanted to look away from, but then he spoke.

'Thank God,' he said and leaned sideways into the aisle. 'I had big plans for today.'

The tops of my cheeks rose slightly, and I murmured a half-hearted agreement before turning away from him and staring straight in front, the fear of what lay ahead steadily filling me with unease. My pulse raced; I didn't want to wake up. I couldn't. What would be waiting for me? But more than that, who? Sorrow clenched around my heart, and the sting of a single tear crept down my cheek.

I WOKE ALONE, MY body numb with dread, but somehow I managed to sit up and place my feet on the ground.

My jet bracelet sat on the table beside my bed. I had no need to wear it today; no deaths were witnessed last night. The white gemstone band Tyler had given me wasn't beside it, and it took a few seconds for the implication to hit me like a sledge hammer, and I caught a sob in my throat. I picked up the jet and placed it on my wrist.

I rubbed the goose bumps on my arms, and dressed slowly in my school gear, I only had one place to get to this morning. On unsteady legs, I made my way downstairs, each agonising step ramming the jagged knife further into my heart.

I wasn't sure I could bear to face anyone so early in the morning and scribbled a quick note to leave on the table.

Walking to school today.

In a haze, behind blurry eyes, with no life in me to run, I waded through fog and inched toward his house. Music – always my companion – walked with me. Billie Eilish and Khalid's 'Lovely'.

I rounded the corner to his street, and the large blue 'For Sale' sign that'd been erected for months, perhaps even years, before Tyler showed up, stood once again on the front lawn of the red-bricked house. I remained there for what felt like hours in silent denial. The day before it had been a house full of life; not happy life, but still...life.

Except it wasn't yesterday at all.

It had never happened.

His days with me were merely a drop in an existence vaster than the oceans, and yet the heaviness of the loss weighed as much as eternity itself. A weight that pressed in on my sides, constricting any breath left in me.

I pressed my hand upon my chest, desperate for an easy breath that didn't want to come. I turned up the music, and my body trembled with the graceful swirl of the violin, echoing like the sorrow growing within me. I willed my feet away from the house and through the path toward our hill. I sat on the grass and, finally able to let out what had been building all morning, I raised my face to the sky and screamed out in agony to relieve an ache I couldn't describe. The cows watched as I yelled and cried, and tears and pain fell.

When at last I had nothing left in me, I lifted myself up and dragged my legs, bit by aching bit, back down the path. I reached the top of the road and stopped, as I often did, to reflect on a simpler time, a happier time before life chewed us up and spat us out as only a semblance of what we'd been.

It'd been six years ago, our whitest winter in a long time, and it had snowed heavily overnight during one of Granny Tess and Pop's visits. We woke to the most magical display right outside our doorstep. The silence was heavenly, and it smelled of happiness.

Pop darted out the door before us, and together we made our way to the end of our street, rounded the bend and climbed the steep road, moments before the rest of our crew joined us.

Pop laid down his homemade sled – the cardboard packaging

from our new fridge.

'Hop on, Lucy Lou,' he said with a grin, holding it still above the pearly white snow for me.

I didn't need much encouragement and jumped on with a wide grin to match Pop's. Max climbed on followed by Sean and Cal and we were all set. My cold fingers gripped the thin piece of rope attached to the front of our sled.

We all turned as Jake and Richie wedged themselves on the ugly, green plastic toboggan Richie had 'borrowed' from the ski resort the year before. Jake had dared him to break the law, and it was the least dishonest thing he could come up with, because he always planned to return it. He never did.

'You guys are mince,' Jake called. He sat behind Richie, who had his tell-tale beanie pulled tightly on his head, his white face sporting the same entire-face-grin his brother often wore.

'No we're not, we're the awesome foursome, right guys?' I said over my shoulder.

'Impossible!' Jake yelled.

'Raise the starting flag, Pops,' Richie called from his driver's seat – he always called him Pops.

'Nothing's impossible,' Pop whispered in my ear and stood to raise his arm. Max's hands dug into my sides, and I fixed my eyes on the bottom of the hill.

'Ready. Set...' Pop lowered his arm. 'Fly!'

*****

I STEPPED INTO THE school building and walked toward an eerily quiet, early morning library. The lump in my throat quivered as I remembered the first dream I shared with Tyler, here in these corridors.

Once in the library I headed straight to the section I'd seen many times before. I ran my fingers along the spines until I bumped into a large book: *Queen Victoria*. I plucked it out and sat at the table. I placed my trembling hands on either side of the book and stared at the gold hardcover, at the face of the Queen staring back at me.

I thumbed the pages until I reached fifty-five. I could still hear his voice as he called the words to me. His smooth, always calm voice, giving me one last thing to hold on to. My pulse sped at the awareness that the words in front of me might be the last thing I ever received from Tyler. I inwardly thanked him for his forward thinking. Always my Robin.

I closed my eyes and drew in a large breath.

On the page were words Prince Albert had written to Queen Victoria before they married, dated November fifteenth, eighteen-thirty-nine – one hundred and seventy nine years past.

'Dearest deeply loved Victoria,'

According to your wish, and by the urging of my heart to talk to you and open my heart to you, I send these lines. We arrived safely at Calais, and Lord Alfred Paget is to re-cross in a quarter of an hour, and will arrive at Windsor early tomorrow. The state of the tide and strong wind forced us to start at half past two in the morning and we reached here at about 6 o'clock. Even then the firebrand could not approach the quay, so that we decided to go ashore in a smaller boat. We both, Schenk, and all the servants were fearfully ill; I have hardly recovered yet.'

I couldn't imagine why Tyler had directed me to this page, what kind of code breaking skills did I need to decipher the hidden message in all these words? And then I read on...

'I need not tell you that since we left, all my thoughts have been with you at Windsor and that your image fills my whole soul.

Even in my dreams I never imagined that I should find so much love on earth. How that moment shines for me still when I was close to you, with your hand in mine! Those days flew by so quickly, but our separation will fly equally so.

Ernest wishes me to say a thousand nice things to you. With promises of unchanging love and devotion, your ever true Albert.

Tears streamed down my cheeks and dampened the page, and the words from the borrowed love letter sank in. He'd gone. He no longer knew me. A dizzying pulse raged in my temple. The memory of me might've faded from his mind, but it didn't lessen the pounding clarity of all the memories I had of him.

Like the years since Albert had written to Victoria, my months with Tyler had vanished, now etched into the subconsciousness of time, but as real to me as the stars threaded in the night sky. Just as real, yet equally unreachable.

And with his promise of unchanging love through our cosmic separation, he gave me a small measure of comfort, while at the same time calmly reached around into my breast pocket and stole every breath he'd ever given me.

After a moment, or maybe a thousand years, I brushed the drying tears from my cheeks and scraped my chair out. I gathered up the book and carried it to the photocopier at the far end of the library and placed it face down on the glass.

I read the words again. And again. Pulled out a pen from my bag and traced a line under the words, *'our separation will fly equally so'*. Was it possible? I wanted to believe it was. I *chose* to believe it was.

Just as Tyler taught me to ignore the fear of travelling when the only detail required was Canada, I needed to ignore the niggling doubt of impossibility buzzing through my foggy brain, because the only detail I needed to focus on was Tyler. With his voice in my head telling me I was going to be great, that I could do this, I trusted him.

I returned Victoria to the shelf, folded the A4 sheet of paper in four and held it to my aching chest, each inward breath pinching around my heart. I clenched my eyes closed, this was all I had of him now. A whimper escaped and I opened my eyes. No. I had so much more than this letter.

Tyler gave me his love. He gave me the ability to change my dreams – to save people's lives. He gave me wings.

I staggered a step, steadied myself on the table, and focused. I could do this. I was ready and set...

To fly.

Acknowledgements

When I first decided to write a novel, I had this crazy idea it'd be easy, that I could write a few words, tweak things a bit and tadaa, I made a book. Every writer who ever lived is laughing at me right now. This book has become far more than I ever hoped or imagined it to be and it's because of so many wonderful people in my life. I am truly blessed.

Firstly to my daughter, Ajah, my first supporter and reader. Thank you for always being honest with me about what worked and what didn't. And for sharing with me your dreams – the very first inspiration for this story.

To the best mum ever, for lifting me up when I struggled, for showing me what perseverance looks like, and for your undying support, even after reading those horrid early pages. Thank you.

Stephanie Childs, Danielle Walsh, and my fabulous sister Naomi Buick, thank you for being brave enough to read those crappy first drafts and still cheering me on the whole way. Your feedback and honesty has been invaluable.

Kate Bradley, the emails you sent after reading each chapter gave me more encouragement than you'll ever know. Thank you.

Thanks to my wonderful mother-in-law, Judith, for your quiet support and feedback. Fine, I'll use more commas!

To Jessica Cassada, my overseas writing buddy. Who knew you could make such good friends with someone you've never met. Thanks for all your early morning encouragement.

To Sam Fairlamb for reading an early draft and composing

music for me to write to. That my words have become an inspiration to some of your song writing makes it extra special. Thank you.

Ursula James, Melanie Smith, Ruth Ralph, and Deb & Isabelle Augur. Somewhere along the way you each read my words – that means a lot. Thank you for your feedback and the little boost you all gave me.

To my husband, Joe, without whom this book would not exist. Not once did you hesitate when I suggested taking on something as ludicrous as writing a book. Even when it meant you went without a decent meal or clean socks! Thank you for valuing what I do and continuing to go to work every day so I can sit at home and daydream.

To my boys, Marley & Oskar, for being quiet when I said 'Shhh', for willingly spending more time on the computer so I could bash out some words. Your 'sacrifice' means the world.

To my dad. Thank you for the bedtime stories you created out of thin air. They gave me a love of storytelling and sparked a desire within me to create magic too. 'I'm closing my eyes, but I'm still listening.'

To Ian Hugh McAllister, his expertise for the flight and ATC scenes was enormously helpful and I'm ever so grateful. And Holly Richter for her medical knowledge and experience, which helped bring truth to the hospital scenes, thank you. Both professionals in their field, but I'm the writer and take full responsibility for any fault in these areas.

Huge thanks to Kate Foster for believing in me and loving my story. For seeing in my words what I only ever dreamed someone else would. For helping shape and mould the story into so much more than it originally was. Your advice, wisdom and support are way more than I ever thought I would get from a publisher and editor. I truly am the luckiest girl in the world.

To my other editors at Lakewater Press, Jodi Gallegos and Rebecca Carpenter, you made my words shine, thank you for sharing your talents with me.

To everyone who took a chance on this debut author and read *Lucid*, thank you. If you enjoyed it, please consider leaving a review so other readers can hear about my story. And if you're eager to read the sequel, know I am just as excited to share the next instalment with you all. Keep reading for a sneak peek.

About the Author

Kristy Fairlamb is an Australian author of young adult novels with high stakes and heart. She enjoys spending her days drinking coffee and torturing her characters with loads of tension – both love related and the nail biting kind.

Long before her days of writing began, she spent half her childhood in a make believe world, daydreaming about growing up, falling in love, and travelling the world.

She's worked as a nanny in country England, a junior matron in a boy's boarding school south of London, a governess in East Timor, and made coffees and cleared tables in the New South Wales snow fields.

She lives with her husband, teenage daughter, and two sons in the beautiful Adelaide Hills where they're lucky enough to get occasional visits from the local koalas.

She's terrible at gardening, likes her bookshelves sorted by colour, and recently checked off a lifelong dream of jumping from a plane.

When she's not writing or daydreaming about her stories you'll find her reading, cooking for her family, or doing anything to avoid the housework.

To keep up to date with Kristy's author news visit her website:
kristyfairlamb.com
On Facebook: KristyFairlambAuthor
On Instagram: kristyfairlambwriter
On Twitter: @kristy_fairlamb

A Heartbreaking Choice
A Chilling Consequence

KRISTY FAIRLAMB

Excerpt from

LUMINOUS

Lucid Series: Book 2

— 1 —

MY DREAMS BROUGHT ME love, and then they stole that love away. Yet the hope of seeing him once more surfaced in all its heart-breaking vibrancy. I drew in a sharp breath; every one of my six hundred and fifty muscles tensing in unison. He was so beautiful. He always had been, not that I ever expected that to change. In all the days, weeks, and months since I'd lost Tyler, I never truly imagined what it might be like to see him again. But there I stood, diagonally across the road, a mere twenty meters from the boy who meant the world to me yet didn't know I existed.

A confusion of emotions – ecstasy, satisfaction, sorrow – raced through my veins at the sight of him. His hair flicked down his forehead, shadowing eyes I knew were as dark as night. A lump formed in my throat; an accumulation of all the things I wanted to say, but couldn't, and all the things we'd been, but in truth hadn't.

Not since the moment I'd been ripped from his arms.

He walked beside his friends; friends he hadn't lost to the awkwardness that followed death like a bad scent. His laughter filled the air, the kind of easy laughter you find so effortlessly when you don't have a care in the world. His stride was light, his load unburdened from loss and responsibility.

School was out for the day, and as the group paused their scramble along the footpath and kids continued to drift around them, his gaze lifted to mine.

I resisted the urge to smile and wave, to acknowledge how familiar he was to me. So familiar that I knew if I stood in front of him, I'd see the small dimple on his chin, and above that, the most perfect lips – lips that no longer knew mine. Mine hadn't forgotten his though, they never would.

His eyes bored into mine, reminding me of the first time I'd seen him in the dream at the airport. I'd like to assume the curiosity in his eyes was in fact recognition, but I think it was just a reflection of the glimmer of hope in mine. Something I'd held so tightly to for so long; it was the life raft that'd kept me afloat in my sea of pain, too afraid to let go, because if I did I'd sink slowly and heavily to the bottom of the ocean.

*****

Seven weeks earlier...

THE FRONT YARD OF the school sat still and empty. A blue hatchback cruised along the road beyond the school's low iron fence. A growing hum of teenagers in the rooms behind me indicated class was almost over. I sat alone at the table, normally occupied by my four friends, but for a few more minutes would be mine alone.

I slid the crumpled paper from my uniform pocket and unfolded the page to read the words for the thousandth time. The corner fluttered in the gentle breeze, I held my palm flat across the sheet, holding it in place.

Even in my dreams I never imagined that I should find so much love on earth. How that moment shines for me still when I was close to you, with your hand in mine! Those days flew by so quickly, but our separation will fly equally so.

The scrawl underlining the last line had smudged a little since I drew it two days ago, but the meaning remained clear. As vivid as some of Tyler's final words to me, 'You're going to be great.' Words that'd carried me through the constant doubt I'd done the right thing.

How do you know if you've made the right choice? I'd battled with the question for two long days. I lost the one person who meant the world to me when I'd brought back to life all those people who didn't. My head knew it was right, but my heart screamed wrong.

I'd never known pain so agonising. How could something unseen feel so physical? I reeled from a beating as if I'd been kicked repeatedly in the guts with a metal-toed boot and stabbed in the heart by a serrated knife, the only thing missing was the blood. He'd been gone for two days and I still couldn't fill my lungs, not with the permanent vice tightened around my chest, making it near impossible to get enough air in.

I grabbed my sketchbook from my bag, immediately desperate to see him. I flipped to the page where the lines of Tyler's face peered up at me, and I wished with more than the stars that I hadn't had to make that decision. I closed my eyes, hesitated, and turned the page reminding me why I had.

Satisfaction seeped through me as I peered at the old lady who'd sat beside me and the man from across the aisle. She'd made it safely home to the people who needed her, and the man, with his weird grin, went on to fulfil the plans he'd been so eager to the last time I saw him. He still gave me the creeps, but even he deserved life. Like each of the three hundred and twenty-seven souls on board, including Tyler's dad.

Tyler might not be here, and I might be missing what felt like half a lung, but I knew what I needed to keep doing. What I was always meant to do. Help others. Bring people back from an early grave when they still had life to live.

I'd had my mope, now I needed to get back to business, to fly.

COMING MAY 2020

www.ingramcontent.com/pod-product-compliance
Lightning Source LLC
Chambersburg PA
CBHW050140120726
47903CB00002B/426